Viva Lost Vogus

A Comedy Sci-fi Adventure

Pelham and Blandings Book 1

Gary Blaine Randolph

This is a work of fiction. Names, characters, businesses, events, and incidents are the products of the author's imagination. Any resemblance to actual persons, living or dead, or actual events is purely coincidental.

Copyright © 2023
by Gary Blaine Randolph

All rights reserved. No part of this book may be reproduced or used in any manner without written permission of the copyright owner except for the use of quotations in a book review.

ISBN: 978-1-7379299-7-0 (paperback)
ISBN: 978-1-7379299-6-3 (ebook)

Dedication

One of the most memorable people in my childhood, though I only met her a few times as a small boy, was my great-aunt, Auntie Gladys. She had left the farm for the world of business and ended up the head of housekeeping at the famous Flamingo hotel in Las Vegas. In our world of denim and flannel, Auntie Gladys wore furs, which was a thing in those days. She may have met Dean Martin, Jerry Lewis, Sammy Davis Jr. who were frequent guests at the Flamingo. And since this was in the heyday of Vegas's mob-connections, she almost certainly knew the infamous Bugsy Siegal and Moe Sedway, who ran the hotel. Oh how I wish I could have heard her stories. So once I came up with the idea for *Viva Lost Vogus*, I knew I had to dedicate this to her and to slip her somehow into the story.

Oh, and also to Victor and Blaine who at one time called their stuffed flamingo a mingo.

Contents

A Word of Explanation for Readers of The Galactic Detective Agency vi
Chapter 1 Aunt Agutha Barges In 1
Chapter 2 Pelham Receives Disappointing News 8
Chapter 3 Bally Donovians 16
Chapter 4 The Fabulous Pink Mingo 23
Chapter 5 Pelham is Introduced to Jack Black 31
Chapter 6 The Exhilarating World of Trade Negotiations 39
Chapter 7 Suspicious Minds 46
Chapter 8 A Revolting Development 54
Chapter 9 Helping the Colonial Security Force with their Inquiries 61
Chapter 10 All Shook Up 69
Chapter 11 Caught Between a Rock-Headed Sergeant and a Hard Aunt 76
Chapter 12 No Joy with Mountjoy 83
Chapter 13 Hail, Hail Bononia 90
Chapter 14 You've Got to Know When to Hold 'em 96
Chapter 15 The Amazing Mystico 103
Chapter 16 Fools Rush In 110
Chapter 17 No to the Handholding 117
Chapter 18 Are You Lonesome Tonight? 123
Chapter 19 The First Item on the Agenda is the Split 131
Chapter 20 Pelham Makes the News 138
Chapter 21 Awkward Conversations 144

Chapter 22 Start the Revolution Without Me 151
Chapter 23 A Hunka Hunk of Busted Stone 159
Chapter 24 The Inimitable Blandings.. 166
Chapter 25 The Code of the Totleighs.. 174
Chapter 26 The Advantages of Keeping Expectations Low 181
Chapter 27 It's Now or Never... 188
Chapter 28 One for the Money, Two for the Show 195
Chapter 29 Jailhouse Rock (With Real Rocks).. 203
Chapter 30 Don't Be Cruel 210
Chapter 31 Heartbreak Hotel 216
Chapter 32 Carry On, Blandings 222
Chapter 33 Return to Sender 228
Chapter 34 Leaving Lost Vogus 235
Last Word and Something Free... 242
Other Books by Gary Blaine Randolph 243

A Word of Explanation for Readers of The Galactic Detective Agency

I hate to intrude on the beginning of my own book, but I wanted to offer a quick word of explanation to readers of my Galactic Detective Agency series. If you haven't read those books (and for the love of Pete, why haven't you?), feel free to skip on to chapter one.

When I was working on *Murder on the Girsu Express*, book five of that series, I got a tremendous kick out of writing Pelham G. Totleigh and Blandings. They were, and still are, modeled after two of my all-time favorite fictional characters, Bertie Wooster and Jeeves. I enjoyed them so much, I decided to spin them off in their own adventure, which became this book.

For sticklers of chronology, *Viva Lost Vogus* takes place after *Murder on the Girsu Express*. It is set in the Galactic Detective Agency universe with the same alien worlds and species (plus some new ones) but doesn't feature any of the ongoing GDA characters. It isn't even a mystery. Call it a sci-fi comedy, an alien world adventure with an unlikely hero.

You don't need to have read *Murder on the Girsu Express* to enjoy this book. But, of course, I wouldn't mind at all if you happened to pick it up sometime.

So, without further ado, prologues, or forewords, ladies and gentlemen, *Viva Lost Vogus*.

Chapter 1

Aunt Agutha Barges In

"Pelham!"

Pelham G. Totleigh rolled over in his bed, indulging in a vague, wishful notion that a realignment of the limbs and joints might transport him into a better dream — a dream where there wasn't someone shouting his name.

"Pelham G. Totleigh!"

The voice was harsh, demanding. It sounded for all the moon like his Aunt Agutha's. Which made no sense. Why would he dream of Aunt Agutha? Unless, of course, this wasn't a dream but rather a nightmare.

"Sir."

Now, that was the voice of his man Blandings, and Pelham knew Blandings would never take the liberty of entering his dreams. Such a thing would not be proper, and his valet was always proper.

Which could mean only one thing. With profound regret, Pelham realized this chorus of voices echoing around him was not part of any dream, but rather grim reality interrupting his slumber. He propped open one eye to find his bed surrounded. Blandings stood on one side, a serene expression on his face. Aunt Agutha was on the other side, leaning on a cane and glowering with a steely glare.

Pelham, like Blandings and Aunt Agutha, was a Haplor, a species shorter than the average galactic citizen, with long dexterous fingers, huge circular eyes, and stubby noses. They were covered everywhere except for their faces with sandy-colored, spotted fur. The fur on top of their heads grew longer, and Aunt Agutha kept hers coiffed into a stiff bouffant, each hair terrorized rigidly into place.

"Pelham," Aunt Agutha said in a voice capable of stripping insulation from wiring, "why in the name of Gort are you still in bed?"

Pelham's own hair hung down his face in a tangle. He swept it to one side and gaped at her, eyes bugging out. If he had been intending to arise from bed at this hour, which he most definitely had not, he felt he could scarcely do so now. Her shrill voice reduced his spine to mush.

He ran his tongue around his mouth and mumbled, "Good morning, Aunt Agutha."

Blandings handed Pelham a cup of tea, which seemed to have magically appeared in his hand. Pelham pushed himself to a sitting position and took the cup, breathing in the aroma before taking a sip. Perfect as usual. Precisely strong enough, warm enough, sweet enough, creamy enough. Incredible chap, that Blandings, Pelham thought to himself not for the first time.

"Good morning? Good morning?" Agutha banged her cane on the floor. "It is long past the forenoon, Pelham. I ate my lunch on the way over to see you?"

Pelham yawned. "May I ask, Aunt Agutha, where you stopped?"

"What?"

"For lunch, I mean."

"Why do you ask?"

"So I can avoid the establishment in the future. Their food doesn't seem to have put you in much of an agreeable mood."

"Hmph! If I am of a less than cheerful disposition, my half-witted nephew, it is solely because of you."

With a slightly shaking hand, Pelham took another calming sip. "Excellent tea, Blandings."

"Thank you, sir."

Ordinarily, it would be Blandings' job to prevent random people from bursting into Pelham's bedchamber. But Pelham couldn't fault him this time. One had to make allowances in cases such as Aunt Agutha. One might as easily prevent a tsunami from sweeping ashore … on planets, that is, where they have sufficient aboveground water to generate such phenomena, which they did not here on their little moon Sonus.

"May I offer you some tea, Aunt Agutha? I'm sure Blandings could conjure up another cup."

"I didn't come here for tea."

Aunt Agutha Barges In

"If I dare to ask, what does bring you here ... into my bedchamber ... in the wee hours? Don't you normally summon me to your office like a stern headmistress?"

"I did attempt to summon you, you nincompoop. I called your office this morning. You remember your office, don't you? The place where you are supposed to go to work?"

"I do make it in most days, Aunt Agutha. In fact, I was planning to put in a full normal workday today."

"Normal workday? It is well past midday, Pelham."

"I meant *my* normal workday. I've always found a day is best faced in the post meridian hours when it's already busy and can be sneaked up on unawares. Facing a morning bright and early is only asking for trouble."

Bright and early was, in this case, merely an expression. On a moon that was tidally locked — another imprecise expression since, again, Sonus had no aboveground water — in its orbit of the planet Nuggies, a lunar day lasted a full forty-two days and nights as time was measured on their home world of Haplor.

These dual, conflicting meanings of the word day were a constant source of confusion on Sonus and the cause of people missing some truly epic parties or, in some cases, showing up for them months early. The colony tried to standardize on a Haplor home world day and compensate with carefully timed artificial lights and luminescence dampeners, but the effect was never more than partially successful. Some colonists, including even Pelham, who had lived here his whole life, felt continually sleep deprived.

"Let me assure you, Aunt Agutha," Pelham said, "all is well down at the office of the Investigator of Exports."

Blandings cleared his throat. "Inspector of Imports, sir."

"Ah. Right, Blandings," Pelham said. "Quite the tongue twister, what?"

"Indeed, sir."

"Indeed not," Aunt Agutha said with a noticeable tinge of scorn. "One would think you would know your own job title. I have always believed Haplors to be among the most intelligent, energetic, and industrious species in the galaxy."

"Yes, Aunt Agutha," Pelham said.

"Granted, exceptions and individual differences are bound to occur."

"Of course."

"And yet you, Pelham, you make me doubt my beliefs."

"Say what?"

She bobbed her head. "Well, of course, it isn't that you completely lack backbone or intelligence."

"Thank you ... I think."

"But you so rarely use either of them that they have atrophied like unused muscles."

"Now see here, Aunt Agutha."

"Do you even know what your job is, Pelham?"

"Of course, I do. I contact chappies on other planets to make sure Sonus has all the thises and thats it needs to continue eating and breathing and terra-whatchamacallit ..."

"Terraforming, sir."

"Thank you, Blandings. Difficult to think of words at this early hour. As I was saying, Aunt Agutha, to continue terrafirming and building up our colony."

"Terraforming," Agutha said.

"Right."

"You said terrafirming."

"Did I?"

"Yes, you moron."

"I say, that's a tad strong, what?"

Aunt Agutha grimaced. "In any event, catch up on all your work this afternoon. Tomorrow I am sending you to an important trade conference ... against my better judgment, I might add. Close your mouth, Pelham. You look like a laundry chute."

"Sorry, but I'm a bit befuddled, perplexed. Did you say a trade conference? You mean one of those gatherings of stuffed shirts where they sit around in uncomfortable seats all day while boring speakers drone on about tariffs and trade routes and what all?"

"Exactly. At a minimum, it will be a better use of your time than idling about with your idiotic friends all night."

That was an assertion Pelham highly doubted. Sonus, despite being a terraforming colony, or possibly precisely because it was a terraforming colony, had a vibrant nightlife. The public houses all competed to put on the most entertaining shows and reviews. And in catering to pipe fitters, metal workers, soil technicians, and other colony builders, the acts tended toward the boisterous side. Case in point: those two comedians Pelham had seen only a few hours before who told jokes while juggling personal solar panels and simultaneously attempting to hit each other with those same panels. The well-lubricated audience loved it, as did Pelham and his friends.

"And let me be clear," Aunt Agutha said, "I expect you to attend the sessions and learn something. I also expect you to network with people and project a positive image of Sonus to the best of your limited ability. And most of all, I expect you to conclude a trade agreement with the Bononian delegate who will be attending."

"Bononia?"

"Yes. I assume even someone of your minimal intelligence is familiar with Bononia."

"Well, yes. It's a planet."

"Astonishing. Bononia has fertilizers we need for the next phase of development."

"Who is this delegate? The Bononian?"

"Someone named Emer. I've never met him. Now don't let him set the price too high."

"I won't, Aunt Agutha."

"And make sure all the terms are clearly spelled out."

"I will, Aunt Agutha."

"Don't make a hash of it."

"Now when have I ever —" Pelham stopped himself from finishing the question. Aunt Agutha, if pressed or even mildly prodded, could unquestionably come up with a long list of things Pelham had allegedly hashed, not least of which was the infamous incident of the stolen hat and the drainpipe back on Haplor. He had always insisted the kerfuffle had been a simple misunderstanding. But just try persuading Aunt Agutha to see it that way. Instead, he asked, "Where is this tedious yawn fest of a symposium being held?"

"On Vogus."

"Vogus. Vogus. Ah yes. Say, that's a bit better. Isn't Vogus where they have the posh Earth-themed casinos?"

"Yes." Agutha said the word as if she had discovered it stuck to the bottom of her shoe.

Pelham tried without success to suppress a grin. A few days away from the old grind spent in lavish surroundings with games of chance from the mysterious planet Earth intrigued him. "Sounds like fun."

5

"Fun? You are not going to Vogus for amusement. You are going there to strike a trade deal and to learn how to do your job better … or at all, for that matter, which would be a pleasant change. You won't have time for the casino." She sniffed in disgust. "An Earth-themed casino. Of all the crazy ideas. Why anyone would want to mimic those tall, ugly, nearly hairless mammals from Earth is beyond me. If they were worthy of emulation, the galactic alliance wouldn't have placed the entire planet under quarantine."

"It is the glamour of the thing, dear Auntie, the mystique, the allure of a strange and forbidden world. You know, I understand the Earthlings are absolutely huge on gambling. They wager on games, sports, politics. I hear they're even taking bets on whether there is life on other planets. Pretty funny, what?"

"It's ridiculous if you ask me. Betting away good money that could be spent on practicalities. Now, you have your instructions. It is settled then, eh? You'll go?"

"Absolutely."

She frowned, appearing suspicious of her nephew's enthusiasm. "And you'll attend to business?"

"You can count on me, Aunt Agutha. What could possibly go wrong?"

"With you, Pelham, anything." She spun on her heels and tottered out of the bedroom, calling over her shoulder with a wave of her hand, "I'll arrange your transport."

"Toodle-oo, Auntie."

Blandings followed and saw her to the door. He returned to find Pelham staring at the ceiling.

"I apologize for the intrusion, sir," Blandings said. "Dame Agutha was rather insistent."

"No doubt she was, Blandings. No doubt she was. My aunt has a special talent for being insistent, for bossing people around. She's been bossing me for as long as I can remember. She bullies my Uncle Spence something terrible. I think it was because she excels at the skill that the colony elected her governor, giving her free reign to boss around everyone on Sonus as well as a fair number of people back on Haplor. Blandings?"

"Yes, sir?"

"What is a bally trade agreement anyway? If something is for sale, one hardly needs an agreement to buy it. What I mean to say is, we don't have to sign an accord with the green grocers to pick up a head of cabbage, do we?"

"No, sir. However, trade agreements are of use in interstellar trade. They specify the obligations of each trading partner and ensure quality standards, protections for property rights, economic policies, et cetera."

Pelham blinked at the valet. "Seems a decidedly silly thing, if you ask me."

"If you say so, sir. Are you ready for your breakfast?"

"Is it time to rise and shine?"

"It rather depends, sir. The hour is indeed appreciably earlier than your usual time of rising. However, the governor did indicate that you needed to catch up on your work today. You might desire extra time at the office."

Pelham sighed. "You are correct, of course, Blandings. Yes. Bring on the feedbag. I will indeed storm the castle early today. There is much I will need to delegate to my assistant."

Chapter 2

Pelham Receives Disappointing News

Humming an old Haplor melody, Blandings began setting out Pelham's clothes for the day. Morning, especially given Mr. Totleigh's expansive definition of it, was the valet's favorite part of the day. To Blandings, mornings were a time of new beginnings, of starting off on the right foot. He had already exercised both mind and body, taken his first cup of tea, and straightened up the flat, all while his employer slept. Blandings pulled from the closet Mr. Totleigh's gray striped jacket and brushed the shoulders, admiring its elegant lines.

"One moment, Blandings," Pelham said, speaking from the bed where he was daubing jam on a piece of toast. "You'll note a new red checked jacket hanging there."

Blandings had, in fact, noticed the blazer with more than a trace of alarm. "Yes, sir. I assumed it was for an upcoming costume party."

Pelham chuckled. "Then you assumed incorrectly. No, I spotted that gem in a shop window yesterday, and, you know, it spoke to me."

"Did it? Fascinating. One supposes it would speak in a rather grating voice."

"I said to myself, 'Pelham, old chap, you would look awfully sharp in that.'"

"I fear I cannot agree with your assessment, sir."

Pelham regarded Blandings with a pinched expression. This was not their first disagreement over clothes. "Blandings, I must remind you that you are the valet, and I am your employer."

"I should not forget it, sir."

"I admit you are in many ways a marvel."

Pelham Receives Disappointing News

"I appreciate you saying so, sir."

"Astoundingly well read. Amazingly intelligent. However, if you have any fault, and I must say you have scarcely any, it is your fashion sense. It tends toward the old-fashioned, you know."

"Does it, sir?"

"It does if I'm being honest. Not that it's difficult to grow out of date on this backwater of a moon."

"Yes, sir, though I feel it is my duty to guide you in —"

Pelham cut him off with a raised hand. "Nonsense, Blandings. Now I admit I have often needed your guidance in the past when I or my friends have got into scrapes."

"Yes, sir."

"Like that matter of the drainpipe. How you extricated me from my predicament was nothing short of miraculous."

"Thank you, sir."

"Or that time old Binky wanted to marry that Penelope Widdershins, and you figured out how to put it past her legal guardian."

"I endeavor to give satisfaction, sir."

"Nevertheless, in this case, Blandings, I must eschew your guidance. I say, is eschew the word I want to apply here? Or is eschew what I'm doing to my breakfast?"

"You employed the word correctly, sir … in the first case, that is."

"Ah. Then please pull out the new red checked number. I will wear it today."

"As you wish, sir." Blandings left the room, seeking the solace of another cup of tea.

He returned sometime later to find Pelham sonic showered and dressed, the fur on his head brushed. His employer stood in front of the mirror wearing the offensive jacket and a disgruntled countenance.

"Is something the matter, sir?"

"Yes, it's this blasted jacket. I look like a cross between a circus performer and a used shuttlecraft merchant."

"I do note the resemblance, sir. I had feared as much."

Pelham slipped out of the red checks and into the gray stripes. "Don't gloat, Blandings."

"I shouldn't dream of it, sir."

***

Pelham left the apartment and made his way through underground corridors, emerging at last into the translucent main dome of the colony. Above the dome, a tiny red sun hung in the sky. But it was the huge planet Nuggies, which Sonus orbited, that dominated the view, its blue rings slicing across the dark sky like a monstrous saw blade.

In between them, a stream of wispy clouds stretched across the sky, a clear sign of the atmosphere beginning to coalesce. People could now breathe outside the dome ... provided they didn't exert themselves much. With a bit more atmosphere, one soon might be able to go outside without freezing off one's bum.

The business district was buzzing with busy Haplors marching here and there. Pelham nodded in greeting as he passed them, a holdover custom from the days before he was born when everyone in the colony knew everyone else.

He was glad those small colony days were gone. With the expanded population had come more shops, more restaurants, more of the things to bring enjoyment to evening hours spent with chums.

Pelham passed through the streets to the towering and dismal gray government building, one of the first large buildings built in the colony back when the emphasis had still been on severe functionality. He took the lift to his floor, followed the hallway around, and entered a dingy cubicle with two desks.

A gray-furred man, small even by Haplor standards, was peering at a screen through glowing green circles that ringed his eyes. He glanced up at Pelham and blinked twice. The glowing circles dematerialized.

"Good day, Mr. Totleigh. You are in early."

"What ho, Munson. Wearing refractors now, eh?"

"I had the chip implanted last week. The eyes aren't what they used to be."

"Hope it helps." Pelham rubbed his hands together. "Well, we have much to accomplish today."

"We do?"

"Indeed, we do. Apparently, I will be out of the office for a few days. Going to a trade conference, you know."

"I see. How many days will you be gone, Mr. Totleigh?"

"How many? Days? Dash it all, Aunt Agutha didn't say. How long do those types of thingamajigs last?"

"I'm sure I wouldn't know. They've never sent me to a conference. Possibly three or four days?"

"Four days of boring seminars. Ugh. Fortunately, this particular torment will be inflicted on the planet Vogus."

"Ooh, Vogus. Quite the stylish place, Mr. Totleigh. I was hoping to take the missus there for our anniversary. I understand the casino complex was designed and constructed based on Earth surveillance performed by the Grays."

Being quarantined — for obvious reasons, if you knew anything about the planet's culture — Earth was cut off from the rest of the galaxy. It did, however, need to be watched, especially in recent decades when the Earthlings had developed a space program of sorts. The galactic alliance delegated the job of conducting Earth surveillance to the Grays, a species with a keen inclination toward exobiology. Pelham had never been comfortable around Grays. You couldn't have a friendly conversation with one. They would tilt and twist their heads and scrutinize you as if you were a test subject, a set of data. They were like the creepy stalkers of the galaxy.

In exchange for keeping an eye on Earth, the Grays were allowed to profit from the intelligence they gathered. They sold videos of the planet. They licensed interesting Earth technology, such as bicycles and slinkies. There were rumors of them doing more than simply observing Earthlings, but most felt it prudent not to ask too many questions.

"Did I ever tell you, Munson, I met an Earth person once?"

"You have, Mr. Totleigh. Several times, in fact."

"Tremendous chap, this Earthling."

"So you have said."

"Helped me out of a dreadful jam ... well, along with the Galactic Detective Agency. You know, he wore a particularly snappy hat, a fedora, I believe he called it. Someday I hope to make it to Earth myself and pick up one of those fedoras. If all Earth people are like that one, then I don't see why we even need the quarantine."

"Perhaps they aren't all like him. I have read they have violent tendencies ... and nuclear fission bombs."

"What? Why would anyone use fission to create weapons when there are so many better uses for it?"

Munson shook his head in apparent bafflement. Pelham stepped to the office's single window, which looked out through the main dome to smaller domes scattered across the surface of the moon and dedicated to hydroponics, soil maintenance, atmospheric development, and more. Between them, tufts of grasses grew here and there, another sign of the progress of terraforming. Across the plain, a stand of short trees grew outside any of the domes. A party of three Haplors were scaling the trees, performing some sort of agricultural task.

"The workers are in the orchard today," Pelham said.

"Hmm?"

"The workers. In the meido orchard."

"Yes, and you'll notice, Mr. Totleigh, they aren't using oxygen tanks. The atmosphere is getting stronger."

"Ah. Quite."

"They do have to keep the tanks nearby, though."

"Well, one can't be too careful."

"What was it you wanted to accomplish today, Mr. Totleigh?"

"Accomplish?"

"Before your conference."

"Ah. Well, whatever needs to be done. What is on the docket, Munson? What is the special of the day, as it were?"

"The shipment of purification filters coming in from Yindaron has been delayed. As I understand it the ship couldn't launch due to the layer of space junk around the planet."

"Space junk?"

"Old satellites and bits and bobs of that nature."

"Couldn't they just blast the ruddy things to smithereens?"

"That's what caused the current problem, Mr. Totleigh. They blew up several satellites and, as a result, created a thousand times more junk from the bits."

"Golly."

"Now they are unable to navigate past it at all without having an odd bolt or shard of metal slicing through the ships. We're going to have to find a new supplier."

"Does anyone else make these petrification fillers?"

"Purification filters. I haven't looked into it."

"Sounds like a perfect job for you, Munson. Find out, will you? Check into who supplies these doodads."

"I will add it to my list. Also, we received a shipment of Antarean barley rice last night. It needs to be inspected."

"Again, another responsibility I feel certain you can shoulder."

"Inspections are supposed to be done by the Inspector of Imports, not the Assistant Inspector of Imports, Mr. Totleigh."

"Yes, yes. But part of my function is to bring you along, so to speak. To help you grow in the job."

"Oh, I think I have already grown well beyond the scope of my job description, Mr. Totleigh."

"Absolutely. And may I say you are doing a fine job."

"But …" He didn't finish the thought.

"But what, Munson?"

"Nothing. I will attend to the inspection directly, and you can sign off on the paperwork. Speaking of which, there are several other inspection reports and supply requests you need to endorse. I put them on your desk."

Pelham's eyes went to his desk, finding it covered by a mound of tablets and clipboards. "For Zahn's sake, Munson, you can't dump everything on my desk."

"All those items require your signature, Mr. Totleigh."

"Can't you sign them?"

"My signature would not be official. Unless you are suggesting I engage in the illegal act of forging your name."

"No, no. We can't break the law … of course. Can we?"

"No."

"Ah. Well, then I suppose I have my morning's —"

"Afternoon, sir."

"I have my afternoon's work cut out for me. I will pitch myself at yonder pile. Fetch me a cup of tea, would you?"

Munson exhaled. "Yes, sir."

"You may have to bring me mountain climbing gear as well."

His assistant blinked.

"That was a joke, Munson. To take on the heap, I mean."

"Ah. Yes. I'll fetch the tea then."

Hours later when Pelham returned home, wearing a weary expression, he found luggage stretched across the couch and Blandings preparing clothes to take. It was a process that involved running garments through the pressing cabinet, followed by hanging them in the particle charger to stiffen them for transport, and then placing them in suitcases.

"Good evening, sir. Would you like a drink?"

"What ho, Blandings? No, don't want to interrupt. You seem to have matters in hand. I'll fend for myself."

"Thank you, sir."

Pelham massaged his fingertip, the one used all day long to tap the signature box on the mound of documents. "Grueling day, Blandings."

"I am sorry to hear it, sir."

Pelham began mixing himself his usual Amurru fizz. "Speaking of packing, did the mauve tunic I ordered happen to arrive?"

"Yes, sir. I sent it back."

"What? I was planning to wear it at the conference."

"The color would not have suited you, sir."

Drink in hand, Pelham dropped into a chair, disappointed about the tunic but conceding that what was done was done. Blandings probably knew best.

"I took the liberty of reading up on the planet Vogus, sir." Blandings slipped a black tunic into the presser. Pelham couldn't help but think the mauve would be more stylish.

"They don't have a problem with space junk, do they?"

"Space junk, sir?"

"Parts of ships and satellites. Odd bolts and whatnots orbiting about."

"I don't believe they do, sir."

"Ah. Excellent. You were saying, Blandings?"

"The hotel and casinos were built by the Zurks, who colonized the planet several years ago. They built in the midst of an existing indigenous population known as the Okcho."

"Ah, nice to hear of different species living together in harmony, isn't it Blandings?"

"It is indeed, sir, though in this case I understand —"

Pelham cut him off. "Have our tickets arrived yet? I wonder what sort of transport Aunt Agutha has arranged for us. I say, it would be grand to travel on that new Fornaxi star liner, what?"

"I rather doubt Dame Agutha would pay for —"

This time he was interrupted by a *ding* sounding at the apartment door. The valet broke off from the clothes to answer it. Outside, a drone hovered. It dropped a memory card into Blanding's outstretched hand, and he returned to the apartment.

"This may contain our travel arrangements, sir."

Pelham Receives Disappointing News

"Thanks." Pelham took the card and pulled out his personal electronic device. He tapped the card to the screen to initiate a download. Pelham's jaw dropped. He gaped at the screen. "What? No, Blandings. There must be some mistake."

"What is it, sir?"

"Our travel arrangements. They are aboard Donovian military transport. Bally Donovians."

Chapter 3

Bally Donovians

"Donovians. I can't believe it, Blandings."

Pelham had no idea how many intelligent species there were in the known galaxy, though he suspected Blandings could rattle off the exact number. There were blue-skinned Rhegedians and green-skinned Dierens. Srathans have scales. Avanians fly with feathered wings while Snuuls glide about on their bellies with four arms swaying in the air. Kolrabie resemble tall leafy plants. The Yindi have eyes embedded in about a dozen tentacles with no discernible face. So many ways to make a person. And then there were Donovians.

"Donovians," Pelham repeated.

"So it would appear, sir."

"You know, Blandings, I like to think of myself as a person open to other cultures, a citizen of the galaxy."

"You have often said as much, sir."

"I've enjoyed friendly relations with everyone from Arsawans to Zosmi. But Donovians … Donovians get under my fur."

"It is possible, sir, you are prejudiced against them since one of their number once arrested you for murder."

Pelham scoffed. "And on the flimsiest of evidence. That officious copper from Girsu Space Port."

"Yes, sir."

"Large blobs of purple fur with spindly arms and legs. Eyes sticking up on top of their odious heads, rolling this way and that — the eyes, I mean, not the heads."

"Yes. I have met them, sir."

"I know you have, Blandings. But did you know they actually enjoy paperwork?"

"I did, sir."

"Give those chappies a form to fill out, and they will while away any number of enjoyable hours. But if you or I were compelled to help them do it, ho-ho, why a person could go stark raving mad with the tedium of it all. And now we have to fly on Donovian military transport. I can't believe it. It's like being bashed on the head with a sock full of marbles. No, I take that back."

"It does not resemble being bashed, sir?"

"No. I mean I bally well do believe it. This sounds precisely like something my dear Aunt Agutha would conscript me into."

"The arrangements do epitomize Dame Agutha's characteristic disdain for your comfort. Granted, sir, Donovio is in the same star system as Sonus. One supposes this method of transport was convenient."

"And cheap."

"No doubt, sir."

"A whole crew of those purple blighters organized into a command structure with procedures and rules. It sends shivers down my spine."

The next morning, Blandings loaded their luggage into a three-wheeled taxi, one of many that roamed the colony, and the pair set out across the dome toward the space terminal. Pelham's thoughts bubbled in a stew of eagerness to reach their destination mixed with a large dollop of apprehension as to the particulars of the impending journey. They entered the sprawling space terminal, bustling with vendors and shops and people heading out on excursions.

Pelham blinked at the reservation on his device. "Concourse X? I've never heard of Concourse X, Blandings." He gazed up at signs for Concourses A, B, C, and D. Nowhere among the listings was X.

"I presume it is through there, sir." Blandings pointed with his head as his arms were busy holding four bags.

"Where?"

"The doorway there."

"The washroom?"

"No, sir. Beside the washroom."

"Looks like a service closet, Blandings."

"Nevertheless, sir, there is an X above the door."

As they approached, the gray portal rolled open to reveal a gloomy and eerily silent corridor.

"Are you sure about this, Blandings? This place gives me the creeps. It brings to mind the sort of passageway they shove into those horror vids where, without warning, a Srathan boasaur springs out from the shadows."

"The hallway does produce a certain unsettling effect upon the nerves. However, I detect a light at the end."

Blandings was not speaking metaphorically. At the end of the hall, it turned toward a dull light glowing from somewhere. They headed hesitantly in that direction and came out into a small seating area filled with Donovians in brown jumpsuit uniforms. A group of four was sitting around a table with a board game stretched between them, one of their number gleefully reading through the rules while the others listened in riveted attention. Other Donovians were scattered in groups of twos and threes, talking, eating, and drinking.

Blandings pointed through a door to the outside, one of the original revolving doors previously ubiquitous on Sonus back when one needed a pressure suit to even step outside. "That should be our ship there, sir."

"That orb-shaped monstrosity? Or should I say, vaguely orb-shaped?"

The ship's plating was indeed severely dented in several places. The whole thing leaned a bit to one side. And something was venting out the side of the ship, probably something important, Pelham thought. "The thing looks like it's been struck by a meteorite ... repeatedly."

"I agree, sir, the craft is unlikely to be fresh off the assembly line."

"I'll say. I doubt if any of its builders are even still alive. I shouldn't be surprised if its last crew have all passed away as well, screaming in terror."

"It can't be as bad as that. It surely passed space port inspection."

Pelham regarded his valet doubtfully, remembering times when his own inspections of imports were less than painstaking and exhaustive. "Before I board that rust bucket, I'll need a bracing drink."

Pelham scanned around the small room and spotted a Donovian standing behind a counter. "That must be the publican there." He approached the bar. "Amurru fizz, if you please," he said, relying on translator bots to make his meaning clear to someone of another species.

Translator bots were in many ways the single most important technology in the galaxy. The microscopic nanobots attached to brains to translate any language, written or spoken, into the host's native language. Everyone in the known galaxy had them implanted, which made everything from travel to trade so much easier.

The fuzzy purple pear of a bartender stared at him a moment, then grabbed a mug and held it under a tap. The tankard began filling with a golden, frothy liquid.

"Excuse me, old sport, but I asked for an Amurru fizz," Pelham said.

The Donovian shrugged. "We don't have drinks like that. We only serve Donovian lager."

"But I don't want a Donovian lager."

The barkeep continued filling the tankard. "Sorry."

"Well, then cancel the order."

"Sorry, you ordered a drink, and I already started pulling it."

"But I didn't order that drink."

"It's the only drink we have."

"But …"

Blandings appeared at Pelham's side, and handed a payment stick to the barman. He took the lager and passed it to a Donovian in a smart uniform sitting at a nearby table. "Complements of Mr. Totleigh, who will be your guest today, Captain."

The officer stood, lager in hand, and walked toward Pelham, who was still standing at the bar looking dumbfounded. "Thank you for the drink. Mr. Totleigh, is it?"

"Hmm? Oh right. Pelham G. Totleigh. This is my man Blandings. You're most … um … welcome."

"Captain Kwint of the Donovian space cruiser *Proviso*. I recognize you from the description I was given. Young, well-dressed, eyes bulging."

"Bulging eyes? I don't know about that. Though I am known far and wide for my stylish togs."

"You must have been pretty anxious to ride with us," Kwint said.

"We were?" Pelham asked.

"I can only assume as much. As soon as we filed our flight plan, someone from your governor's office contacted us and asked if we could drop a couple of Haplors off on Vogus. Well, we were headed for the Chalawan system anyway for an asteroid survey, so I said why not? We can chrono jump to Vogus and then burn ions to the asteroid belt."

"Ah, well, um … glad it could all work out."

"Taking passengers is a new market for us. Normally, we transport only dry goods and fertilizer. We aren't a luxury boat, Mr. Totleigh, but we'll get you there. Welcome aboard … that is, when you actually board."

"Right. Say, I don't suppose you could dig up an Amurru fizz during the trip, could you?"

"Afraid not. No alcohol is allowed aboard the ship. But they serve a fine Donovian lager here." He held up the mug, smiling.

"Yes, well …"

At that moment, a badge on Kwint's chest chirped. He tapped it and said, "Kwint here." He turned and walked off.

Pelham said, "Well, Blandings, since we can't dredge up a proper drink here, I suppose we should board and find out precisely how far from luxury the next hour or so will be."

They moved through the revolving door into the chill air of Sonus. Gasping in the weak atmosphere, they crossed the tarmac to board the ball-like transport ship. At the top of the ramp, they were met by another uniformed, though younger-looking, Donovian, who stared at them with wild googly eyes and held up a stick-finger hand.

"Admittance to the ship is limited to crew only."

"We're passengers. I'm Pelham G. Totleigh, and this is Blandings."

"I was informed of no passengers."

"I have the information right here." Pelham pulled out his device and punched up the reservation.

The Donovian goggled at the screen, eyes rolling around once before again focusing on Pelham. "I'm sorry. That form doesn't give me authorization to allow you to board."

"It doesn't? Can you call somebody? I was speaking with Captain Kent only moments ago."

Blandings said, "I believe the name was Kwint, sir."

"Ah. Thank you. Yes, Captain Kwint. He welcomed us aboard and all that."

The googly eyes widened, growing even googlier. "The skipper welcomed you aboard without a completed form Y15-87A? Everyone has to fill out a form Y15-87A."

"Uh-huh. So if we fill out this Y-thingy, we can board?"

"Yes. Well, once it has proper approvals from the captain, and the Sonus space port authority, and the defense minister back on Donovio."

"Who what now?"

Blandings said, "Excuse me, sir, but you appear to be gawping."

"Gawping?"

"Yes, sir."

"He's right," said the space cadet blocking their entry. "I've never seen anyone's eyes bulge out that much."

"And well they may bulge out," Pelham said with emotion. "I have cause to gawp, to gape. I may even start to glare. See here, I need to get to Vogus, and I understood all arrangements had been made."

Even as he said it, Pelham realized he should have taken this obstacle to boarding as a gift from the universe. He could have told Aunt Agutha the Donovians had refused him passage and then proceeded to book more commodious accommodations. But in the heat of the moment, he was too annoyed at the hindrance to think of anything except getting past it.

A voice came from behind them. "What's the problem, Ensign?" It was Captain Kwint ascending the ship's ramp.

"These passengers don't have the proper forms filled out, sir," the ensign said.

"The forms have been filled out and approved, Ensign. I completed them myself last night. Enjoyable form, the Y15-87A."

"Oh unquestionably, sir, but I didn't find it on file."

"Look in the folder called Forms, then Transit Forms, then Completed Forms, Approved Completed Forms, Y-Forms, and then under my name."

"Ah, there it is. Sorry, Skipper." The ensign looked up at the Haplors. "If you gentlemen will follow me, I will show you to the ... um ... guest cabin."

It soon became clear the word cabin was something of a euphemism. To Pelham the word closet seemed more appropriate, or cupboard, or cubbyhole. In fact, he reckoned, the word cell wouldn't be too far afield. The floor was stacked with crates, the walls lined with pipes. One of the pipes was dripping a mysterious red ooze. The whole place had a moist, foul smell. There were no seats. Pelham perched on one of the suitcases. Blandings took another.

Pelham said, "So this is what it feels like to be cargo."

A voice sounded from a tinny overhead speaker. "Prepare for launch. All hands strap in."

"I say, Blandings, I don't suppose this luggage comes with built-in seatbelts."

"I'm afraid not, sir. Hopefully the ride will be smooth."

"You're quite the optimist, aren't you, Blandings?"

A small screen in the corner of the cabin flashed on. The camera angle appeared to be from the side of the ship looking out across the Sonus landscape onto a long orange track.

"What do you think the track is for, Blandings? I thought we were going up, not out, eh?"

His question was soon answered when the ball-like ship began rolling along the track. The camera spun with it, whipping around from a view of the track to a view of the ground, then an upside-down glimpse back at the space port, then a quick peek toward the dark sky before flashing another brief look down the track and then on around again.

Pelham and Blandings were thrown from their luggage. Blandings grabbed hold of a pipe. Pelham grabbed hold of Blandings. They stayed clutched together until the centrifugal force of the rolling took hold, pressing them firmly against the outside wall.

"Glad I had a light breakfast," Pelham said.

From brief glances ahead, they saw the track undulating up and down. The ship slowed on the ascents and accelerated on the descents. Cresting the last rise, the ship speeded toward an upturned ramp.

"Ah," said Blandings, "I understand now."

"What? What do you understand? What the blazes is going on?"

"You see, sir, the ship has been moving along this track, gaining momentum. Soon it will shoot off from the ramp into Tucana Canyon where —"

"Where it's nearly bottomless!" Pelham said, stress cracking in his voice.

The spacecraft shot off the end of the ramp into the thin Sonus air.

"Quite right, sir. However, I expect they will choose this moment to ignite the launch engines. Yes, there they are now. The impelling force of the ship coming off the ramp will enable it to achieve orbit while employing significantly less thrust. It is a fuel-efficient maneuver."

"Not so efficient on my nerves, I dare say."

The ship took to the skies and climbed toward space, though Pelham got the distinct impression that not all of the craft agreed with the plan. With the engines roaring, the whole ship began to shake and groan, at the height of which a bolt jiggled out from an overhead clamp and dropped with a *clank* to the floor between the two Haplors.

Pelham shook his head. "Bally Donovians."

Chapter 4

The Fabulous Pink Mingo

Once they achieved orbit over Sonus, the shaking of the transport ship faded away, as did gravity. Pelham floated from the floor. He swatted at a crate to grab hold but only managed to push off from it and sailed on toward the ceiling. Passing a beam, he wrapped arms and legs around it and clung on. Blandings, on the other hand, by remaining as motionless as possible, managed to hover serenely not far above the floor.

Pelham looked around, wild-eyed. "This weightlessness is all well and good for now, but without harness straps, what will happen when we land and gravity kicks back in?"

"Not to worry, sir." Blandings dug an arm into one of the suitcases floating beside him and came out holding two mag-belts. The valet slipped one on and let it pull him back to the floor. He tossed the other belt to Pelham, who snatched it from the air and affixed himself to the beam.

Moments later a buzz started up as the chrono drive kicked in to jump across the light-years. Only a few minutes after that, they heard an announcement. "We are now orbiting the planet Vogus. All crew, prepare for landing."

"What's this bally ball of a ship going to do when it lands?" Pelham asked. "Bounce a few times and roll all the way around Vogus?"

"We shall soon see, sir."

Which was a rare instance of Blandings being mistaken, at least about the soon part. While the Donovian crew ticked through checklists, followed procedures, and filled out in triplicate all necessary — and several unnecessary — forms, the ship orbited … and orbited.

Pelham continued to hang from the beam by the mag-belt. "You know, Blandings, this reminds me of a story about my great-grandfather. We Totleighs have always been pioneers, and before there were Haplor colonies in space, great-granddad Eustace explored the jungle of Tharsis."

"Indeed, sir."

"Indeed, indeed. And this one time he was chased through the bush by a roonaceros. Well, as he was running and looking over his shoulder at said beast hot on his heels, wouldn't you know, he stepped off a cliff edge. He would have been a goner, except he happened to land in the branches of a tree. The tree began swaying back and forth, back and forth all while old Eustace clung on for dear life."

"Ah, the rockets are firing now, sir. You might want to begin working your way down."

Pelham switched the mag-belt to minimum force and slowly spider-walked down the wall.

"What of your great-grandfather?" Blandings asked. "How did he manage the descent from the tree?"

Pelham blinked. "Hmm. Now that you mention it, that part of the story escapes me. Of course, you know, Haplors are great climbers."

"Quite true, sir."

"We are, I don't know, springier, I would say, compared to most species."

"Possibly, sir. I, for one, do not spring."

The spaceship settled on the surface of Vogus with a minimum of rolling, much to Pelham's relief. The hatch opened, and they stepped out of the ship to a cool, drizzling breeze. A pair of white suns shone through clouds in a greenish sky.

As colonies go, it didn't amount to much — not compared to the enormous settlement on Sonus. Inside a high concrete wall, a single street stretched away from the landing pad. Beyond the wall lay a gray and green plain of rock outcroppings dotted with patches of grass and the shapes of livestock. In the distance rose moody green hills.

What the colony lacked in size, it made up for in flash. The buildings were tall and stylish with stately fountains out front shooting water high into the air. And everywhere were flashing, electric signs.

"Where do we go, Blandings?"

"The information should be included in the travel arrangements, sir."

The Fabulous Pink Mingo

Pelham pulled out his device and punched up the information. "The Pink Mingo Hotel and Casino."

"There it is, sir." Blandings indicated a building glowing in pink lights with a sign over the door confessing to the name.

Inside, the hotel gleamed white and pink with thick pillars, lush potted plants, and people of all species milling about. Blandings led the way to a shiny, black counter and then stepped aside, allowing Pelham to assert his leadership.

Behind the counter stood a thin person, significantly taller than the Haplors. The person wore a green uniform, the jacket buttoned up to the neck. The person's skin, where showing, was as yellow as butter with green veining running through it. Instead of hair, the top of the head was crowned by a yellow bony crest with a dozen or more spiny points sweeping back.

The person regarded Pelham with deep set, baggy eyes and said in a monotone, "Welcome to the Pink Mingo. My name is Urdi the Unfortunate. I am your hotel and casino host. How may I help you today?"

"Urdi, you say?" Pelham asked.

"Urdi the Unfortunate."

"Ah. Well, Urdi —"

"The Unfortunate."

"You keep saying that."

The host stared vacantly. "It is my name."

"Quite a moniker. Doesn't exactly trip off the tongue, eh?"

Urdi sagged visibly. "Perhaps not."

"Um … I don't suppose you go by Urdi for short?"

"No, sir. Going by part of a name has the potential for confusion. You see, there is also Urdi the Honest, Urdi the Dishonest, Urdi the —"

'Golly. How many Urdis are on this list?"

"I am not sure of the total number. I can count them. There's Urdi the Honest, Urdi the Dishonest, Urdi the —"

"I get the picture. Urdi the Unfortunate then."

"That's it, sir."

"I mean, is that what your spouse calls you when you return home after a long day's work?"

"I am not fortunate enough to have a spouse, sir."

"Oh. Sorry, Urdi."

"The Unfortunate," Urdi inserted.

"I am un-mated myself. Personally, I rather prefer the single life. Not trying to minimize your feelings or anything, of course. Then again, I have Blandings here to look after me. But none of that is relevant. We have reservations at the hotel. The name is Pelham G. Totleigh, and this is my man Blandings, as you might have already inferred."

The unfortunate Urdi bobbed a heavy head in Blandings' direction and tapped on a device mounted on the counter. "According to this you are attending the G42 Interstellar Trade Conference."

"Indeed, we are ... or I am. Blandings will no doubt be using the time to improve his mind or some such." Pelham gazed around the elegant lobby. "Quite the place you have here, Urdi."

"The Unfortunate. Thank you, sir. Well, Lord Bugzee owns it. We Okcho are only employees."

"Ah. Well, then quite the place Lord Bugzee has."

The host took a deep breath and let it out wearily. Then, as if someone had pressed the play button on a vid screen, Urdi the Unfortunate launched into an uninflected, memorized monologue. "Everything before you," he swept out a hand mechanically, "is based upon eyewitness reports from the Grays who monitor Earth. There is an actual Pink Mingo hotel and casino on Earth in a city called Las Vogus. When Lord —"

"Pardon," Pelham said, interrupting him. "How did the Earthlings come to name a city after this planet?"

"Hmm?" Urdi looked confused. "Oh. That is believed to have happened by coincidence. However, the Grays' reports of Earth are sketchy. Odd people, the Grays. Now where was I?" Urdi began muttering, "Casino on Earth in a city called Las Vogus ... ah." Urdi's voice came up again to full volume. "When Lord Bugzee heard the name of the city, he decided to replicate the experience here on the similarly named planet Vogus, launching the Zurk colony years ago. Today we have all this."

Pelham waited a moment before speaking. "Um ... thank you. Are you finished?"

"I am, Mr. Totleigh."

"Didn't want to interrupt again."

"Much appreciated."

"One question, though. What *is* a mingo?"

"It is a bird."

"A bird?"

Urdi's head nodded slowly. "A bird is a vertebrate animal with wings and feathers generally with the ability to fly."

"Right, I know what a bird is."

Urdi pointed to a mural painted on a wall of a bright pink bird with legs and neck so long as to strain credulity. "Here is one rendered as art."

"That's a mingo?"

"It is pink, sir."

"I can see it is. Why are the legs and neck like that? So long, I mean. Could such a creature even exist? And if so, why?"

"The mingo definitely does exist, Mr. Totleigh."

"And why is the rummy creature standing on only one leg? If I had legs that long and skinny and tried getting by employing only the one, I'd fall over, eh, Blandings?"

"Quite possibly, sir."

"Take my word for it, Urdi, that beastie is mythical."

"Again, Mr. Totleigh, the name is Urdi the Unfortunate, and I promise you the mingo is native to Earth and so highly regarded among the locals that many Earthlings place statues of them in their yards."

"You don't say."

Urdi nodded solemnly in affirmation. "Now, how will we be handling payment, Mr. Totleigh?"

Pelham fished from a pocket a thumb-sized payment stick and handed it over.

"Very good." From somewhere beneath the counter, the host pulled out two black square screens about the size of Pelham's hand attached to elastic straps. "These will take care of everything you need. They will lead you to your suite, notify you of conference events, give you access to gaming in the casino, and allow you to rate our services to enable us to serve you better. The bracelets also serve as your room key, though to give you a more authentic Earth experience, the doors are made of real wood and swing on hinges."

"Hinges?"

"Ancient door technology. Still used on Earth, as I understand. They work by … well, you'll see them in your room. Now, what amount would you like me to load on the bracelets?"

"For what?"

"For gaming, food service, amenities. All bets are placed with funds pre-loaded into the bracelets. All winnings are credited there. They also handle food and drink payments."

"Ah. Can I get the funds back at the end of my stay?"

"Yes, you can. Or leftover credits can be redeemed at our gift shop for a wide range of souvenirs." Urdi waved an indifferent arm toward a tiny shop behind him where a shirt emblazoned with the picture of a mingo hung in the window.

"Uh-huh. Well, I'm not sure what Blandings would think about that." Pelham glanced at the valet and saw him tremble.

"What amount would you like me to load from your payment stick?" Urdi asked again.

Pelham hesitated. If he spent too much of the colony's funds on this junket, Aunt Agutha would go off on him like a charging crocoraptor. "Oh I don't know. One hundred?"

Urdi raised a green eyebrow.

"Two hundred?" Pelham ventured.

"Most guests start out with three hundred, Mr. Totleigh."

"Three hundred bills?"

At that moment, the sound of excited electronics and loud cheering erupted from another room.

Urdi said in a deadpan, "Someone has just won in the casino. The excitement never stops at the Pink Mingo."

Pelham's insides began to vibrate. His lips flickered into a smile. "Sounds thrilling. Well then, three hundred it is."

Urdi the Unfortunate placed the bracelets on top of the tablet device and tapped. The device made a sort of sad *wah-wah* sound.

Urdi frowned. "Oh dear. I appear to be having difficulty getting these to load with your information." He tapped again and received another *wah-wah*. "This always happens to me." He flipped the bracelets over and tried again and again. "I am truly sorry for the delay, gentlemen. I don't understand why —" The bracelets dinged. With a relieved shake of the head, Urdi handed them over. "Again, sorry."

"Quite all right my good ... my ..." Pelham wasn't sure if Urdi was male or female, or if indeed Okcho had gender as such. Someone had once told him about a species with seven genders. He couldn't remember which one it was.

The Fabulous Pink Mingo

Pelham's mind floated away, wondering how seven genders even worked. Urdi cleared his throat, and Pelham's mind snapped back to the present. "Um ... my good person."

"Arrows will appear on the bracelet screen to guide you to your room."

A red glowing arrow on Pelham's bracelet pointed to the right. "Well, thank you, Urdi."

"The Unfortunate."

As Pelham and Blandings stepped away from the counter, their bracelets vibrated. A message popped up on the screens: *Urdi the Unfortunate*. Under the name flashed the outline of five mingos.

"What's this, Blandings?"

"It would appear, sir, the intent is to provide you with a method for rating Mr. The Unfortunate's service."

"Oh. Ah. You mean how well the chap did for me."

"Precisely, sir."

"What do these implausible birds have to do with it?"

"One presumes, sir, you express the rating by selecting the number of mingos, five of them representing excellent service."

"Well, Urdi was a bit of a wet blanket, what? But I'm guessing he probably gets paid based on these rating whatsits. Wouldn't want to ding him. He seems to have it tough enough as it is." Pelham slid his finger along the line of birds, lighting up the whole flock in pink.

They followed the arrows on their bracelets through a doorway into a long, noisy room with a high ceiling. The middle of the room was filled with tables where Okcho in crisp uniforms, a match to Urdi's except in black, served up games to well-dressed people of all species. Around the outside of the room, other more casually dressed and mainly older people sat in front of brightly lit machines, repeatedly pressing big red buttons. A sign on the wall above them read: *SLOTS*.

"I say, Blandings, I thought these bracelet gizmos were going to lead us to our suite."

"I suspect, sir, the path to our quarters leads through the gaming hall."

"Daft layout, don't you think?"

"Perhaps not from an economic standpoint. I imagine it is meant to entice one to play the games."

"Tell me, Blandings, do you ever try your hand at games of chance?"

"Rarely, sir. Typically, the odds greatly favor the house."

They proceeded through the casino, Pelham's interest drawn to one of the tables where, with an excited *bloop-bloop-bloop-bloop*, the bracelet of a blue-skinned Rhegedian began flashing. The Rhegedian cheered and ordered drinks for everyone at the table. Pelham ogled the scene with interest.

Their bracelets led them out a door on the other side of the casino to a line of transparent tubes.

"Oh no, Blandings, not pneumatic lifts. First Donovians, now pneumatic lifts."

"Such appears to be the case, sir."

"Of all the ways to move vertically through a building, this has to be the most nerve-racking. Give me a solid elevator floor any day."

"I agree, sir."

"Or an escalator."

"It is said the Delusians employ a catapult mechanism, though I understand the device does require a substantial amount of padding to be added to walls and flooring."

"It might still be better than being sucked up through one of these ruddy tubes like something going through a drinking straw."

"Nevertheless, this conveyance appears to be our only option for getting to …" Blandings checked his bracelet. "… floor thirty-five."

"Thirty-five, Gort help us."

Blandings sent the luggage up first. They watched it shoot up the cylinder with a *whoosh*. Then, as Blandings slid into one tube, Pelham stepped into another. A hiss began, building in intensity until Pelham shot upwards, air breezing past his face, fur standing on end. The suction slowed as he approached their floor, and Pelham stepped out with a shaky gait.

They found the suite well-appointed with a common sitting room, kitchenette, and two bedrooms. Pelham dropped onto the couch to recover while Blandings began unpacking. Something beeped, and an unwelcome apparition appeared on the wall screen — the face of Aunt Agutha.

Chapter 5

Pelham is Introduced to Jack Black

From the screen, Aunt Agutha scowled at Pelham with a glare of annoyance. "Hmm. Lying about, I see."

"What? No," Pelham said. "I haven't lied about anything. I've been entirely truthful with you ... for ages and ages."

"I meant, you dimwit, that there you are lying about in your suite when there is work to do. Have you contacted the Bononian delegate about the trade deal?"

"We only just arrived, Aunt Agutha."

"Nonsense! What took you so long?"

"What took us this long was being sent on a blasted Donovian ship. Those blighters have to fill out forms merely to request permission to fill out other forms. They have procedures specifying in detail how they need to follow other procedures. They orbited Vogus so many times today their ship could have been re-classified as a space station. Not to mention the atrocious accommodations we had to endure. Blandings and I were treated like cargo."

Pelham noted with irritation a momentary smile flitting across Aunt Agutha's face. "Yes, yes, Nephew. We all know about Donovians. But now that you're there, what have you accomplished?"

Pelham stared at the screen nearly too dumfounded to say anything. "I ... I found my room."

"And I am sure for you it was quite the accomplishment, though you probably needed Blandings' assistance. Now get to work. Contact the Bononian. Secure that trade deal. And learn something from the conference."

The screen went blank.

"Blandings!"

The valet glided in from one of the bedrooms. "Sir?"

Pelham flapped a hand toward the blank display. "Aunt Agutha. She materialized on the screen, seemingly for the sole purpose of berating me."

"Yes, sir. By chance I overheard the exchange."

"She was a bit ... I don't know ... overwrought, don't you think, Blandings?"

"Thunderous, one might say, sir."

"Indeed, Blandings. I am shaken by the encounter. Any chance of you scrounging up an Amurru fizz for me?"

"Of course, sir." Blanding set to work on the drink.

"Now how do I find this Bononian delegate, Blandings?"

"The name, I believe, was Emer, sir."

"Yes, Emer. How do I dig up this chap?"

A lilting voice sounded from Pelham's bracelet. "Dig? Would you like to visit an archaeological site? A team is currently on Vogus from Zurk to uncover ruins of an ancient Okcho burial mound."

Pelham jumped from the couch and gawked at the armband. "I say, I didn't know this rummy thing could talk."

The voice said, "I am VICTOR, the Visitor Intelligent Concierge to Order Recreation, Refreshment, and Relaxation."

Pelham said, "They certainly packed a lot into that one R."

"That is true, and I have a lot of service packed into my programming. I am available to assist you in booking entertainment and dining and to answer any questions you may have about the planet and the Pink Mingo. I am programmed to serve."

Pelham's eyebrows shot up like pneumatic lifts. "Serve, you say? I don't suppose you could help me locate another hotel guest, could you, VICTOR?"

"I am allowed to locate other members of your party. For example, guest Blandings is northeast of your present location in the same room as you."

"Ah, well, I already knew that. I was trying to chase down a fellow attendee of the trade conference, a Bononian chap named Emmett."

"Emer, sir," said Blandings.

"Emer."

"I am sorry," VICTOR said. "For security reasons, I cannot provide information about other guests."

"Oh, come on. Be a sport." On occasion Pelham had cajoled chums with similar words and a friendly nudge. His elbow instinctively shot out, even though this time he was dealing with an un-nudge-able, disembodied AI.

"I *am* sorry, Mr. Totleigh, but the request is contrary to my programming."

"Can't do it, eh?"

"Well, I have the ability, of course."

"It would help me out awfully."

"I cannot."

"You would be doing a great service."

"Well … I *am* programmed to serve.

"Yes?"

"Here's what I can do. I can give you a tiny hint. Twenty seconds ago, Emer came into some money."

Pelham scrunched up his face. "How does that help?"

Blandings said, "The casino, sir."

"Ah, the casino."

VICTOR said, "I did not say that, Mr. Totleigh."

Pelham tapped the side of his nose. "Most assuredly, VICTOR. I did not hear it from you. Thanks loads. Blandings, I'll be popping off now."

Pelham downed his drink and headed out of the suite, the heavy wooden door slamming behind him and giving him a start. Hazarding another trip through the pneumatic lift, he landed back on the ground floor and strode into the casino, looking around for a Bononian. Which was when he realized he had never met a Bononian and didn't know what they looked like. He didn't know if they had feathers or fins.

"Say, VICTOR, what can you tell me about the appearance of Bononians?" he asked.

The melodious voice answered, "Bononians, from the planet Bononia, are a species of mammal with copper-colored skin. They have hair on the tops of their heads along with eyebrows and eyelashes. They have four fingers on each hand. In terms relative to your species, their average height is one-and-a-half times that of a typical Haplor."

"Much obliged, VICTOR."

Pelham scanned the immense room but saw no one fitting the description. He set off on a ramble around the outside of the gaming tables, head swiveling left and right. He scrutinized the row of people mechanically pressing the red buttons at the glowing, beeping slot machines along the wall. No Bononians there. He passed a food court where a group of white-feathered people were eating seeds from bowls.

He had made one complete circuit of the room without success when he came to the bar area. A barstool, he thought, might give him a better view of the place. He climbed on one and scanned the room.

A voice behind him said, "What can I pour you?"

Pelham turned back to the bar to find an Okcho. This one was not much taller than himself. "A drink? You know, a stiff one might be just the thing to buck me up. Amurru fizz, please."

The bartender moved to prepare the drink while Pelham watched. "Pelham G. Totleigh," he said with a nod.

"Shay the Shorter." This Okcho had the same yellow skin as Urdi the Unfortunate, though this one wore a seemingly younger face, and the green veins were thinner, less pronounced. Pelham wondered if the green was somehow a function of age.

"Shay the Shorter? That's your name?"

Shay nodded. Pelham also had a strong suspicion this Okcho was female. The body was leaner than Urdi's, the movements more fluid. Then again, that could also be age. Aunt Agutha, whom he always assumed was female, was built like a barrel and moved like a bot in desperate need of servicing.

"Shorter than what, if I may ask?"

"Shorter than Shay the Tall. Not as short as Shay the Shortest."

"Interesting. Did they line up all the Shays to make the determination?"

The bartender laughed. "Nothing as formal as that." She — if she was a she — slid the glass across the bar to him.

"What's the damage?"

"It's on your bracelet."

Pelham checked his wrist and was shocked to see fifteen bills deducted from his total. Another message flashed on the screen: *Shay the Shorter* with the same five pink birds he had used to rate Urdi. Irked by the high price of the drink, he came close to punching in a mere four-bird rating, but he figured the price wasn't the bartender's fault. He gave Shay a full five mingos, downed the drink, and moved on.

He decided next to make a zig-zag circuit through the tables. As he was passing one, someone from the table called out, "Jack Black!"

Pelham is Introduced to Jack Black

Pelham twisted around. A woman in a long sequined dress sat at the table. She was one of the furless mammalian species, her skin reddish brown.

"Sorry," Pelham said, "you may have me confused with someone else. Pelham G. Totleigh is the name, not Jack Black."

The woman laughed. "Jack Black is the name of the game and something you yell when you hit a perfect score."

"Astounding."

"Do you know the game?"

"I do not."

"I'll teach you."

Pelham stepped to the crescent-shaped table beside the woman. Opposite her, in the center of the table, an Okcho female — or so he reckoned — shuffled a huge stack of rectangular pieces of cardboard.

"What are those?" Pelham asked.

"The cards," the woman in sequins said.

With lithe movements, the Okcho slipped two of the cardboard pieces to each of the players.

"Odd-looking cards," Pelham said, more used to the round variety, "and decorated with all those red and black doodads."

The woman in sequins said, "The cards with an Earthling's face on them are worth ten points. The ones with a single big shape are worth either one or eleven, your choice. The others with numbers are worth whatever the number says. You try to score as close to twenty-one as you can without going over."

Pelham inspected his companion's cards. One was a five. The other showed a bearded chap wearing a crown and holding a sword behind his head. Dodgy place to hold a sword, Pelham thought. Not an ideal defensive position, or so he assumed from his limited knowledge of fencing.

"Why is it called Jack Black?"

The Okcho dealer said, "The game is named after an Earthling vid actor. The story is that he invented it to help pass the time on vid shoots. Or at least that's what the Grays told us. They brought back all these games from Earth. Of course, I don't know if I swallow everything the Grays say. The way they tell it, Earthlings serve another species, a small furry creature called a gat, spending their own money to feed and take care of their gats for no apparent reason. Now is that any way for a supposedly intelligent species to act? Hello, by the way. I'm Kiz the Chatty."

"I'll say, you are," Pelham said.

Kiz nodded to the players. "Place your bets."

As the players tapped wagers into their bracelets, holographic piles of chips appeared on the table in front of them.

The Okcho dealer looked to the first player, a short alien with a dark round head dominated by huge white eyes with tiny black pupils. Pelham recognized the species as Axan. "Card?"

"Hit me," the Axan said in a pinched, high-pitched voice.

Pelham's head jerked to face the copper-skinned woman. "He wants to be struck? What kind of game is this?"

"That's Jack Black lingo. It means he wants another card."

The dealer issued the Axan a card displaying a seven. With his other two cards, it added up to twenty-three. The player's pile of holographic chips evaporated. The Axan shook its dark round head and walked away. The dealer then turned to the woman in sequins.

"Okay," she whispered to Pelham. "I have fifteen right now, which doesn't generally win. But if I pull another card, and it's anything over six, then I go over twenty-one and lose." She glanced at the dealer. "Be gentle with me, please, Kiz."

"Kiz the Chatty," the dealer said with a smile. "I'll be as gentle as I can, sweetie." The dealer pushed a card to the woman and flipped it over to reveal a four.

Pelham ran through the math. "That's nineteen. Is that good?"

The woman in sequins chewed her lower lip. "We'll soon find out. It's not bad."

"What about you?" the dealer asked the last player, a green Dieren female who towered over everyone and barely fit under the tall ceiling. She had eighteen showing and refused a card.

Two cards sat in front of the dealer. One of them displayed a ten. The other was face down. Kiz now turned it over to reveal a seven. "I hold on anything above sixteen. Your nineteen wins."

The woman in the sequined dress bounced in her seat. Her bracelet lit up and made the *bloop-bloop-bloop-bloop* sound. She gave Pelham a hug, leaving him slightly dazed.

"Hors d'oeuvre?" Pelham became aware of an Okcho at his elbow holding a tray of something that smelled delicious.

Pelham is Introduced to Jack Black

"Don't mind if I do." Pelham picked up one of the goodies and took a bite. It tasted as wonderful as it smelled. He halted mid-chew as it dawned on him this snack would likely incur a charge. He checked his bracelet. Five bills! Five bills, for a couple of bites? A rating request popped up, and he gave the Okcho server five mingos. Despite the price being outrageous, he had to admit the food and the service had both been excellent.

Kiz the Chatty scooped the used cards into a pile and swept them into a box beside her.

"Thank you for the lesson," Pelham said to the woman in sequins. "I should move on. I'm looking for a chap."

"Stay and play. You're my good luck charm."

"Well, I really —"

"We have the spot the Axan left open."

Kiz the Chatty chimed in. "Come on. Try your luck. Everybody has fun at my table."

"Oh … I suppose it wouldn't hurt." Pelham sat in the vacated chair.

"What's your name, love?" Kiz asked.

"Pelham G. Totleigh."

"Welcome to my Jack Black table, Pelham G. Totleigh." She dealt him a ten and an eight, his sequined friend a six and a four, and the Dieren a face card and a seven. The one card of Kiz's that he could see showed a bearded face.

"Ooh, good hands all around," Kiz the Chatty said. "Place your bets, everybody."

Pelham needed a moment to think this through. He drummed his fingers on the table.

"It's hard to decide sometimes, isn't it?" Kiz the Chatty said. "I always tell people to go with their gut."

"My gut?"

"You know, instinct, intuition, what are you feeling?"

"I'm feeling a bit stumped." He decided to venture ten bills and tapped the wager into his bracelet. The hologram of a single green chip with the picture of a mingo bird and the number ten appeared beside his cards.

"Card?"

"Golly. I don't know. I have eighteen at present, which means … um … I could only take a three or less. Am I right with the math, there?"

"You are," Kiz said.

"Then perhaps I had best not."

"Suit yourself, sugar."

"I'll take a card," his sequined friend said. She received an eight, giving her the same eighteen as Pelham."

The Dieren said, "hit me." She was dealt a six to put her out.

"Okay," Kiz said. "Let's see what I have." She turned over her other card. Two cardboard faces now stared back at her. "Dealer wins with twenty. Too bad, Mr. Totleigh. You were so close. You'll get 'em next time."

Pelham grinned. "You know, I think I might."

Kiz the Chatty dealt again, this time passing Pelham a picture of a feminine face and another with a person holding a spear. He didn't know what the different faces were supposed to represent, but he knew in Jack Black they meant twenty, which was a good thing indeed. The other players were dealt totals in the mid-teens. Feeling optimistic about his chances, Pelham tapped in a wager of thirty bills and when offered, refused a card.

The woman in sequins tapped the table and received a nine, putting her over twenty-one. The Dieren stared down at Pelham's twenty and then bobbed her head to the dealer. She received a seven, also going over.

Kiz the Chatty, already showing a ten, flipped up a nine. Pelham's bracelet went *bloop-bloop-bloop-bloop* and flashed a message saying he had won enough to cover his prior loss plus the drink and hors d'oeuvre. His new friend gave him another hug.

Which was when Pelham noticed each of her hands had four fingers. "I say, are you Bononian?"

"I am."

"You wouldn't happen to know a fellow going by the handle of Emer, would you?"

Chapter 6

The Exhilarating World of Trade Negotiations

The woman in sequins grinned down at the little Haplor. "Emer? Well, of course, I know him. He's me. Or she's me … and not a fellow."

Red flushed into Pelham's face. "Oh! Ah. Frightfully sorry. I seem to have been tragically misinformed. I've been looking for you. No wonder I didn't pick *him* out from the crowd. My name is Pelham G. Totleigh. Wait. Did I previously say that?" Shaking off the embarrassment, he produced a formal bow.

She bowed back. "No need to apologize. I should have given you my name sooner. Are you from Haplor?"

"From Sonus, a Haplor colony."

"I'm supposed to work on a trade agreement with someone from Sonus."

"Ah yes. I'm your contact, and said agreement is the exact wheeze I wanted to discuss with you."

"Wheeze?"

"Well, not a wheeze as such, you know. The scheme, the plan, the piece of business, I should say."

"Um … right. I have a draft agreement prepared. Would you care to join me in my suite to work on it?"

"Doesn't sound as enjoyable as Jack Black, but seeing as I am under strict orders to conclude this agreement, yes."

As they stepped away from the gaming table, their bracelets lit up with rating requests. Emer gave Kiz the Chatty a full five mingos and noted Pelham doing the same.

Kiz called after them, "Thanks, folks. You have a great evening now."

As they approached the pneumatic lifts, Emer said, "Floor thirty. Meet you there." She stepped into a lift and *whooshed* away. She waited for him at the top and led him to her room where she waved toward the sitting area. "Have a seat. Tea?"

"Gosh, yeah."

While replicating it, she caught her reflection in a mirror and realized with alarm that her attire was altogether too flashy for a business meeting. Should she excuse herself and change? No, that didn't sound professional either. This was her first big assignment, and she couldn't escape the feeling of being adrift at sea. She tried to think, but all she could come up with was an image in her mind of her mother staring at her with a disappointed frown.

What must the Haplor be thinking, invited to her room with her dressed in sequins? She glanced at Pelham and was both gratified and somewhat puzzled to notice that he didn't seem to be thinking anything. He was perched on her couch with a sort of dazed expression on his face. Oh well, she thought. For all she knew, this might be business attire for Haplors. The replicator dinged, and she served the tea."

"Thanks awfully," he said, as she sat in a chair opposite the couch.

"I think you're the first Haplor I have met."

"And you are the first Bononian I've known. You know, you look a dashed lot like Earthlings … or at least the one Earth person I met. More or less the same size, though I think their ears sit a bit lower on the head. And I'm almost certain the one I saw had an extra finger or so. Of course, he was male … I think. It is possible the males might feasibly have extra digits."

As he spoke, Emer found herself gawking at his bulging eyes. "Is there something wrong with your eyes, Mr. Totleigh?"

He blinked a couple of times. "What about them?"

Tingles of embarrassment swept up the back of her neck and across her cheeks. "What? Nothing. Forget I said anything." She grabbed up her tablet device. "Let's get to business. May I send you my draft, Mr. Totleigh? I've been reading up on Sonus. I think I've included all the goods and services we might be able to supply for you."

"Call me Pelham, please. And by all means, send away." He pulled out his own device. A *ding* sounded on both gadgets. He turned his eyes toward the screen, stared, then squinted and bit a lip. "Hmm. Bilateral Bononia Sonus Free

Trade Agreement. There's a mouthful for you. And potentially a mistake right off the bat. We don't intend to trade for free. I assume there will be charges on both sides."

"Charges? No ... um ... free trade means without unnecessary restrictions. You see —"

"And I don't know about bilaterals. I'm fairly certain we have never imported bilaterals, nor do we need them. What are the bally things anyway? Are they those two-wheeled contraptions people ride around on? What we're looking for is fertilizer, agricultural equipment, clothing, and what not."

Emer opened her mouth, then closed it again. "Um ... yes. We can supply those. They're in the document."

"Excellent then. We're making progress already. Pelham scrolled through the draft, his long finger flicking up and down. "Hmm. Tariffs. Investment. Intellectual property. Uh-huh." He blinked at the screen. "Uh-huh."

"Maybe it would be better if we talked it through," Emer said.

"Right. Except ... um ... I'm not sure where we should start. For instance, listen to this little gem. 'On the request of either party, the participants shall consult for the purpose of considering the reduction or elimination of customs duties as set out in Schedules 1-15. An agreement between parties to reduce a customs duty on any class of product shall supersede any duty rate or staging category determined pursuant to said schedules for such product when approved by both parties in accordance with their respective applicable legal procedures.'" Pelham looked up from the screen with a blank expression.

Emer said, "Did you have a concern about that clause?"

"Well, my initial concern is, um ... what in the moon does it mean?"

"Hmm?"

"Tell you what. Would you mind terribly if I summoned my man Blandings? He's exceedingly skilled with words, and there certainly are a lot of them in the document."

"That would be fine. The more thoughts we can pull in on the BiBoSo FTA, the better."

"The who now?"

"The Bilateral Bononia Sonus Free Trade Agreement. The BiBoSo FTA. That's what we're calling it back at the office."

"Ah ... right. The BiBo-whatsit." Pelham looked down and said, "Blandings," triggering an audio connection between their linked translator bots.

Emer saw Pelham nod, though she couldn't hear the response of this Blandings person, obviously a close associate, probably an assistant in the import office.

"What ho, Blandings," Pelham said. "I located the Bononian bloke, and much to my surprise, he's female. I mean, she's female. Quite a pleasant person as well and not too shabby at Jack Black from all appearances. We've been going over her ideas for the trade thingamabob, and, well, the long and short of it is I wouldn't mind letting you take a crack at it. It uses a great number of oversized words, and I know how much you enjoy that sort of thing. Wondering if you might stop by soon as poss, and all that."

Pelham nodded again, then looked to Emer. "What's the room number here?"

A few minutes later the door dinged. Emer called, "Come in." Nothing happened. She tried again. "Open." More nothing. "Oh! I keep forgetting about these Earth-style doors." She hopped up from the chair and swung the door open.

Blandings glided in while Pelham handled the introductions.

Emer asked, "Mr. Blandings, what is your role in the Sonus Office of Imports?"

Pelham made a nervous chuckle. "Oh, no official capacity. Blandings is my valet, my gentleman's gentleman."

"You want your valet to advise you on a trade agreement? You want the person who presses your clothes to set economic policy for your entire colony?"

"Don't be misled by Blanding's station in life. He's as smart as they come. Many a time he has come up with the perfect plan for extracting me or one of my friends from the soup."

"Soup?"

"You know. A predicament, a dilemma, a fix."

"I see," she said, telling a fib.

"There was this one time when my pal Corky had accidentally got himself engaged to a girl named Muriel Belcher. What a specimen she was. Had a voice like a foghorn. Well ... would that be proper to say, Blandings?"

"Unlikely sir, but the simile does to a degree fit."

"I'll say. Well to make a long story shortish, Blandings came up with a scheme to entice the Belcher female to call off the engagement herself. And thus, old Corky was saved."

Emer looked back and forth from one Haplor to another. "How does one get accidentally engaged?"

Pelham chuckled. "That's a story a bit too convoluted for present circs. My point, though, is I often rely on the old Blandings noggin. He and I are of one mind … and Blandings has most of it."

The valet said, "I have an extensive range of interests, Ms. Emer, trade policy being one of them."

"I see," she said, another lie. However, her government had instructed her to negotiate with the Sonus delegation, and this Blandings appeared to be taking that role. She bobbed her head and returned to her seat.

Pelham sat back on the couch and handed off the tablet. "Dig in, Blandings. Emer, I don't suppose you have any more of that excellent tea, what?"

While Emer replicated more tea, Blandings set to work on the document. He would read a section, then look up and slowly nod his head. He highlighted sections, added notes in the margins, crossed out entire paragraphs.

Pelham's eyes began to blink and grow heavy. Before long they quit opening at all. His head dropped to his chest. This Haplor was a funny little fellow, Emer thought, but likable and seemingly without pretension.

***

Sometime later Pelham stirred at the sound of voices. He opened his eyes to find Emer and Blandings going back and forth on the terms of the agreement.

"Now," Blandings said, "on the amount of fertilizer stipulated in the agreement, I am not positive Sonus can agree to purchase as much as that. It depends in large measure on the pace of the soil enrichment process."

Emer said, "We can lower the required amount, but not at the stated rate schedule. However, with a fifteen percent price increase, we can let you order as much or as little as you want. If you eliminate the tariff entirely, we can make it ten percent."

"Would you commit to the purchase of hydroponically grown meido fruit in lieu of cash payments?"

"We could agree to payment half in meido fruit and half in galactic bills."

Pelham's lids fluttered shut again. Everything seemed to be in hand. He drifted off into quite a nice dream about shenanigans with his chums back on Sonus.

It was Blandings' voice that ended the dream. "Excuse me, sir."

Pelham opened his eyes to find Blandings standing over him.

"Hmm? How did we do, Blandings?"

"If you are referring to the trade negotiation, sir, I am pleased to report significant progress. There are a few matters left to iron out."

"Well, ironing is one thing you excel at, Blandings."

"It is kind of you to say, sir."

"What are these sticking points, if I might ask?"

"I believe it best, sir, for us to discuss the details back in our suite."

Pelham pulled himself up straighter on the couch and glanced at Emer. "Yes, yes. I suppose we should be going in any case."

"Yes, sir. There is also the opening session of the conference this evening."

"Ah. Right. I should make myself presentable."

"Indeed, sir."

Pelham smiled at Emer and stood. "If you will excuse us for the nonce, we will respond with further proposals."

Emer stood. "I look forward to it. Thank you, Mr. Totleigh, and you too, Mr. Blandings."

Returning to their rooms, Pelham said, "Blandings, where in the moon did you pick up on all that gobbledygook about tariffs and quotas and suchlike?"

"I have, on occasion, sir, out of curiosity and a desire for personal improvement, perused materials you bring home from your office. I hope I haven't overstepped my purview."

"What? No, Blandings, by all means, carry on. It appears a fellow needs to possess a goodish bit more behind the forehead than I do to deal with such notions. My current bedtime reading, as you may know, is an amusing little tale called *The Adventures of Bongo*, which follows the exploits of the aforementioned Bongo, who is a Fornaxi youngling, along with her pet tumpta. I found the prose in this trade agreement decidedly more complex. I don't mind saying, I was … baffled, even befuddled."

"Such is often the case with legal phraseology, sir."

"Tell me, what are the remaining points of contention in the agreement?"

"The first, sir, is exclusivity. The Bononians wish to be our sole supplier for all agricultural inputs and equipment."

"Did you explain to her the Haplor home world requires us to purchase a certain percentage of goods from them as a condition for their continued support?"

"I did, sir."

"How did she respond?"

"She said she looked forward to our counterproposal."

"Did she now? Anything else?"

"Yes, sir. There is the method of transport. They would like all shipments to be sent on Bononian ships. We would, of course, prefer to use Sonus ships when possible."

"Is that the entire list?"

"A few other minor issues remain. There is work still to be done."

"Do you think we can come to terms?"

"I feel sure of it, sir."

"Splendid. Then apply that prodigious bean of yours to working out a compromise. Between you and me, it's all I can do to get the right number of whatsits delivered on time. Can't say I truly care about the details and fine print. I'd rather just eat the meal than worry about all the ingredients, if you take my meaning?"

"I do, sir."

Pelham took a shower of real water, which was a treat coming, as he did, from a world where a lack of atmosphere and ground water made sonic showers the norm. He dressed and was giving himself a final once over in the mirror when Blandings entered.

"Most stylish, sir."

"Thank you. I suppose I'm ready. My evening will likely be composed of a cheap dinner followed by a lengthy lineup of boring speakers."

"It is fortunate then, sir, that this afternoon you were able to get in a nap."

Chapter 7

Suspicious Minds

Pelham left the suite, his bracelet guiding him through the casino, back to the lobby, and then down a corridor to a conference room filled with a long table set for dinner. He spotted Emer beside an empty seat, now changed from the sequined gown to a more conservative red number. He headed for the vacant chair.

"Hullo-ullo-ullo. May I join you? Friendly face among strangers and all that, what?"

She smiled and gestured toward the chair. "Exciting, isn't it? Being here with all these people from all these worlds." She shook her head. "Sorry. You can probably tell this is my first trade conference. You're likely an old hand at these things."

"Oh, not really. They don't let me out much. Work, work, work, you know."

A person with a flat, almost non-existent nose and short horns sticking out of long, scraggly hair slid into the seat on the other side of Pelham. "Hi." The person slowly nodded several times before continuing. "I'm Syd Duncil from Cunedda."

"Pelham G. Totleigh from Sonus. Call me Pelham. Should I call you Syd or Duncil or Syd Duncil?"

"That's a matter of opinion. Some people call me Duncil ... or Duncilrino ... or Your Duncilness."

"Quite the range of options there. Um ... Duncil, this is Emer from Bononia."

"Greetings," Emer said.

"Hey." Duncil closed his eyes, grabbed the lapels of his floppy sweater, and took a deep breath.

"Are you all right?" Pelham asked.

The Cuneddan opened his eyes. "Yes, I am, as it turns out. It appears this is where the universe wants me right now."

"The universe told you that ... just this instant?"

"Something like that, man."

Two Mucs with stubby noses and shaggy hair and beards took seats on the opposite side of the table. The other spaces filled in with Arsawans, Delusians, and a few other species Pelham couldn't name.

Okcho servers entered, gracefully flowing through the room as they bore platters of plates to the guests. They served each person a different dish according to the tastes of the various species. Emer was brought a leafy salad. The Mucs were given a dish of a purple, oily kind of rice. Pelham received fruit and nuts. Duncil was served a brown, round griddle cake with syrup soaking into a grid of indentions across the top.

Pelham stared at it. "Is that a waffle?"

"It is," Duncil said. "They are most sublime."

"Don't I know it? I've had waffles, but I thought they were Earthling food."

"Oh, they are. They were only recently introduced to Cunedda after a planet evaluation mission returned from Earth."

"Is Earth's status being re-evaluated?" Pelham hoped to visit the planet sometime. Lifting the quarantine would mean he could travel there without taking the chance of getting called before some petty galactic alliance official to explain himself.

Duncil shook his head and ran a hand through his long hair. "It was, but the mission ran into trouble with the Earthlings or something. The planet remains off limits for now. But their waffles have taken Cunedda by storm."

"I can imagine. Delightful dish. I had one once. I've even met an Earthling."

"You did?" Duncil leaned over and whispered. "What do they look like?"

"Compared to you? More nose, but less in the horn department. The fellow I met was an excellent chap."

The Axan who earlier had lost at Jack Black now stepped up to a raised platform at the head of the table and rang a small bell. Conversation stopped and all heads swiveled in that direction.

"Good evening, trade delegates, and welcome to the G42 Interstellar Trade Conference. I am Jasper Jadarite, your conference chair. For the next few days, the galaxy is one, and we of the participating forty-two worlds are all siblings." The Axan bobbed his dark, globe-like head, blinking his huge eyes.

Pelham said to Emer from behind a hand, "The galaxy one? Not likely. The Oecanthus keep to themselves, the Snuuls dislike us Haplors for reasons I can't fathom, and nobody trusts the Thomians."

Emer responded with a shush.

"Before I deliver my keynote address," Jasper said with a pompous grin, "I want to introduce our host, the owner of the fantastic Pink Mingo Hotel and Casino, Lord Bugzee."

Pelham slouched back in his chair in resignation. The doors to the banquet hall were flung open by two waiting Okcho, and in walked — or perhaps waddled would be a better word — a, well, how to describe this person?

A pear past its prime sprang to Pelham's mind. The Grays had introduced pears to Haplor after one of their survey missions to Earth, and Pelham had once seen one that had apparently been forgotten on a windowsill for far too long, its skin rippling and folding as the pear began to collapse down on itself. Yes, take that pear and color it gray, stick on a couple of chubby arms and legs, then on top of it place a head about two sizes too small with a long floppy proboscis and two sizeable black eyes.

How somebody could look like that and still wear a self-satisfied expression was a mystery to Pelham, but somehow Lord Bugzee managed it. He tottered to the stage, struggled up the step, and turned to face the delegates. His head rotated left and right to take them all in, so far to the left and right, in fact, it made Pelham's neck hurt to watch it. Could this bloke turn his head all the way around? If so, Pelham didn't want to see it. Different species were always … well, so extraordinarily different.

"Welcome to Vogus," Lord Bugzee said in a deep, smug voice, "the jewel of the Greater Zurk Protectorate. We are proud of what we have built here on Vogus, taking a backward planet and turning it into a thriving world where the native Okcho can find employment, and you from many worlds can come to meet together and enjoy our fabulous Earth-themed facilities. I hope during your time with us you even learn something of the mysterious planet Earth. If any of you need anything during your stay, don't hesitate to ask any of our Okcho staff or your VICTOR system. Enjoy your stay."

The delegates applauded politely. As Bugzee doddered off the stage and out of the room, Pelham leaned toward Emer and whispered, "A lord, eh?"

"The Zurks are obsessed with titles. I've had a lot of dealings with Zurks, and they all want to be lord this or baron that or the most noble whatever."

"How did a blighter like that nab one?"

"I read up on that. They called it service to the Greater Zurk Protectorate. I think mainly it was awarded for making piles of money."

"Ah, of course. Since the title is lord, I take it this bloke is male?"

"Zurks don't have gender. They use masculine pronouns and titles as a default."

"Only one gender, eh? Sounds a bit dull."

"The Zurks consider it efficient."

The Axan was talking again. "And now I have prepared some introductory remarks."

He launched into the longest string of incomprehensible gibberish Pelham had ever heard, all about regulatory environments and asynchronous copartners and knowledge outsourcing protocols. The trade agreement document had been interesting compared to this speech. After some minutes, Pelham signaled one of the Okcho and requested a drink to keep himself awake. Duncil seconded the motion, and others around the table followed suit.

The Axan droned on. Pelham was beginning to despair of the speech ever coming to an end when he at last heard the words, "Thank you," followed by scattered applause.

Jasper Jadarite said, "And now, in keeping with the Pink Mingo's Earth theme, it is my privilege to present to you, for your enjoyment, an impersonator of the most famous Las Vogus entertainer on Earth. Fellow delegates, I give you the king of rock and roll. It's Elfus!"

Peppy music started up from somewhere as spotlights roamed back and forth across the room. They settled on a figure jogging in from the back. The person was a Kabar, an amphibious species from the ocean planet Piscina, that looks like a walking fish with eyes stuck on the sides of their heads where most people keep ears.

Though Kabars don't have hair or fur, this one wore a big mop of a wig, thick and black, tufted up on the top of his head and even streaming down the sides of his face to where other species have chins. He was wearing a white jumpsuit with a high collar, gold sequins, and a cape.

The musical riff kept repeating over and over, growing in intensity, as the Kabar approached the stage. He ascended the platform, lifted a microphone to his mouth, and began to sing in a rich baritone.

The theme of the song was difficult for Pelham to follow. It was all about being confined in some sort of trap caused by suspicious minds. The protagonist of the ballad claimed to be unable to extricate himself due to his great love for someone he called Baby. Given the baby part, Pelham assumed the song must be a lullaby of sorts. He had once been roped into watching a friend's youngling and had himself felt trapped when the tot wouldn't go to sleep on schedule. However, why that had anything to do with suspicious minds was beyond him.

The song went on, and Pelham, though confused by the lyrics, found the performance remarkably entertaining. Whenever there was a break in the lyrics, the Kabar Elfus would wiggle his hips and mug for the crowd. It ended with the fish-faced singer saying in a resonant voice, "It's a trap."

As the audience applauded, Kabar Elfus pulled a piece of cloth from a pocket, wiped his sizeable fish forehead, and flung it into the crowd. Several trade delegates quickly scooted their chairs in an attempt to distance themselves from the thing.

The singer raised a hand and said, "Thank ya vury much. That song has much to teach us about Earth culture — love, mistrust, the many challenges of Earthling relationships. It must be exhausting being an Earthling. This next song is one of Earth Elfus's most iconic hits."

Elfus began belting out a lyric to a driving beat. This song was addressed to the singer's pet dog, specifically a hound. Pelham had heard of the Earthlings' love for their pets. In this case, the relationship between Earthling and dog appeared to be somewhat strained. The lyrics repeatedly accused the dog of crying and never catching a rabbit, which led to the dog no longer being regarded as a friend. To Pelham the sentiment seemed a bit harsh. Yet by the end of the song, those concerns had fallen away as Pelham delightedly tapped his toe to the beat.

When the concert ended, Emer asked, "Do you want to work some more on the trade agreement?"

Pelham said, "Bit late for work, what? How about we see what's happening in the casino?"

"Want to try a different game?"

"What do they have?"

"There's one called Roll It."

"Roll what?"

"Roll It. It gets its name from the little marble that rolls around a spinning wheel."

"Sounds fun. I'll give it a spin. Ha!"

She led him to a rectangular table with a wheel at one end and a grid of colored squares stretched out from it, some of which displayed stacks of holographic chips.

The two Mucs were there. One said, "I bet black," as he tapped on his bracelet. The other said, "I'll take red," and tapped on his. As each person placed a wager, chips appeared on the table in corresponding squares.

The Okcho attendant said, "No more bets," and pressed a button. The wheel started revolving one way while a white marble popped out from somewhere and began spinning around an outside track in the opposite direction. When the marble lost its momentum, it fell into a slot on the wheel marked with a red nineteen.

"I win," said the one Muc with a good deal of enthusiastic snorting as his bracelet went *bloop-bloop-bloop-bloop*.

"I'll give it a try," Pelham said. He stepped up to the table and nodded to the attendant. "Oh, hello. You're ... you're ... Shay the Smaller, right?"

"Shay the Shorter. How are you doing, Mr. Totleigh?"

"Me? I'm topping. Last time I saw you, you were tending bar. You run the gaming tables as well?"

"We all do whatever they tell us. Do you want to play?"

"I believe I will. Do you deal cards or something?"

"No cards. You simply bet on where you think the ball will end up. You can select a certain number, a range of numbers, odds, evens, or red or black. The more specific the wager, the more it will pay off."

"I think I have it," Pelham said.

Shay spoke to all the players. "Place your bets."

As the other players tapped in wagers, Pelham took a flutter on odd numbers and saw his holographic chips appear on the grid.

"No more bets," Shay said. She pressed a button to spin the wheel and drop the marble.

It rolled and rolled and slipped into black twenty-one. Pelham's bracelet announced the payoff. He glowed with the thrill.

He kept playing odds, and for a few spins, he continued to win. Then his luck changed, and his winnings began to slip away. In desperation he switched to evens. He tried playing red. He gave black a whirl. Nothing was working. He blew through his initial three hundred bills and more. His bracelet was now showing a balance of negative five hundred forty-two.

He looked to Emer. "This game is cleaning me out."

"My turn then," she said. "Red fourteen. I'm wearing red and fourteen is my lucky number."

She placed her bet while Pelham abstained after the bruising he had received. The wheel spun, the marble rolled and dropped neatly into red fourteen. Her bracelet blooped. She tapped it again. "I'm letting it ride and betting more."

Red fourteen hit a second time.

"Again," Emer said, her copper face flushed in excitement.

Pelham couldn't help himself. He tapped in his own bet on red fourteen. This time the ball dropped into black thirty-five.

Pelham and Emer were giving each other disappointed shrugs when, unexpectedly, both their bracelets lit up and went *bloop-bloop-bloop-bloop*. Other bloops began blooping all around the casino followed by cheers from every corner. There were celebrations at other Roll It tables, at Jack Black tables, all along the line of slot machines. It seemed everyone had won at the same time.

Shay's eyes darted around the room looking uncertain. Other Okcho glanced back at her with the same expression. Finally, she said, "Place your bets."

Emer tapped on her bracelet. "Let's try it again."

Pelham joined her in taking another whirl on red fourteen. Shay pushed the button to spin the wheel and drop the marble. It fell into black seven, but Pelham and Emer's bracelets again recorded a win. And with this win, Pelham's balance, though still negative, had climbed to a number a lot less negative than it had been. Other bracelets across the floor also blooped and lit up. Everyone had won again.

Before anyone could place more bets, all the lights at all the gaming tables and slot machines went out. All the bracelets fell silent. A minute later, Lord Bugzee strode into the room followed by a tough-looking Zurk.

"Friends," Bugzee said, his voice sounding through everyone's wrist device, "we appear to have a problem with our bracelet system. The odds of these massive simultaneous payouts happening naturally is … well, frankly, it is astronomical. We believe our system has been hacked. The house cannot pay out to everyone at once, and we have no intention of paying out to cheaters. Therefore, all winnings of the last ten minutes have been revoked. You may be confident we will discover the perpetrators of this insidious attack on the integrity of gaming here on Vogus. Thank you."

Amid a wave of grumbles from the crowd, Lord Bugzee waddled back toward the door. The bracelets of everyone in the casino dinged, displaying new, lower balances of credits, wiping out their recent winnings. Incredibly, the notification was followed by a request to rate Lord Bugzee in pink mingos.

Chapter 8

A Revolting Development

It's a rum thing, Pelham thought, looking around the room, how various species react in such divergent ways to a given situation, especially an adverse situation. This was now the case as casino patrons stared at reduced balances showing on their bracelets.

Some who had evolved from predator species, reptilian Srathans and feline Pardiuns, for instance, began shouting and rushed to block Lord Bugzee's exit like a pack on the hunt. Other species, whose ancestors had tended to end up as prey, seemed to simply accept this setback as an inescapable fact of life, standing there in dejected but peaceable disbelief.

As a Haplor, Pelham was squarely in the latter group. He sniffed and shook his head, reminding himself that he had not, in truth, bet on the winning numbers and wasn't entitled to the payoffs now taken away. Several others, however, were not as circumspect.

"What do you mean my winnings have been revoked?" a tall Arsawan asked, the violet patches on his bald, gray head growing more scarlet.

"You can't do that!" a Yutronan yelled, its black eyes flaring beneath its beehive forehead.

The two Mucs locked arms in front of the door. One sneered, "I've done nothing illegal. I want my money."

"I'm never coming back here again," growled a Thomian, throwing aside other people in an effort to get to Bugzee.

Lord Bugzee scowled at the angry crowd, his proboscis curling and uncurling defiantly. The tough-looking Zurk beside him pulled out a blaster and raised it above his head. Bugzee's eyes widened. Whether that was due to the threat of violence or to the risk of blaster damage to his casino Pelham couldn't be sure. Bugzee forced his comrade's arm down and raised his own hands in a gesture of peace. His voice again came through everyone's bracelets, shaken but confident.

"You all make valid points, and the Pink Mingo Hotel and Casino always listens to its customers. We are sorry about the inconvenience, but I am sure none of you would want to collect winnings that were awarded because of someone cheating the system. That would not be fair, would it?"

Murmurs swept around the room, many of them expressing the opinion that they didn't have a problem with accepting winnings under any conditions. One of the Mucs at the door yelled, "If you were hacked, then that's *your* problem." Several others voiced their agreement.

With a frown, Bugzee motioned to quiet them again. "I assure you we will launch an immediate investigation. When we find the culprit behind this, that person will be prosecuted to the full extent of the law. Everyone else will be paid what they are due … assuming we can work out which winnings are legitimate."

This was greeted by no small number of grumbles. Someone called out, "What will be your criteria for determining the legitimate winnings?"

Bugzee took a step toward the door, staring like a deeply disappointed aunt at the Mucs still blocking it. The glare failed to dislodge them.

With a low growl, he spoke again. "All right. Listen. For the time being, I will restore your winnings." He was forced to wave both hands to cut off the resulting cheers. "However, no one will be cashed out until we complete our investigation. In the meantime, you may use your winnings to purchase any of our food and drink services, plus souvenir merchandise in our gift shop. You can also use them in the casino … when it reopens … which I hope will be tomorrow." Bugzee tapped on a device in his hand.

Amid a round of bloops, everyone's balances jumped back to what they had previously been. In Pelham's case, that meant going from a deeply negative number to one not so negative but still on the wrong side of zero.

Despite a few remaining mutters of discontent, the crowd now seemed relatively pacified. However, even as he shuffled toward the door, a circle of customers formed around Lord Bugzee shouting questions and comments. The casino owner attempted to answer them, his face alternating between pasted-on expressions of empathy and genuine annoyance, until at last, he abruptly reeled away and fled the room.

Pelham hooted. "Well, I'll be blasted. What do you think about all that?"

"Lord Bugzee is in a fix," Emer said. "Like it or not, he's going to have to pay out most of the winnings or risk alienating clientele from dozens of planets."

"What do you think? Was this the work of a gang of desperate criminals? Have we witnessed a real live casino heist?"

"Desperate, perhaps. A heist, maybe not." She jerked her head in the direction of a group of Okcho leaning against the wall. "They don't appear upset."

It was true. Several of the Okcho were smiling, joking with each other. Pelham said, "I imagine they're happy to be able to clock out early and return home to their families."

"That is one possible explanation. How informed are you about the situation here on Vogus?"

"Well … um … I was thinking about reading up on it tonight." Truthfully, though, *The Adventures of Bongo* sounded much more enjoyable.

Dings sounded on the bracelets of everyone in the room. A message popped up: *Tonight's winnings courtesy of the Okcho Liberation Force. Support Okcho Rights!*

"Is this the situation on Vogus you were referencing?" Pelham asked.

Emer nodded. She started to make a comment but was interrupted when a squad of Zurks in uniform burst through the door holding blasters. They rounded up every Okcho in the room and led them away.

Emer said, "Well, there goes the entire staff. Now how are they going to reopen the casino?"

"Or serve breakfast," Pelham said.

"I hope they straighten this all out before the end of the conference. I want my winnings."

"You have winnings?" He flashed a sly smile. "As far as I'm concerned, they can keep my sub-zero tally. Drink?"

Emer cast her eyes toward the empty bar. "No one to pour it."

"Hmm. Still, there is Blandings. He'll fix me an Amurru fizz. Want one?"

"Can he mix an Antarean sour?"

"I shouldn't be at all surprised. You know Blandings. Performs wonders daily."

They took the pneumatic tubes back to Pelham's suite and found Blandings reading and enjoying a cup of tea. He set down his tablet and cup and stood as they entered.

"Blandings," Pelham said, "do you know how to make an Antarean sour? Ha! Cutting him off in traffic would do it, eh?"

"Beg pardon, sir?"

Emer said, "The drink. Can you make an Antarean sour?"

"I am familiar with the beverage, miss." Blandings glided to the kitchenette.

"Amurru fizz for me," Pelham said, "and you might want to mix something bracing for yourself as well. We have shocking news to impart."

"Indeed, sir?"

Blandings returned with two drinks on a silver tray, apparently opting to stick to tea himself.

"Sit, sit," Pelham said.

Blandings hesitated, then perched stiffly on the edge of the chair. Pelham gave him the rundown on the evening's events, leaving aside for the time being his losses at the Roll It wheel.

Blandings' response was a single grave nod of his head. "I have heard, sir, of a certain amount of dissatisfaction on the part of the Okcho with the current state of affairs."

Emer tsked.

Pelham turned to her. "You tsked?"

"You bet I did. The Zurks came here years ago and took over the planet, reducing the Okcho to a servant class. No offence, Blandings."

"None taken," Blandings said with another nod.

"Now some are fighting back."

Pelham said, "You mean this Okcho Libation Forks group? What is that anyway, some culinary fraternity?"

"I assume, sir," Blandings said, "you mean the Okcho Liberation Force. It is one of several groups attempting to pressure the Zurks into granting the Okcho more rights."

"What rights do the Okcho lack?"

"That depends on whom you ask. According to the Zurks, they lack for nothing. The Zurks and Okcho control separate governments. Each has free elections. The Okcho maintain their own communities as they have for thousands of years."

"Then what's the problem?"

"The problem, sir, appears to be in what each government is permitted to do and in the relationship between the two species. Beyond that, I am somewhat uninformed."

"You, Blandings, uninformed about something?"

"The Zurk government, which controls the media, has not released detailed information on the issues involved."

Another tsk from Emer. "They dominate the entire planet, a planet where the Okcho are the indigenous people and yet do not control their own destiny. I tell you —" She stifled a yawn. "The two cultures are —" Another yawn. "Oh my. I'm afraid I'm done in with space lag. Perhaps we should take up this topic in the morning. Thank you for the drink. I think it's time for me to turn in."

Blandings showed Emer the door, then returned to where Pelham still sat on the couch.

"You appear disquieted, sir. Would that be due to the Okcho situation or is there something else?"

Pelham shook his head in awe. "Blandings, you read me like a tablet. There is another matter. I seem to have got a bit carried away in the casino."

"Oh dear."

"I'm down either a few hundred or several hundred bills, depending on what the management decides to do about this hack."

"Dame Agutha would not be pleased."

"My exact thoughts. She will not be pleased in the least. She will, in fact, be monumentally displeased. She will be chafed, angry, riled. She will have daggers drawn, as it were. The question remains, what should I do about it? I can keep playing in the hope that my luck will turn. But what if it doesn't? What if I lose even more?"

"A vexing problem, sir. I will give it some consideration."

"See that you do, Blandings."

"In the meantime, sir, I suggest you stay away from the casino."

"Sound advice, Blandings. I will give the place the skirt. Which won't be a problem since the casino is for the moment closed for business."

"So you said, sir. However, I doubt it will stay closed for long. The casino is far too profitable to management."

"No doubt. Exhibit A being my negative balance. Say, do you think you could assemble another Amurru fizz?"

"Coming up, sir."

Blandings, however, didn't get to make the drink, and Pelham was never able to drink it because at that moment a *ding* sung out from the door.

Pelham let out a sigh. "Now who could that be?"

Blandings provided the answer by opening the door to reveal a Zurk wearing a green uniform and matching beret. He stepped in without being invited.

"My name is Sergeant Humstuggle of the Colonial Security Force. Which one of you is ..." He consulted a tablet device, his whole head dropping to change his line of sight. "... Pelham G. Totleigh?"

"That would be me." Pelham waved from the couch. He turned to examine the specimen in the doorway. Something about these Zurks reminded Pelham of a species of giant seal, the snuffle-something seals, back on the Haplor home world that flopped around with the same kind of long proboscis trunk thingy. You know, he thought, if you took off the fins and plopped on some arms and legs, you would nearly have one of these Zurk chappies.

There was something else rummy about Zurks, something he hadn't noted of Bugzee when viewed from a distance — the eyes. They were absolutely lacking in the white parts, merely two large orbs of black. And when the sergeant looked around, he moved his entire head, his eyes seemingly fixed in place.

Sgt. Humstuggle said in a formal tone, "Our records indicate you were in the casino at the time of the cyberattack."

"You have records of where I've been?"

By way of answering the question, the sergeant smirked and rotated his head toward Pelham's bracelet.

Pelham's eyes bulged. "This thing tracks me? I say, what about my privacy?"

Humstuggle raised his head as if performing a recitation for a school program. "Tracking allows us to better serve you, Mr. Totleigh."

"Oh? How is that?"

The sergeant consulted the tablet again, his head once more dropping. "Would you like an Amurru fizz, sir?"

"Hmm? An Amurru fizz? I dare say I would. I was just having my man Blandings fix me one."

"There you go, sir. We know you ordered one at the bar. For the rest of your stay here, you can expect offers of Amurru fizzes to follow you around the establishment."

"I can? Well, that's jolly good. I don't suppose you have one on you now, do you?"

"No, sir. Sorry, sir. Right now, I am asking you to come with me for questioning."

"Questioning?"

"You know what questioning is, don't you?"

"Indeed, I do. I've been questioned on numerous occasions, more than once by my Aunt Agutha, which is a horrid experience. Tell you what, why don't we talk here? Have a seat. My man will fix us something. It will make the whole thing much more pleasant."

"Sorry. I have orders to bring you to security headquarters."

Pelham let out a long breath. "Couldn't this wait until the morning? I've had a full day. Flew fifty-some light years and all."

"Sixty-two to be precise," Blandings said.

"Let's not split hairs, Blandings."

"Forgive me, sir."

"Quite all right."

Sgt. Humstuggle regarded their exchange with a scowl, his head bobbing back and forth between them. "I am sorry, Mr. Totleigh, but I have my orders. We need to get to the bottom of this attack as quickly as possible so we can pay out any legitimate winnings. I'm sure you can understand our position."

"I suppose," Pelham said. "But I have no information that could possibly help you."

"Nevertheless, you are on the list."

"And I'm guessing you have to follow the list."

"I do, Mr. Totleigh."

Pelham responded with annoyance. "Well, if we must."

"Should I accompany you, sir?" Blandings asked.

"No, Blandings. You stay here. Catch some shut-eye. And if I don't appear in the morning, come looking for me."

"I intend to, sir."

Sgt. Humstuggle led Pelham away.

Chapter 9

Helping the Colonial Security Force with their Inquiries

Lieutenant Commander Leopold Mountjoy leaned back in the stiff desk chair and gazed around at his office tucked away in the labyrinth of halls beneath the Pink Mingo Hotel and Casino. The walls, windowless in this underground warren, at least had plenty of room for pictures and mementos of his thirty years of service — regimental photos; his service award; his fragment from the *Encounter*, the ship he had served on as lieutenant before it was destroyed in the Kahari campaigns. His office was his sanctum … or it would have been if it were not stuck down in this dingy hole.

His security force should have better digs. Of that he was certain. They should be ensconced in a respectable command center along the strip … and at ground level, for Zahn's sake. Instead, they had been stashed down here along with the hotel mechanical plant while Lord Bugzee enjoyed a penthouse suite. In effect, it turned them from a military unit into something not much more than glorified hotel detectives.

Then again, protecting the interests of the hotel and casino was their primary mission as dictated by Colonial Command back on Zurkannia. Hence, their proximity to the hotel. This was their duty, and Zurks always did their duty.

A *buzz* sounded from the hallway. Sgt. Humstuggle entered, bringing with him a short furry alien, mouth open, eyes bulging, wearing an expression of bewildered astonishment. Through the open office door, Mountjoy watched them thread their way through the half dozen empty desks of the outer office. He adjusted his peaked cap, straightened the green uniform stretched tight around his middle, and began pretending to read a report from an electronic device on his desk.

Humstuggle knocked on the doorframe.

Mountjoy looked up. "Yes?"

"I have Mr. Pelham G. Totleigh, sir."

Mountjoy trotted out his cheery voice to answer. "Bring him in, Humstuggle. Bring him in."

The sergeant ushered in the Haplor, saluted, and departed.

Mountjoy waved toward an uncomfortable chair on the other side of the desk. "Mr. Totleigh, come in and have a seat. I do apologize for dragging you away from your bed, but we need to sort out this frightful business."

"Um ... yes." The little Haplor's large eyes darted around the office.

Mountjoy tried to put him at ease with a broad smile. "I am Lieutenant Commander Leopold Mountjoy. I'll try not to take too much of your time."

"Pelham G. Totleigh."

"Yes. Yes. Of course." Mountjoy picked up the tablet device and tapped it a few times. "You arrived from Sonus, correct?"

"I did."

"A Donovian cruiser, I see. Well, at least no one can question your courage, eh?" Mountjoy smiled at the Haplor, the curve of his thin lips extending out on either side of his plump proboscis. The Haplor stared back with a blank expression, seeming not to grasp the joke. "Um ... what do you do on Sonus, Mr. Totleigh?"

"I am the inspector of ... um ... whatsits ... um ... you know ... goods, merchandise ... um ... wares we bring in ... oh, imports. That's the term I was fumbling for. I'm the inspector of imports for our little colony."

"Ah. Then we both labor for our respective governments, you and I. How long have you worked there?"

"Oh I don't know. Quite a while. Ever since my Aunt Agutha said I had to apply myself if I wanted to amount to anything in life. What about you? Been with the constabulary long?"

Mountjoy's jaw tightened. "It's not a constabulary."

"Oh. Sorry. My mistake."

"We are a provisional military agency with broad security powers operating within the greater Vogus sphere of operations."

"A what now?"

Helping the Colonial Security Force with their Inquiries

Mountjoy massaged one hand with the other. This Totleigh seemed to have trouble understanding even the simplest of explanations. Haplors must be an inferior species, Mountjoy thought, both in size and intelligence. He decided to move on. "The reason I've asked you here —"

Totleigh scoffed. "I don't recall that asking was involved."

Mountjoy's proboscis curled. When he spoke again, the words came more slowly. "My point is that perhaps we can help each other out, one colonial government employee to another. What do you know about this attack on the casino?"

"What? Me? Nothing!" Totleigh's eyes bulged out even further.

Mountjoy had never seen anyone's eyes protrude like this. They reminded him of the bulging eyes on those odd purple creatures swimming around in Lord Bugzee's office aquarium. "Excuse me, did … did your species evolve from fish, Mr. Totleigh?"

"What? What?"

"Insects possibly?" Or, Mountjoy wondered, was this bulging a sign of guilt or fear? Always difficult to tell with these foreign species.

"No, Commander. I guarantee we're mammals, primates all the way."

"Interesting. In any case, you were there, correct?"

"Where?"

"In the casino at the time of the attack. How is this confusing you? It's a simple question."

"Well, our conversation has bobbed around a bit. And I've had a long day what with bally Donovians, and getting settled into the hotel, and all. But no, I'm not confused … I don't think so anyway."

"Good. Now as to the attack."

"I … I don't know anything. I was playing Roll It and was finally starting to do well after a frightful streak of bad luck when everything around the room started beeping and blooping, et cetera, et cetera."

"Yes, that was the attack. Did you notice anything unusual before it happened?"

"Um … no. I was only watching the Roll It ball."

"You didn't take note of anything suspicious?"

Totleigh chuckled and leaned in. "Only the price of the drinks, what?"

Mountjoy took a breath to calm himself. "Then after the attack. Then what happened?"

"Then Lord Bugzee tootled in and said the casino wasn't going to pay, and, let me tell you, that did not go over well with the crowd, not one bit. Reminded me of this one singing act I once saw. The blighter hadn't the least notion of rhythm or melody. Sounded more like the cries of a wounded animal, I thought. The poor vocalist was booed from the stage, as nearly was Lord Bugzee."

"Uh-huh."

"At first, I thought this — and by this I am again speaking of the hubbub in the casino — must have been a heist pulled off by a sophisticated crew of thieves. I said as much to my friend Emer, but she said perhaps it wasn't."

Mountjoy sat up straighter, his proboscis twitching. "You don't say? Who is this Emer?"

"A fellow delegate to the trade conference … from Bononia."

"I see." Mountjoy stretched out the word. He was well familiar with the formal protests the Bononian government had lodged against their colony regarding their handling of the Okcho situation. All the pieces were fitting together. "Who did Emer believe was responsible for the attack?"

"I gathered she thought the Okcho were behind it."

"Now where could he have gotten that idea?"

"He?"

"This Emer."

"She's a she. Female."

Gender. Mountjoy's proboscis curled in disdain, and he felt his face flush. Why did these alien species always insist on talking about gender? The topic was distasteful, especially since gender had to do with … well, to put it indelicately … fadoodling, amorous congress, dancing the jig as his granddad used to say. He refused to allow more graphic terms to enter his mind. Mountjoy cleared his throat. "Let's not get into …" He waved a hand in a circle rather than say more. "Now, when Emer said the Okcho were behind the attack, was this before or after the Okcho Liberation Force claimed responsibility?"

The Haplor seemed to freeze for a moment. "Golly, you know, it all happened so fast. Let me think. We heard the beeping, then Bugzee —"

"Lord Bugzee."

"That's the fellow."

"Titles are important, Mr. Totleigh."

Pelham shrugged. "If you say so. I don't go in much for the ruddy things myself. *Lord* Bugzee said there had been an attack, and everything was in an uproar, and I said to Emer, 'blah blah blah,' and then she said ... Yes, she mentioned it before the whose-its put up their message."

"All right. How long have you known Emer?"

"I met her today."

"For the first time?"

Totleigh chuckled. "You know, I believe you can only meet someone once. Well, of course, not my great uncle Mortimer. He went a little funny in the head in his old age and couldn't recollect anyone from one time to the next."

Mountjoy feigned a weak smile. "You met Emer today."

"Yes."

"What else did Emer tell you about the attack?"

"Oh, not much. This and that."

"Please be as specific as you can."

"Oh ... ah. She told me relations between Okcho and Zurks were strained."

"She said that?"

"Something along those lines."

Mountjoy's proboscis curled up into a ball, for once showing his full mouth. "Well, for your information, our relations are not strained. The vast majority of Okcho get along fine with Zurks. You know how it is, Mr. Totleigh."

"I do?"

"You live in a Haplor colony. This is a Zurk colony. I don't need to tell you about colonizing planets. One always steps on a few toes, no matter how carefully one treads."

"Well, when we came, Sonus didn't have any toes to tread, no indigenous life, not even microbes. The moon was devoid of anything organic."

"But that isn't always the case with Haplor colonies now, is it? What about Tucana Three?"

"I'm a bit fuzzy on the history. I was told the Tucanans welcomed us with open tentacles. They dwell in the sea, you know. We dwell on land. There was no conflict."

"Yes. It is much the same with Zurks and Okcho. We live inside our colony. They dwell on those windswept, rocky plains and hills."

"But there do seem to be a fair number of them working in the Pink Mingo. I met Urdi first thing."

"Which Urdi is that?"

"Beg pardon?"

"The Okcho are fond of their indicative names."

"As you are of your titles."

Mountjoy's eyes narrowed. "It's hardly the same thing."

"No? In any case, it was Urdi the Unfortunate. That's who I met."

"Ah yes. Poor man. Seems to have the worst luck. But it's not like the Okcho are forced labor. They come in for the jobs. Can you blame them? Who wouldn't rather work for steady wages in a climate-controlled casino rather than struggle for survival out on a cold hardscape with soil so poor it can barely grow crops? If we weren't here, the Okcho wouldn't have those jobs. They would be dining on bog rat ... when they could catch one. There's only a small handful of malcontents who resent our presence. They cause all the trouble."

"Ah. Then why did you round up the entire Okcho staff after the attack?"

"That was nothing but routine questioning. Obviously, the gang had someone on the inside working with them. I assure you the staff have all been released. Well, most of them. Now then, what did Emer tell you about the attack before it happened?"

"Before? Nothing. How could she know about it beforehand unless ... Wait. You aren't suggesting ..."

Mountjoy saw understanding at last register in Totleigh's eyes. This Emer was looking like a collaborator in the attack. Took him long enough, Mountjoy thought. Unless, of course, this idiot persona was an act. If so, it was a good act.

"You said Emer suspected the Okcho and said as much even before the terrorists claimed responsibility."

"Well, sure, but —"

"Did Emer express any sympathy toward the Okcho terrorists?"

Pelham pursed his lips and leaned back against his seat. "Not really."

"Not really?"

"No."

"Which implies that Emer voiced at least some kind of tepid support."

"Oh, not really."

"What precisely did Emer say?"

"She ... she tsked."

"Tsked?"

"You know." Pelham made a tsk sound to demonstrate. "Tut-tut and all that."

"When was that?"

"Ah … well, I think it was after Blandings related how he had learned about the Okcho being dissatisfied with the existing state of affairs."

"Who's this Blandings character?"

"My man. My valet. Emer and I adjourned to my suite for a drink."

"And how did you interpret this tsk?"

"Well, you know, a tsk could mean anything. It might imply she disagreed with Blandings. It could mean something was off with her drink, though that's unlikely since Blandings made it. She may well have had regrets of the day. I often tsk after I've made a mistake. There was this one time when I —"

"What did *you* think the tsk meant?"

"I wasn't sure. If I'm being honest, I must admit I often have trouble following conversations. Grab the wrong end of it sometimes. Well, unless I'm with my mates down at the club, joking and making merry. I navigate those conversations fine, and they flow like a babbling stream in spring. Do you have streams here on Vogus? I haven't seen any. We don't have them on Sonus, not yet. But we're terraforming, you know. Someday it will be near enough to Haplor, or so my Aunt Agutha says. She says —"

"Mr. Totleigh."

"Yes?"

"Would you like a cup of tea?"

"If I had my druthers, I'd prefer to go to bed."

"Yes. I apologize for keeping you up. However, we need to talk some more about Emer and also about this Blandings. It may take a while. Tea? I'll have Sergeant Humstuggle make some."

Pelham nodded with a wince.

"On second thought, let's not have Humstuggle make the tea. He always makes it weak as dishwater, though how he manages to do that with a replicator is a mystery to me. I'll make the tea, and while I do, you can wait in one of our interview rooms."

Mountjoy stood and led the Haplor to a drab little room fitted only with a table and two cold straight back chairs. "Make yourself comfortable."

"How?" Pelham asked, staring at the sparse furnishings.

Mountjoy locked the door behind him, relishing how the bolt always clicked with a certain degree of menace. He wobbled to the kitchenette to replicate two cups of tea. He hoped the combination of the friendly cup along with the forbidding interrogation room would produce the desired effect.

Mountjoy made Pelham repeat everything once more. Here and there he stopped him with follow-up questions, pressing for ever more detail. And then, after they had talked through each of the evening's events, Mountjoy made the Haplor go through it all again.

Chapter 10

All Shook Up

Hours later, Pelham stumbled back to his suite to find the lights low but left on. Blandings was asleep in a chair in the sitting room.

Pelham considered trudging on to his bed and leaving Blandings peacefully snoozing where he was. But he worried the valet might wake in the middle of the night not knowing Pelham was in the other room. At the same time, he reckoned it terribly unfair to wake anyone from restful slumber as Aunt Agutha had so recently done to him. He compromised by plopping down on the couch in his clothes, where he promptly fell asleep.

He awoke to the scent of eggs fresh from the food replicator. His eyes opened one at a time, and there was Blandings holding a tray of mushrooms, beans, and bangers, as well as two over-easies staring back at him.

"Good morning, sir."

Pelham pushed himself up to a sitting position and yawned. "Gad mung."

"Here, sir." Blandings handed him a cup of tea from the tray.

Pelham took a long grateful sip, then motioned for Blandings to set the tray on his lap.

"I was glad to discover you here this morning, sir, after the long interrogation."

"Long and tedious, Blandings. Long and tedious. I thought this Zurk bloke, Commander Mount-something … um … Mount … joy, was never going to release me even though I clearly had nothing to do with the attack and possessed scarcely anything in the way of information concerning it. He was relentless, Blandings."

"Zurks are known for their resoluteness. Now, if you eat up, sir, I judge you will have time to shower, dress, and make it to your conference session."

"The last thing I need right now is some blasted conference session."

"I would remind you, sir, Dame Agutha expects a report of the proceedings."

Pelham scowled back despite knowing the abysmal situation was anything but his valet's fault. "All right, Blandings. Give me a chance to engulf an egg or two and get myself on the outside of this excellent tea. Then I will strive to face the day."

Pelham showered, changed, and endured the pneumatic lifts once more to reach the ground floor. The casino was again open for business, though it was currently only sparsely populated by lonely patrons at scattered slot machines, who were repeatedly tapping the buttons like lab animals at a feeding station.

Still, the casino was fully staffed even at this lonely hour. That said something, Pelham thought, though he wasn't sure exactly what. Maybe that the Okcho weren't paid particularly well. Or maybe that the casino made a lot of money off gamblers. Or both.

"Amurru fizz, sir?" the bartender called to him as he passed.

"Oh, no thanks. Bit early, what?"

He followed the arrow on his bracelet out the casino and around the hall to the conference room to find the proceedings in progress. The long table from the night before had been replaced by rows of seats in various widths and heights for the different species. He scanned the room for Emer without luck before taking a seat in the last row beside a Siriun, a canine-like alien with wide floppy ears and a long, pointed muzzle. The Siriun gave him a broad, friendly smile, with tongue hanging out. Pelham acknowledged it with a nod.

From the platform, a blue Rhegedian was addressing the group, describing a pilot program in which industry from Rheged Prime was being transferred to businesses on Rheged Minor owned by native Nojava. Charts detailed how Rhegedian Primers opposed the plan for economic reasons while the Nojava were wary of it due to environmental concerns.

From what Pelham could gather, the project seemed to be an unmitigated failure. Then again, he couldn't be entirely sure, since every sentence out of the speaker's mouth was peppered with incoherent terminology — market access, logistics, countervailing duties, and the like. During one particularly jargon-laden section, Pelham caught himself with eyes closed, listing toward the shoulder of the Siriun. He jerked back upright, and fortunately, the session ended soon thereafter.

As the conferees stood and filed out of the room for a break and refreshments, Pelham stood on the chair to try to spot Emer. She was nowhere to be seen. He figured she too had been kept up half the night by the Colonial Security Force. She would probably appear later, but he wanted to check on her, if only to be sure.

He took the pneumatic tube up to her room and knocked gently on the door. She didn't answer.

"Emer." He knocked again.

"I say, Emer, are you awake?" Still no answer.

Pelham knocked more loudly with no result. Then he had an idea. "VICTOR?"

His wrist lit up. "How may I be of assistance, Mr. Totleigh?"

"My friend isn't answering her door. I'm concerned."

"What would you like me to do?"

"Could you let me in?"

"Let you into someone else's room? Oh no, Mr. Totleigh, that is not allowed."

"But this is something of an emergency. She could be sick … or injured."

"Oh my. The situation does sound worrisome. However, Zurk Colonial Statute ten dot eighty-nine dash one hundred fifty-three states that guests at premises licensed for transient lodging with twenty or more sleeping rooms are permitted to enter only public rooms and the rooms they have tenanted during the period of their occupancy."

"What's that again?"

"It means I cannot let you in, Mr. Totleigh."

"But what if my friend is in there at death's door? Isn't there something … what was it? Blandings would know. Stay on the line a moment, VICTOR. Say, Blandings?"

The valet's voice sounded in Pelham's ear. "Yes, sir?"

"Blandings, didn't you tell me something once about those AI chaps being programmed not to harm people?"

"Yes, sir. It is an axiom of AI programming that an artificial intelligence shall not harm a member of any sentient species or allow such a person to come to harm by the AI's inaction."

"Inaction. There's the snippet I was looking for. VICTOR, did you hear that?"

"Hear what, Mr. Totleigh?" VICTOR asked.

"Oh right. Blandings voice was in my ear, translator bot to translator bot. Well, the long and the short of it is, as I understand it, you are programmed to not allow anyone to be harmed through ... um ... inaction. Is that how the tune goes, Blandings?"

"I believe you are quite near the mark, sir."

"Right. Well, what do you have to say for yourself then, VICTOR? We're standing here in the hallway in a complete state of inaction while Emer could be inside in who knows what kind of condition."

"I must admit, Mr. Totleigh, you make a persuasive argument."

"I do? I mean, I do, VICTOR. Yes. Decidedly so."

"Still, I cannot let you in."

"Isn't there any way?"

"Well, I suppose ... if you promise not to snoop around or remove anything."

"You have my word, VICTOR, and the word of a Totleigh is not to be doubted."

"All right then."

The door clicked, and Pelham rushed in. Emer was not there, but somebody had come and gone, leaving the suite in a shambles. The cushions of the couch and chair where Pelham and Emer had sat yesterday were now tossed across the room. Drawers were pulled out, end tables overturned. Pelham gawked at it all. He stepped to the bedroom door to find the mattress pulled off the bed, clothes strewn across the floor. Some of Emer's unmentionables lay at his feet, freezing him in his tracks.

Then a *whirring* sound started up from all over the room at once, and cleaning bots emerged to do the daily room tidying. A wedged-shaped robotic vacuum slid out from a wall, wheeling over the scattered clothes and sucking up a few of them. Arms extended from the bedposts, reaching for sheets and blankets and failing to find them because the bedding had been tossed across the room. A flying drone descended from the ceiling, lowered a hose, and began sucking dust from the top of the dresser, only to get clogged with clothes and papers piled on top. After a few seconds of fruitless work, every cleaning bot stopped. Lights flashed, and their alarms all began to blare.

Pelham rushed back to the sitting room and made a beeline for the door, hearing the *click* of a lock in the moment before he reached it. The alarms fell silent. Pelham jiggled the old-fashioned doorknob. He pulled and pushed. The door refused to open.

"VICTOR?"

The AI didn't answer. Pelham hoped persuading the expert system to break the rules hadn't resulted in a shutdown of the software. He would hate to be the cause of VICTOR being deleted.

"Blandings?"

"Yes, sir?"

"Ah. Yes. Good to hear your voice. It appears I am locked inside Emer's room."

"Is Ms. Emer there with you, sir?"

"No. That's the rum thing. I haven't seen her all day. I came up to check on her, but she's not here, and her suite has been ransacked. Then these deranged cleaning bots trundled in and set off alarms. The next thing I knew, I was locked in."

"A troubling scenario, sir."

"Troubling fails to cover it, Blandings. I'm incarcerated here, trapped, cut off from the outside world."

"Does the food replicator work, sir?"

"The replicator? Why should I care if the dashed replicator works?"

"I suggest you fix yourself a calming drink and make yourself comfortable. If the cleaning bots set off alarms, then one assumes someone from the hotel will be along shortly to check on the problem."

"You mean you can't extract me from here, Blandings?"

"Highly unlikely, sir. You'll need to wait for the hotel staff."

"I suppose you're right, Blandings. Fine. I'll wait here and keep you posted."

"Please do, sir."

Pelham replicated himself a cup of tea. He located the cushion that went with the sitting room chair and reunited the two. He sat and waited.

The person who finally opened the door was neither a Zurk nor an Okcho. Instead, she looked almost like an Earthling, except her skin was gray. Her short hair was set in wavy curls with almost the same precision as Aunt Agutha's, and she wore a grave expression that would fit nicely — or rather not so nicely — on the Sonus governor's face. Pelham hopped from the chair.

"What have you done to my room?" the person asked.

"Your room? This is Emer's room."

"They are all my rooms. I'm the head of housekeeping. My name is Gladiss."

"Pelham G. Totleigh. Pleased to meet you." He produced a formal bow.

Gladiss stared him down. "What's going on here?"

"Ah. Yes. I found it like this. My friend Emer was a no-show at the conference this morning, and I was worried about her. See, once a chum of mine, Bunko Tiddlesley, went missing and, well, as it transpired, he had taken ill — eaten some moldy cheese, as I recollect, though why he did so I haven't a clue. In any case, the pals and I never thought anything of his absence. What Bunko did was Bunko's business, that was our philosophy. In the meantime, the poor guy was suffering, and he really could have used —"

Gladiss stopped the flow of words with a look. "And you found the room like this?"

Pelham nodded solemnly.

"And this Emer person wasn't here?"

Pelham shook his head.

"You weren't looking for her in the drawers and under the cushions?"

"She would hardly fit."

"Does this have anything to do with the attack last night?"

"I have no idea. She was there at the time, as was I. And when whosehisface … um … Commander Mountjoy interviewed me, long into the night I might add, he expressed a marked interest in Emer."

Gladiss sighed. She picked up a couch cushion and slid it back where it belonged before sitting on it. "That explains it then."

"What?"

"This is the Zurks' work. I imagine they've detained your friend and tossed her rooms in search of evidence."

"They didn't tell you about it? You said you were the head of housekeeping."

She pointed to her face. "As I hope you can tell, I'm not a Zurk. I'm a Porta. The Zurks wouldn't admit to tearing up a room, not to an outsider. It wouldn't fit with their cultivated image as benevolent overlords."

"I thought everyone who worked here was either Zurk or Okcho."

"I'm one of the few exceptions. They brought me in because of my expertise. I've worked in hotels across the galaxy. I can reprogram a cleaning bot in thirty seconds flat."

"Then perhaps I might ask you how you would classify the relationship between Zurks and Okcho? Some say they coexist quite nicely. Others take a different perspective."

"No comment."

"Eh?"

"I'd like to keep my job." Gladiss stood. She picked up a table and righted it. "I need to straighten all this up. This is well beyond what a cleaning bot can do. Too bad I don't have my Univac working yet."

"What's that?"

"Universal Vacuum." She stooped to pick up the remaining couch cushions and slid them into place. "It's something I've been tinkering with in my spare time. It will wash, dust, clean, pick up, everything. It will revolutionize the housekeeping industry. That is, if I ever get it working. Since it isn't, I'll have to clean all this by hand."

"I hate to see you do it all by yourself," Pelham said. "Tell you what, I'll call my man Blandings."

Chapter 11

Caught Between a Rock-Headed Sergeant and a Hard Aunt

"Thank you, Blandings, for coming to our aid," Pelham said as they left Emer's suite. Between Blandings and Gladiss, along with nominal help from Pelham, the suite had been restored to its former arrangement.

"My pleasure, sir. I do enjoy tidying up. I find it a way to put to rights at least one small part of the universe, to fight back, as it were, the inevitable march toward disorder and entropy."

"Well, let me say, Blandings, you hold the line against end trophies quite formidably. I doubt any will slip through on your watch."

Blandings let the malapropism pass. "If I could make a suggestion, sir, possibly we should inquire with the authorities concerning Ms. Emer."

"We should, Blandings. In all the hustle and bustle of resetting her rooms, I had forgotten about her mysterious disappearance. Truth be told, I may be responsible for her ending up in this predicament."

"Indeed, sir?"

"Oh, you know the thing. Under the pressure of police interrogation — hot lights in your face and all that — it is possible I may have let slip something about her not being surprised by the attack, and ... well, you know how those blighters think."

"Blighters, sir?"

"The police, the constabulary, the gendarme. That Mountjoy chap. He's the one who questioned me. Smooth operator, this Mountjoy. All 'tut-tut, we're both colonizers, eh, Mr. Totleigh?' but underneath always probing for weaknesses."

"That is their job, sir."

"But perhaps with your brain power engaged, we can remedy the situation. Let me lead you to the security office. I suspect Humstuggle will be the weak link."

They took the pneumatic lifts down and strolled through the casino where, seeing as they had business ahead, Pelham declined an offer of an Amurru fizz from a passing server. They strode out into the main lobby, nodding toward Urdi the Unfortunate as they passed the front desk, and continued down the hallway past the line of shops to a pair of elevators at the end.

"Is the security office not on the ground floor, sir?"

"Indeed, it is not." Pelham punched a button beside the elevator doors. "The place is subterranean, buried within an ominous, eerie maze of hallways. I would hesitate to return if it were not to help a chum. I say, Blandings, shouldn't this elevator have beeped or booped or lit up or something?"

"Lift buttons do in most instances provide some type of feedback, sir. Are you sure this is the conveyance you took during your earlier visit to the security office?"

"I am. That Sergeant Humstuggle pressed this exact button. No wait. He did something before that. What was it? Ah. He scanned his badge. Yes, he waddled right up to the control panel nose to wall, so to speak. Then the bally thing dinged, and that was when he pressed the button."

"The lift must require an electronic security code, sir. We shall have to request assistance."

They retraced their steps to the front desk, where Urdi the Unfortunate greeted them with a mournful, "Good day, gentlemen. May I be of service? Most likely I can't, but I'll try."

"I'm hoping you can," Pelham said. "We wanted to have a quick word with that Sergeant Humstuggle bloke, but we can't make the dodgy elevators over there work for us."

"I am sorry, Mr. Totleigh. That is unfortunate. The elevators require authentication to operate. It leads both down to security and maintenance but also up to administrative offices and Lord Bugzee's suite. As you can imagine, we must be careful."

"Well, how do I jolly well get down there, then?"

"I will summon someone to escort you." Urdi tapped a few times on the tablet on the desk. "Oh dear. Now why isn't this sending the message? Sorry, gentlemen, it looks like I'll have to restart the device."

After two reboots and several minutes of waiting, a uniformed Zurk appeared. "Good day, gentlemen. I am Private Stebbins. How may I help you today?"

Pelham said, "We'd like to visit the security office."

"For what purpose, may I ask?"

"We are inquiring about a friend of ours."

"Has there been a robbery? An altercation? I can take the information here."

Pelham was stunned. "There's been a robbery too?"

Blandings placed a hand on Pelham's arm. "Private Stebbins, Mr. Totleigh had the distinct pleasure last evening of working with Sergeant Humstuggle. We need to speak with him again. We have information that may be relevant. Could you please take us to him?"

The Zurk swiveled his head back and forth between them, his proboscis twitching. "All right. Follow me."

They returned to the elevator doors, where Stebbins scanned his badge. A car arrived, and they rode down in uncomfortable silence. The door opened to a long beige hallway with glaring overhead lights.

"Ah, this is the place, Blandings. Lovely, isn't it? Even during the day, it gives me the willies."

They set off down the hallway, their footsteps echoing behind them. At the end of the corridor, Stebbins stopped at a door and again scanned his badge. With a *buzz*, the door clicked open.

***

Sergeant Humstuggle was at his desk writing up the week's uniform violations. Private Dankworth had reported for duty in unpolished shoes. Corporal Turner failed to wear a regulation belt. Private Button had a missing button. Ironic that last one, Humstuggle thought. He heard the door *buzz* and looked up to see Stebbins enter with the two Haplors from last night. Now what were they doing here?

Totleigh strode over to him. "Ah, Humstuggle, old boy, how are you this morning?"

"It's Sergeant Humstuggle," he said with a gruff tone, setting down the tablet.

"Yes, quite. Say, I was wondering if you happened to have my friend Emer in custody."

Humstuggle regarded Totleigh for a moment, shifted his eyes to the other Haplor, then went back to Totleigh. "I cannot comment on ongoing investigations."

"What? Why can't you?" Totleigh looked like he hadn't understood the sentence.

The other Haplor cleared his throat and spoke. "Sergeant, I don't believe we were formally introduced when we met in Mr. Totleigh's suite last evening. My name is Blandings. What Mr. Totleigh means to say is that if Ms. Emer should happen to be in custody, he would like to inquire about posting her bail."

"Bail is not an issue until someone has been formally charged with a crime."

"I see. So you are saying Ms. Emer is in custody but has not been charged."

Humstuggle felt his stomach drop, realizing he had said too much. "No. I said no such thing. What I mean is … um … I cannot comment on the investigation."

"I understand," said Blandings. "Perhaps we did not sufficiently explain the situation, Sergeant. You see, Ms. Emer is missing, and we are concerned for her safety."

Humstuggle said, "I'm sure wherever he is, he's … um … safe."

"She," Blandings said. "Bononians have gender."

Behind his proboscis, Humstuggle's lip rose in a sneer. "They do? Shocking how some of these foreign species operate. Distasteful if you ask me."

"And is she safe, Sergeant? In the aftermath of the attack by the Okcho Liberation Force, anything could happen. Which is why we have come. We would like to formally ask the security force to try to locate her."

Humstuggle stared back at Blandings with annoyance. "You want to file a missing person report?"

"We do."

Humstuggle frowned. A report meant he would have to launch an investigation, assign men, search for someone whose whereabouts he already knew. And all that paperwork. "Are you related to the missing person?"

"Not as such," said Blandings. "We are of totally different species. Is that a requirement?"

"Well … not technically, but —"

"Good. How do we proceed then?"

Humstuggle raised a chubby hand and pointed toward a kiosk hanging on the wall. "All forms are accessible there."

"Perfect. And what will filling out a form cause to happen?"

The sergeant felt a headache coming on. "We'll re-examine the prisoner's room. I mean, we'll *examine* … the *missing person's* room … for the first time. Obviously, we haven't been there yet. If the inspection yields no clues, then we'll send a search patrol through the colony and out into Okcho territory."

"Thank you," Blandings said. "You have been most helpful. You may expect us to check in on your progress tomorrow."

Humstuggle nodded his head in tight motions and dropped his eyes back to his tablet. What was Stebbins thinking, letting those two Haplors in here? Come to think of it, Stebbins wasn't wearing his beret at the proper angle. One more uniform violation for the report.

***

As they left the security office, Pelham asked Blandings, "Did I miss something? Is Emer missing, or do those security blokes have her?"

"I am sure they do have Ms. Emer in custody, sir. However, it appears there is nothing more we can do for her at this time. The missing person form was merely a stratagem to put them on notice."

"Ah … ah. What do we do now?"

"The logical alternatives, sir, would be for you to either return to the conference or eat some lunch."

Pelham laughed. "One of those options is hard to swallow, Blandings, and I don't mean lunch. Should we try one of the restaurants on the main floor?"

"I think, sir, the privacy of our suite would be more conducive to discussing matters at hand."

"Right you are, Blandings. Back to the suite it is. Feasibly you could replicate up some grub?"

"I can manage that, sir."

"I knew I could count on you. By the way, quite the schnoz on those Zurks, eh?"

"Indeed, sir."

Minutes later, while Pelham lounged on the couch, casually watching Blandings instruct the food replicator in the preparation of greens, nuts, and fruit, a *beep* sounded from the room's view screen and the unwelcome countenance of Aunt Agutha appeared. Pelham's first reaction was a startled gasp, but he managed to force a smile to his face.

"Hello, Aunt Agutha. Good day … or night … or whatever it is back on Sonus."

"Why aren't you attending the conference, Pelham?"

"I was there, Auntie. I spent the morning with rapt attention. Merely getting a spot of lunch, what? Who knew learning about tariffs and duties could work up such a prodigious appetite?"

"What have you learned so far?"

"Loads. This and that. Odds and ends. Did you know the most famous singer on Earth is a chap named Elfus?"

Agutha's eyes rolled toward the heavens of Sonus. "I didn't send you there to learn about the entertainment industry, you oaf. How is the trade agreement coming?"

"Yes, that. Fine. Fine."

"What do you mean by fine? Are you suggesting everything is fully worked out?"

"There remain a few … um … outstanding details."

"What details?"

"Yes, what details. Well … um … Blandings, can you … um … locate that note where I wrote down the unresolved issues?"

Blandings slid into view of the screen holding a tablet. At a glance, Pelham could see the device was not, in fact, switched on.

Blandings said, "Yes, sir. Here is what you wrote." He cleared his throat. "The Bononians, you noted, are requesting to be our exclusive supplier for several of the goods under consideration. In addition, here is a further note that they would like to specify that goods be transported on Bononian ships. Is that how you remember it sir?"

"It is indeed, Blandings. It's all coming back to me now. Thank you."

Aunt Agutha scowled. "Well, I hope you told them what's what on those counts."

"Oh, he did, Dame Agutha," Blandings said. "Mr. Totleigh was extremely firm."

She narrowed her eyes. "He was? Pelham? We're talking about Pelham here?"

"We are, ma'am. If I may say so, your nephew is displaying a previously hidden talent for skillful negotiation."

"Hmph! Well hidden, indeed," she muttered. "When are you meeting again, Pelham?"

Pelham swallowed. "Ah, a bit of a hitch there. It seems the Bononian I've been working with is being held by the security people in relation to a minor cyberattack by a group of Okcho."

"A trade delegate from another planet is being held by the police? Outrageous! Somehow this is your fault, Pelham, isn't it?"

"What? Me? No, I had nothing to do with the attack. Neither did Emer. It's only that she seemed to understand some of the social forces at play, and that's when those security blighters seemed to take an interest in her."

"*What* was when they became interested? What are you talking about, Pelham?"

"Oh, when I ... that is to say ... I mean ... um ... they were interviewing everyone. They kept me half the night. And this morning Emer came up missing. We can only assume ..." He stopped mid-sentence, hesitant to continue lest he inadvertently divulge his part in suspicion falling on the Bononian.

"Well, you need to arrange her release. Don't blow this trade agreement. We need it."

"Yes, Aunt Agu —"

She was gone. Pelham's last view of her before the screen faded to black was a frown of disappointment.

Chapter 12

No Joy with Mountjoy

Pelham looked up from the couch to his faithful valet. "Well, now what, Blandings?"

"It appears, sir, we must endeavor to effect the release of Ms. Emer per Dame Agutha's instructions." Blandings brought him the salad with fruit and nuts he had prepared.

While Blandings stood to the side, straight as a tin soldier, Pelham forked a bite and gestured with it. "Yes, yes. I did manage to follow along thus far. What I meant, rather, is how? How do we spring Emer from incarceration? Do we bake her a cake with a file embedded? Do we sneak her out disguised as a plumber or something? You know, I remember hearing about a prison escape where they constructed a boat out of raincoats."

"Unfortunately, sir, we are not near an ocean or other navigable waterway."

"All right, then scratch that one off the list."

"In this instance, sir, I think a direct approach might be more fruitful. Since Sgt. Humstuggle would not help us, I believe we should visit the person who interrogated you. You said his name was Mountjoy, I believe."

"Yes. Commander Mountjoy. No, Commander Lieutenant Mountjoy. No, that's not it either. Lieutenant Commander Mountjoy. There you have it."

"Very good. We can simply ask him what would need to transpire to have Ms. Emer released."

"You mean go back to the security office again? We just came from there, Blandings. Here I am at a lavish resort, and all I seem to do is bounce back and forth between my suite and that underground lair."

"It is most regrettable, sir, but I feel certain this is the best course at this time."

Pelham shook it off. "You're probably right, Blandings, though I think the old file in the cake gag would be more fun."

"No doubt, sir. It is also, shall we say, risky. One can only imagine what Dame Agutha would say should you be arrested on Vogus for participating in criminal activity."

Pelham shuddered. "Oh, one hardly needs to speculate. I've faced down that tempest many a time, and believe you me, it has never been pleasant, not in the least."

"The direct approach then, sir?"

"I suppose so, Blandings." Pelham handed the rest of the salad back to the valet. "Let's get to it. We shall sally forth to call on this Mountjoy menace."

"Excellent, sir. Give me but a moment to clean things up. In the meantime, might I suggest that this time you inquire as to whether VICTOR can secure us an appointment?"

***

Lieutenant Commander Mountjoy eyed the prisoner sitting across the table from him. "Is this your first visit to Vogus, Emer?"

She rolled her eyes. "I already told you it isn't. I came here with friends one weekend when I was at university."

"During that visit, did you meet with Okcho resistance leaders?"

"Not unless they were dealing Jack Black."

"Have you met with Okcho resistance leaders during this current visit?"

"No. I've told you that. I don't know any insurrectionists."

"What have you —" Mountjoy was interrupted by his pocket device ringing insistently. He pulled it out and read the notification, an appointment request from the VICTOR system for: *Pelham G. Totleigh and valet.*

Mountjoy's first reaction was to dismiss the request. He didn't have time for that brainless Haplor. But then he remembered how Totleigh had blurted out about this Bononian under questioning, this person who was now his leading suspect as the inside collaborator for the attack. Possibly in a second interview he could draw even more information out of Totleigh. He accepted the appointment and returned the device to his pocket.

He looked across once more to the Bononian. "Let me get this straight. You're saying this was your first visit to Vogus?"

***

As Pelham entered the lobby, he said, "Blandings, I'll let you see about getting us down to the bowels of the building this time."

"Very good, sir." Blandings approached the front desk. "Excuse me, Mr. The Unfortunate."

"It's Urdi the Unfortunate," Urdi said.

"Ah. Thank you for clarifying. My error entirely. Now, Mr. Urdi the Unfortunate —"

"We Okcho don't go by misters, only our names. Just call me Urdi the Unfortunate. Not that anyone does."

Blandings hesitated. "I … I am not sure I can."

Pelham stepped forward. "What Blandings is trying to say is that addressing someone by title is in his nature. One could as easily ask an Avanian not to fly or a Thomian to set up a charity."

Urdi scratched the crest on his head. "I suppose it doesn't matter."

"Thank you," Blandings said. "Now could we trouble you once more to request someone to escort us to the security office?"

"You know, gentlemen," Urdi said, "there are lovelier sights on our fair planet than the security office."

"Of that I have no doubt," Pelham said, "but duty calls. This time we even have an appointment."

***

Commander Mountjoy was back in his office when the Haplors arrived. Private Stebbins escorted them into his room while Humstuggle glared.

"Hello, Totleigh, good to see you again," Mountjoy said, affixing his best smile to his face. "Have a seat."

"Yes, thank you," Totleigh said, sitting down. "This is my man Blandings." The valet remained standing.

Mountjoy nodded to the new Haplor. "Lieutenant Commander Mountjoy."

This one was not as bug-eyed as Totleigh, Mountjoy thought. And there appeared to be more skull sticking out at the back of his head, possibly suggestive of a larger brain. "How can I help you today?"

"It is my friend Emer," Totleigh said. He took a breath. "We know you are holding her. What you may not know is that we are negotiating a trade agreement, which makes it a priority of both the Bononian government and the Sonus colony for her to be released forthwith, thus allowing talks to resume."

Mountjoy leaned back in his chair. "I see. I sympathize with your situation, I do. But, of course, you realize I'm investigating a terrorist attack on our own colony."

A low, polite cough emanated from the other Haplor, the one called Blandings. Totleigh's eyes went to his companion. "You coughed, Blandings?"

"I confess I did, sir."

"Something to add?"

"I wouldn't want to overstep my place, sir, but it appears I have missed some facts of the case. Specifically, I was wondering why the lieutenant commander would characterize the attack as terrorism. There was no threat to sentient life. There was no physical destruction of property. How exactly was anyone terrorized?"

Mountjoy's jaw tensed. "There was destruction of property all right. Not physical property but the assets and goodwill of the Pink Mingo Hotel and Casino. Illegal winnings are the same as robbery. And when the casino is forced to rescind those winnings, it will cause irreparable harm to their image and good name."

"Thank you for elucidating," Blandings said with a nod. "Still, terrorism is an extreme word. One wouldn't want to dilute its power and meaning by using it lightly."

Mountjoy tried to stare down the valet. However, this Blandings was a domestic and seemed to avoid direct eye contact with anyone in authority. Mountjoy's glare collapsed unseen. The commander found it infuriating.

Totleigh said, "But whatever you wish to call it, Commander, whether terrorism or an attack or a mere fracas, why do you have to keep Emer in custody? Surely, you want the Okcho who are behind it."

"Gentlemen, you don't know the Okcho as I do. They are a simple people, uneducated, unsophisticated. Before we came, they were nomadic shepherds living hand-to-mouth. We've given them stability, prosperity, steady jobs. They would be completely pacified were it not for outside influences stirring them up."

"What sort of outside influences?" Totleigh asked.

"Oh, many groups, I assure you. Some even inside the agencies of the galactic alliance. They push for what they call indigenous autonomy, ignoring the natural symbiosis of inter-species relationships."

"Symbi ...?"

"Mutually beneficial relationships, Mr. Totleigh. For instance, on Zurkannia we have two insect species called hopperbugs and milk beetles. The milk beetles secrete a pasty substance, which the hopperbugs like to eat. So the hopperbugs supply the milk beetles with pollen to eat and protect them from predators. In exchange they milk the beetles, sucking the secretions from their bodies."

Totleigh scratched his forehead. "Interesting. So ... to apply your somewhat distasteful metaphor to Vogus, is it the Okcho or the Zurks who are getting milked?"

Mountjoy's proboscis curled up in annoyance. "Since we are both advanced species, our relationship is understandably more complex. The Zurks benefit from Okcho labor. The Okcho choose to settle down near the Zurk colony and take jobs here rather than living as vagabonds."

"And they like that, do they?"

This time Mountjoy's temper got away from him, escaping in harsh tones. "Of course, they like it. Don't you like having regular meals and a fixed abode?"

"Sorry," Totleigh said, looking abashed. "Didn't mean to offend. Only all this talk of the Okcho benefitting ... see, my Aunt Agutha is constantly telling me how I can improve myself. Trouble is, rarely does her recommended plan of action appeal to me terribly. Too much working and reading of boring things and all that."

"Well, take my word for it," Mountjoy said, "the Okcho appreciate all the Zurkannian empire has done for their planet and way of life. Ask any of them. Well, ask most of them. As I say, outside influences have stirred up a few malcontents."

Pelham said, "Oh, are you Zurks calling it an empire now? Rather a grandiose word for a dozen tiny, scattered colonies, don't you think?"

Mountjoy's proboscis unfurled and stiffened. "We'll call it what we please. What do you call your Haplor ...?" He waved a hand to finish the question.

"A confederation of simi-automatons —"

"I believe, sir, the word is autonomous," Blandings put in. "Semi-autonomous domains."

"That's it," Pelham said with a pleased nod. "All that."

Blandings spoke again. "But to return to Ms. Emer, Lieutenant Commander, you believe she is one of those agitating influences?"

"It is possible. That is why we are interrogating her."

"Have you uncovered any proof of her involvement in the attack?"

"Not as yet."

"Then if you have no proof …" The valet let the sentence hang.

Mountjoy, not accustomed to having his actions questioned by outsiders, glared at the Haplors. "Do you have any proof Emer *wasn't* involved?"

Blandings inclined his head. "We do not. Am I to understand that is how justice works here on Vogus? Is someone presumed guilty until proven innocent?"

"I am trying to protect our colony, to save lives. We can't be too careful. The Okcho troublemakers are extremely shrewd and devious, always planning some assault like this casino attack. We must keep a sharp eye out for them."

"No doubt," Blandings said as if musing to himself. "If these Okcho are at once both cunning schemers and simple folk, one would imagine it must leave your head spinning."

"Oh, it can," Mountjoy said, not catching the irony until after he had spoken.

Totleigh asked, "Can you give us any indication of when Ms. Emer will be released?"

"No."

"Then what do you propose we do about our trade agreement?"

"Frankly, your trade agreement is not my concern."

Totleigh muttered something.

"What was it you said?" Mountjoy asked.

"I said, try telling that to my Aunt Agutha."

Blandings asked, "Is there anything at all we can do for Ms. Emer?"

"Nothing short of bringing me proof that she had nothing to do with the attack."

Totleigh's eyebrows shot up. "You want us to help with the investigation?"

"What? No. I didn't say that." The last thing Mountjoy needed was these two Haplors snooping around and getting underfoot.

Totleigh said, "You know, Blandings, if we found proof of Emer's innocence and got her freed from the guardhouse, that would certainly give us an edge in the trade negotiations."

Mountjoy felt his blood pressure rise. "No. No. We can't have civilians involved in security force business." Especially, not aliens, Mountjoy thought. He could imagine one of these Haplors getting in the middle of a firefight between Zurk forces and the Okcho subversives. If they ended up injured or killed, he would never hear the end of it. He would be recalled to Zurkannia, sanctioned, demoted.

Fortunately, Blandings seemed to agree with him. "Sir, we should leave the investigation to Lieutenant Commander Mountjoy."

"A fat lot of good he seems to be accomplishing," Totleigh said in another slightly louder mutter.

Mountjoy said, "Now listen, Totleigh —"

Blandings said calmly, "Before we go, Lieutenant Commander, could we at least speak with Emer."

Mountjoy grabbed at the request like a lifeline to extract him from the conversation. "Of course, you may. Emer is in an interrogation … I mean, an interview room right now. I would be more than happy to give you a few minutes … provided you don't get any crazy ideas about investigating."

"You can be sure," Blandings said, "nothing could be further from our minds than intruding into your case."

Mountjoy studied the valet, reading openness and honesty in his face. He rotated his head toward Totleigh and read … what? Totleigh's bushy eyebrows furrowed as he looked up and away with a silly grin on his face. Now what was this little Haplor thinking?

Chapter 13

Hail, Hail Bononia

With a fair amount of effort, Lieutenant Commander Mountjoy pulled himself out of his chair and wobbled around his desk to the door. Pelham and Blandings followed him back into the office bullpen and then down a short hallway to a tiny room where Emer sat at a table in a hard, straight-backed chair. Looking around at it, Pelham would swear this was the same room where he had been plagued by Mountjoy the night before. At the least, it must be a twin or triplet of it. Who knew how many of these odious compartments infested the place?

Emer looked up as they entered. Dark circles ringed her eyes. Strands of hair stuck out at odd angles. Her face was drawn, its copper glow faded to a sickly beige. "Pelham. Blandings. What are you doing here?"

Mountjoy said, "They were ... concerned about you. I have granted them a few minutes of visit time. I'll leave you alone."

Mountjoy locked the door behind him, the deadbolt once more ominously clicking in Pelham's ears like the latch of a coffin.

Pelham took the one other chair at the table. Blandings stood behind him, maintaining a rigid formal pose while somehow also exuding concern.

"Well, at least now we know where you are," Pelham said. "Have they given you any indication of how long they intend to keep you?"

Emer shook her head.

Blandings asked, "Have you been given anything to eat or drink?"

Another headshake.

"What?" asked Pelham. "The blighters."

Blandings moved to the door and knocked. Moments later Mountjoy opened it. "Done already?"

Blandings said, "We were hoping, Lieutenant Commander, that Ms. Emer could receive some food and drink. If I am not mistaken, her right to sustenance is guaranteed in the galactic alliance charter, is it not?"

Mountjoy sulked but said, "I'll have something brought around." He closed and re-locked the door.

Pelham said to Emer, "They can't seriously believe you had anything to do with the attack, can they?"

"I think they do." Her words came out devoid of all energy.

"Poppycock! Rubbish! I mean … you didn't, did you?"

Another shake of the head.

Blandings said, "If I may interject, Ms. Emer, you are here on Vogus as an emissary of Bononia. Would not diplomatic immunity apply in this case?"

She propped an elbow on the table and leaned her forehead into her palm. "They say there's a loophole. According to Mountjoy, diplomatic immunity applies only to the Zurk home world, not to their colonies."

"Sounds dodgy to me," Pelham said. "They can't do this to you. We'll stop them. We can stop them, can't we, Blandings?"

Emer looked up from her palm. "Mind what you say."

"What do you mean?"

She lowered her voice. "They are bound to be listening." Her eyes darted to cameras in the corners of the gray ceiling. Pelham's eyes followed.

He whispered, "Have you been able to contact your government?"

"They haven't let me contact anyone."

"Would you like us to do that, Ms. Emer?" Blandings asked.

She looked up, her deep hazel eyes gazing into the valet's huge brown ones. She nodded.

The door clicked open, and a uniformed Zurk appeared, carrying a tray with a bowl of orange soup and a cup of water. He set it down in front of her and left. Emer eyed it but didn't touch it.

"Eat. Eat," Pelham said. "You must be starving."

Emer complied, displaying a less than delighted expression as she tasted the soup. Still, she kept going.

Pelham said, "You know, Mountjoy suggested I might try to find evidence to clear you."

Blandings cleared his throat. "Sir."

"He did. He said I should bring him proof."

"Pardon me, sir, but I do not think the lieutenant commander's intent was for —"

Pelham said, "Nonsense. Imagine the fun of conducting an investigation. What's more, it would all be in service of our orders to conclude the trade agreement, a job we can't finish, I might point out, while Emer is incarcerated."

"I doubt Dame Agutha would view it from that perspective."

"If you will recall, Blandings, I have a bit of experience with investigations." He leaned in toward Emer with raised eyebrows. "A murder investigation, in fact."

"I remember it well, sir. However, you were the suspect in the case, not a detective."

Pelham waved a hand. "I worked in close collaboration with the famous Galactic Detective Agency to clear my name, didn't I?"

"They did ... keep you apprised as to the progress of the investigation."

"Apprised hardly covers it. They consulted with me. Or I with them. Which is it, Blandings?"

"I'm not certain either truly applies, sir."

Emer's eyes shifted from Pelham to Blandings and back to Pelham. "I think if you contact Bononia, it will be more than sufficient. Talk to the Minister of Commerce. That's my boss's boss's boss."

"Righto," said Pelham. "And what will they do?"

"I don't know. Something ... surely." She dropped her head. "I've never been jailed on another world before ... or on my own world for that matter." She reached out and placed a hand on Pelham's arm. "Contact them for me. I would be extremely grateful. It's terrible in here."

At the touch, a tingling sensation raced up the back of Pelham's neck. "Um ... not at all. Think nothing of it. Pleased to help."

The door clicked open again. This time it was Mountjoy. "I'm afraid that's all the time I can give you."

They said their goodbyes and Pelham and Blandings returned to their suite. Pelham dropped to the couch. "I can't help but think, Blandings, this is all my fault. I said too much to that nuisance Mountjoy."

"You mustn't blame yourself, sir. I understand a certain amount of excessive talk is a common occurrence under police interrogation."

"You understand correctly. Those blighters, they ask you question after question until you find yourself blurting out something."

"What's done is done, sir. Best to look forward to what we can do now, such as making that call for Ms. Emer."

"Right you are, Blandings." Pelham stared at the video screen, blinking. "Um ... Blandings, what do you know about this business of placing calls?"

"I should be able to work out how to do it, sir. Allow me." The valet stepped in front of the screen and said, "Place call to the office of the Minister of Commerce, Bononia."

The screen flashed to life showing a picture of the Pink Mingo with a superimposed circle of gray dots, a single black dot spinning around and around.

"Shouldn't be but a moment, sir."

"It's already been a moment. And another one. Looks like that ruddy Roll It wheel. I feel as if I should be placing a bet or something."

The dots dissolved away and were replaced by the copper-colored face of a Bononian man with thin cheeks and dark hair that looked like it had been cut with the assistance of a salad bowl. He wore refractors, circles of shimmering blue ringing his eyes.

"Ah, hello," Pelham said. "Is this the Minister of Commerce?"

"This is the assistant minister. Or I should say the assistant vice deputy minister ... for administrative services. And you are?"

"Pelham G. Totleigh, Sonus Inspector of ... um ... um."

"Imports, sir," Blandings said.

"Definitely."

"May I ask why you are calling?" the Bononian asked.

"Well, it's a bit of a long story, what? It's about Emer, who is representing you at the trade conference on Vogus. Do you know her?"

"I am familiar with the name."

"Good. Turns out she's being held by the local constabulary. Well, not the constabulary precisely. They claim to be a military contingent or some such with law enforcement powers, none of which matters at this point. You see, there was an attack ... not a physical attack, mind you. No blasters or any of the like. This group claiming to be the Okcho Hibernation Flock —"

"Okcho Liberation Force, sir," Blandings said.

"That's it. The Okcho Librarian Force, they did a little ... I don't know ... I suppose you would say they fiddled with the casino's gambling system. Don't ask me how they pulled it off. All that computer gobbledygook goes straight past me. But ... um. Where was I Blandings?"

"You were explaining, sir, how the casino's computer system was hacked, leading to unearned payouts to all the guests. The Colonial Security Force in their investigation has been holding Ms. Emer for questioning for the best part of a night and a day, suspecting she had something to do with the attack. We thought her superiors on Bononia should be informed of her plight."

"Yes," said Pelham. "Yes, well put. Excellent exposition there, Blandings. Couldn't have said it better myself. In short, she's in a fine kettle of fish."

The Bononian on the screen opened his mouth, closed it, then opened it again. "Fish?"

"A fix. A difficulty. A jam."

"Jam?"

"Dash it, man. She's in trouble. She's incarcerated."

"How ... how did you come by this information?"

"From Emer herself. She suggested we call you."

The Bononian switched off the refractors and rubbed his face with both hands. "This is a distressing situation. Let me be clear. Our government does not look highly upon our representatives running afoul of the law on other planets."

"Eh?"

"This will be a black mark on Emer's record."

Pelham threw up his hands. "What? No! She's innocent. She's being wrongfully detained, I tell you. We need to secure her release somehow or another, and we were hoping you could do something."

"Oh. Hmm. That's different then. How is Emer doing?"

"She is drained, haggard, hollow-eyed. She is no doubt being subjected to constant interrogation."

The Bononian shook his head sadly. "Unfortunately, I'm not sure we can do much to ensure her release without coming there ourselves."

"Then, by all means, come," Pelham said. "Hop the nearest spacecraft. Not a Donovian one, though, if you can help it. Take my advice."

"That would be problematic. We are approaching the end of our budget cycle. Emer used the last of the travel allowance for this conference."

"Budget? You're concerned about the budget? The liberty of one of your citizens hangs in the balance. Not to mention what might happen to her should they convict her of involvement in the attack. By the way, Blandings, what *would* happen should they convict her?"

"I am sorry to say, sir, I cannot provide a definitive answer at this time. She has not yet been charged with a specific crime, and I would need to brush up on Zurkannian law."

"Did you say brush up?" Pelham asked. "Do you mean to suggest you have some working, though slightly out of date, knowledge of Zurk law?"

"Yes, sir. Given the number of awkward situations you and your friends end up in, I try to keep abreast of the legal customs of most worlds."

"Blandings, you never fail to astound me. But that is, at present, beside the point." He turned back to the screen. "Are you saying you are going to do nothing for Emer?"

The Bononian's brows furrowed. "I am not saying that at all. I will take this matter to the minister at once. I expect he will immediately write a strongly worded protest to the Vogus authorities."

"Write a protest?" Pelham couldn't believe his ears. "I scarcely think a protest will accomplish much."

"A strongly worded protest, Mr. Totleigh. No doubt unsparing in its condemnation, rest assured." The Bononian nodded his head meaningfully.

Pelham stared at the screen, open-mouthed. "I ... I am flabbergasted, stupefied, confounded. I ... I —"

Blandings took over. "Thank you, Mr. Assistant Vice Deputy Minister. It was lovely chatting with you. We will pass along to Ms. Emer your sincere concern and will be in touch again later with updates on her situation."

The Bononian bowed his head, and the screen went blank.

"Well, I'll be dashed, Blandings. I mean, if I were jailed by the gendarmerie, I shouldn't be at all surprised to hear that Aunt Agutha had cut me adrift, but I never dreamed the Bononians would do such a thing. No, I take that back, Blandings. Remember when I was in that seedy cell on Girsu? Even Aunt Agutha didn't leave me there to rot. She hired the Galactic Detective Agency. I'm astonished. I'm gobsmacked. I'm flum .... um ... what's the flum one, Blandings?"

"Could you mean flummoxed, sir?"

Pelham pointed at his valet. "Bullseye, Blandings. I was certain I could count on you. I only wish we could count on the Bononians."

Chapter 14

You've Got to Know When to Hold 'em

"Now," Pelham said, running a hand across his chin, "what about digging up some real proof that Emer was not involved in the attack?"

Blandings raised one eyebrow, an extreme reaction for him. "You will recall, sir, we dismissed that idea as being impractical and quite possibly dangerous."

"Did we, Blandings? Odd, I don't remember deciding that."

"We did, sir. Such an undertaking could result in any number of unfortunate outcomes."

"Well, if you say so. What's next on the program then?"

"I believe, sir, it would be best for you to return to the conference in case, at a later date, Dame Agutha has questions concerning the proceedings."

Pelham grimaced. "You mean listen to another boring speaker? Say it isn't true, Blandings."

"I fear, sir, it is expected of you."

"Right, right. As much as I hate to say it, you are likely correct." He heaved a heavy sigh and hopped from the couch. "Fine. I will attend another bally session. I don't suppose we have any toothpicks I can use to prop my eyes open."

"I neglected to pack any, sir. However, you might inquire at the hotel restaurant."

"Blandings, I never know when you're joking."

"Oh, sir, jesting would not be an appropriate manner of discourse between a gentleman and his gentleman's gentleman."

Pelham returned to the conference to find the session being led by a Thomian, who was talking about the supposed advantages of other planets allowing Thomian businesses to expand into their worlds, which sounded like anything but a good idea to Pelham. Most of what he knew about Thomians was how they were thugs and involved in all sorts of unsavory enterprises. The way the hulking, scraggly-haired speaker was putting it, with a sneer on his face and using terms like "protection" and "piece of the action," it all sounded more like a threat than a business opportunity. Pelham noticed several of the delegates staring wide-eyed at the speaker, seemingly afraid to move.

"I know a lot of youse have real nice planets," the Thomian said, his beady, red eyes sweeping the room. "We can help youse keep 'em dat way. If youse have elements in your society dat are difficult to control, we can take care of 'em for youse. Get rid of da riffraff and centralize everything under our authority. Now, I know what yer thinking. What do youse have to do in exchange for dese fine services?" The speaker shrugged and flipped over a meaty hand. "Maybe nothing. Or maybe someday youse can return da favor and do a service for us. We're friends — we'd like to be anyway — and dat's how friends operate."

Pelham could see no value in listening to any more of this hokum. He began to cough, prompting stares from the other delegates and an angry glare from the Thomian. He continued coughing, held a finger in the air, and exited the room as quickly as possible.

He wandered into the casino to find it again hopping with activity. Marbles were spinning around Roll It wheels. Cards were being dealt to Jack Black players. Pelham wandered through the tables, scouting for anything that grabbed his interest.

He spotted the horned Cuneddan who had sat beside him at dinner the night before — was it only last night? Hard to imagine after all the hubbub with the attack and interrogation and getting locked in Emer's room and all the trips to the security office.

The Cuneddan was sitting at a table sneaking a peek at two cards face down in front of him. The person's name had escaped him, but Pelham remembered him as a friendly sort.

"What ho!" Pelham said, nodding to his former dinner companion. "How are you doing?"

The Cuneddan looked up. "I'm taking it easy, man. Taking it easy. Mr. Totleigh, was it?"

"Indeed. Pelham G. Totleigh. Call me Pelham. I confess your name is not popping to mind. Sorry. Simply frightful at hanging onto names, what?"

The Cuneddan chuckled. "No worries. It's Syd Duncil. Call me Duncil. Or Duncilrino. Or Your Duncilness."

"Amurru fizz?" came a voice from behind.

Pelham peered around at the question. An Okcho female was there wearing a bright smile and holding a tray of drinks. "Ah, sounds lovely." He took the drink and watched the credit balance on his bracelet sink lower. Hovering in the negative hundreds, it scarcely seemed like real money anymore. He gave the Okcho a five mingo rating.

Drink in hand, Pelham stepped toward the gaming table. "Righto, Duncil. What are we playing?"

"It's called Texas Odin. Texas is a powerful country of Earth that nobody wants to mess with."

"And the Odin bit?"

"An Earth god, evidently a Texas god."

"Must be a popular god to have a game named after him … or her … or whatever they have on Earth. Would this Odin be a god of chance by any chance?" Pelham smiled at his own wordplay.

"Could be. I was thinking more the god of sanitation since the game appears to have something to do with plumbing. People are scoring flushes and straight flushes and full houses. There are cards in the hole. There's even a deuce."

"A what?"

Duncil chuckled. "Never mind. Earth slang."

"And you form all those combinations with only the two cards?"

"These two plus the five the dealer has."

Pelham looked to the dealer, recognizing Shay the Shorter from Roll It and earlier from the bar. "What ho, Shay the Shorter. Say, you get around."

"Hello again, Mr. Totleigh. How are you?"

"A bit sleep deprived but otherwise holding up, thanks." To Duncil he said, "I see only three cards in front of Shay."

"Be patient. More are coming. I have to wager first. There's a lot of wagering in this game." Duncil typed a bet into his bracelet. Holographic chips appeared in front of him.

"Have you been interviewed by the security force?" Pelham asked.

Duncil rolled his eyes. "They pulled me out of bed in the middle of the night, completely disrupting my inner balance. I think that's why my luck is off now."

"They kept *me* out *until* the middle of the night. They still have Emer."

"The Bononian? What do they want with her? Wait. I have to bet again."

Pelham glanced up to notice Shay the Shorter studying him. He smiled and nodded at her as her eyes darted away.

Duncil tapped something into his bracelet. "I'll raise ten. I hope this works."

Pelham said, "They seem to think Emer was in cahoots with those Okcho levitation blokes. I may try to help her with some investigative work of my own."

Shay was eyeing him again. Pelham assumed it must be his blue serge suit. It had a bit of flash. He knew this one was a corker when he bought it.

"How in the galaxy can *you* help her?" Duncil asked, taking yet another peek at his hole cards.

"Less talk, more card playing," said an Arsawan sitting on the other side of Duncil.

Pelham said, "These Okcho lactation people were eager to claim credit for the attack. I hoped if I could contact them, I might persuade them to make it clear to the authorities that Emer had nothing to do with it. Surely, they wouldn't want an off-worlder to be seen as the driving force for their operation."

The Arsawan said, "Fold."

Duncil said, "Raise another ten," while punching the wager into his bracelet. His holographic stack of chips grew taller.

The Delusian on the other side, his chest even with the table, looked up and said, "I'll see your ten and raise another ten."

Duncil bit his lower lip and ran a hand across a horn.

"It's to you, Duncilrino," Shay the Shorter said.

Duncil held up a hand. "Wait. Wait. The universe should be giving me a sign right about now." He closed his eyes. A moment later he opened them and shook his head. "Turns out the universe is not answering right now. Okay, I fold. What do you have?"

"Two queens," the Delusian answered, flipping over the cards. His bracelet went *bloop-bloop-bloop-bloop* and flashed up his winnings.

Duncil's jaw dropped. "No! But I had two pair, fives and jacks." He flipped over his cards, each one matching one in front of the dealer. "I would have beat you!"

"Those fellows are called jacks?" Pelham asked. He wondered what jacks had to do with plumbing. Weren't jacks things mechanics used to prop up other things? Weren't jacks something used in electrical work?

Duncil raised his hands in surrender. "Oh well. Life goes on. Gambling is nothing but money flowing to where the universe wants it to be. Want to play, Pelham? I'm going again."

"Ah, I don't believe I will. I'll stick to Roll It, if you don't mind, where one only needs to know colors and numbers. I'm not up on all the lingo of the skilled trades."

Pelham wandered off in search of other excitement.

***

Upstairs in the suite, Blandings hummed softly as he cleaned Pelham's clothes from the previous day and decided on his clothes for the dinner tonight.

"Oh, VICTOR, what is the theme for the conference this evening?"

VICTOR's melodic voice sounded from Blandings' bracelet. "Tonight the trade conference attendees will dine on an Earth delicacy known as Pete-Za followed by entertainment by The Amazing Mystico."

"And what, may I ask, is The Amazing Mystico?"

VICTOR launched into a publicity blurb. "The Amazing Mystico is a master illusionist from the planet Javid. She has performed before the patrician of Fornax, the interim coalition leader of Antares Five, Queen Scythia and the royal family of Diere, among many others. Her most famous trick was making the planet Gongee disappear, an astonishing feat still under litigation."

"A magician." Blandings shook his head. "One wonders what one should wear to a magic show. VICTOR, what is the recommended dress for the event?"

"There are no dress expectations."

Blandings emitted a soft chuckle. "There are always expectations."

Perhaps the tweed, he thought. He pulled out a green tweed jacket and scrutinized it for dust and lint. Yes, Mr. Totleigh always looked sharp in the tweed.

He hung out the suit, thinking back over his earlier conversation with Pelham. He earnestly hoped he had said enough to dissuade his employer from trying to hunt for more information about the attack. Investigations were not proper conduct for a Haplor of his position, and Dame Agutha would be most displeased should he undertake such an enterprise.

There was, however, only so much he, as a valet, could say, especially with a strong-minded young man such as Mr. Totleigh. Well, possibly strong-minded was not the precise word in this case. Strong-willed, high-strung, easily excitable — those fit better. With all that, the man was sometimes difficult to steer into wise paths. Still, there were techniques for shaping a gentleman's behavior — the gentle word, the guiding hand.

***

The interrogation room door clicked shut, leaving Emer alone once more. She had been there for hours, alternating between mind-numbing boredom when left alone and intense duress while being interviewed. She let her head bang down on the metal table and tried to relax. It didn't work. Sitting up again, she glanced around the tiny room, feeling the walls close in on her. She tried telling herself the space wasn't much smaller than her old college room, and she didn't even have to share it with a roommate. She would have welcomed a roommate right then, even that one majoring in early education who constantly left torn bits of crayon wrappers on the floor.

During her last interview, Mountjoy appeared to be grasping for questions, spending long minutes staring at her in silence. She hoped that meant he was growing tired of her and would soon turn to other lines of inquiry. Even if he did, she might not be getting out anytime soon. With any luck, though, the Bononian government would find a way to gain her release.

What would her bosses think of her getting arrested? Would this trigger a review of her behavior? Would her job now be on the line? Emer had worked so hard to get where she was. Now this. She slouched in the chair, letting her chin drop to her chest. All she had wanted to do was attend this conference, meet some contacts, hammer out the treaty with Sonus. Then all this happened.

***

Not far from the interrogation room, Lieutenant Commander Leopold Mountjoy took a sip of tea and sat back with a self-approving grin. He would yet break this Bononian. But even if he didn't, there was every reason to expect this new plan of his would succeed brilliantly. And when it did, with the resistance crushed, he would bring peace to this restless colony and conceivably earn himself a promotion, maybe even a better posting on a world with fewer troublesome people and an aboveground office. Yes, this plan would work. Those rebels would never see it coming.

Chapter 15

The Amazing Mystico

"So then they place wagers on the various hands they can assemble using the cards in front of them plus the dealer's cards," Pelham said, attempting to explain Texas Odin to Blandings. "They can get them all of the same shape — diamonds or shovels or whatever — or several of the same number, or the numbers in order."

Blandings slipped the tweed jacket on Pelham and gave the shoulders a final brush. "Fascinating, sir."

"Jolly well complicated, you mean. Personally, I think it's for someone brainier than yours truly. I'll stick with Jack Black where there's simple addition."

"Or perhaps, sir, you should steer clear of the casino entirely. You still have that negative balance."

"Ah, well, I'm pleased to report that, thanks to a quick session at the Jack Black table, I managed to drive it significantly upwards towards zero."

"Well done, sir, though I must remind you of the danger of —"

"Until the last couple of hands, that is."

"Oh dear, sir. For this evening I suggest you come directly back to the suite at the conclusion of the magic performance."

"I intend to, Blandings. Well, unless I end up having a quiet drink with a like-minded chap. Duncil seems a nice enough fellow. Tell me, Blandings, do we do much business with Cunedda?"

"If I am not mistaken, sir, Cunedda supplies Sonus colony with plasma synthesizers."

"Ah, good. Then he and I have much to discuss."

A few minutes later, while in the process of whooshing through the pneumatic lift, Pelham's bracelet dinged, and a message popped up. With the wind rushing past his eyes, he struggled to make it out. After several blinks, the letters finally resolved.

If you want to learn the truth, come to the Okcho village beyond the casino walls.

Pelham gaped at the bracelet. Who was messaging him? What truth did they have to report?

The message disappeared as he reached the ground floor. He strode through the casino oblivious to the games, waving off an Amurru fizz, thinking only about what, if anything, he should do in response. Blandings had warned him against getting involved, but, of course, Blandings didn't have the steel nerves of a Totleigh. If this could lead to Emer's release, well, how could he not help a friend in need?

Pelham stepped to the doorway of the meeting room. The only delegates who had arrived were the two Mucs and a Pardiun, who all regarded him with icy stares. He stepped back into the hallway. Across the lobby was the front door of the Pink Mingo. He strode for it and stepped outside, a chilly wind hitting his face as dueling white suns, low in the sky, flooded the street with cold evening light.

Looking to get beyond the casino walls, Pelham walked around the end of the hotel only to find it butted up against a souvenir shop next door. He turned around and walked to the opposite end of the Pink Mingo. There he found a corner, but it led only to a high concrete wall, which appeared to be unscalable, even for a Haplor.

Pelham returned to the hotel lobby and approached Urdi the Unfortunate at the reception desk. "I say, Urdi."

"The Unfortunate," Urdi said in a deadpan.

"Yes. Right. I have a question. I was hoping to visit the Okcho village. I understand there's one right behind the casino."

"Why would you want to go there, Mr. Totleigh? There are no tourist attractions in our little community."

"Oh, you know, I'm something of an amateur anthropologist of sorts. I love learning about other cultures."

"Do you?"

"Absolutely. Old ruins and pottery shards and all that."

Urdi blinked. "Unfortunately, the Okcho village is only for Okcho. It is strictly off-limits to off-worlders. There's not much to see there anyway. Not like all the dazzling sights here inside the fabulous Pink Mingo Hotel and Casino. Have you been to our gift shop?"

"Um ... not as yet."

"We have shirts and tea mugs for loved ones, stuffed mingos for the younglings."

"Right. I'll be sure to check into that. Well, sorry to trouble you."

Pelham stepped away from the desk. He wandered back toward the meeting room, thinking it was just as well he couldn't enter their town. He shouldn't be sticking his nose in. Better to play it safe, as Blandings advised.

Stepping into the room, he spotted Duncil standing in a corner wearing a crumpled, loose-fitting shirt and a bland smile.

"What ho!" Pelham called to him.

"What ho, what ho," Duncil said.

"What ho, what ... ah." Pelham shook it off and sidled up beside him. "How did Texas Odin turn out for you?"

"Ups and downs. Ups and downs."

A bell sounded, and conversation stopped. All turned to see the Axan standing on the raised platform.

"Good evening, trade delegates. It is I again, Jasper Jadarite, your conference chair. I hope you've been learning a lot today and making important contacts with other delegates." He swept a hand toward a buffet table. "I'm pleased to tell you that pete-za is served!"

Pelham and Duncil joined a queue of other delegates. As they reached the buffet, they saw it decked with platters of round crust smothered in a red sauce along with something thick and yellow and bits of green and brown that Pelham couldn't identify. An Okcho stood behind the table, handing out plates, knives, and sporks.

Pelham asked the Okcho, "What is this pete-za?"

"Pete-za is a popular Earth dish. It is presumed to be named after a person named Saint Pete, whom Earthlings believe guards the gates to the afterlife. Which, of course, makes pete-za the food of the gods."

"Interesting. But what I mean is ... what *is* it? What's the bally thing made of?"

"Pete-za consists of a flatbread spread with the pulp of a fruit called maters and covered with the coagulated lactation secretions of dairy animals and other various items."

Pelham twisted his neck, giving the Pete-za a sideways ogle. "Quite the … um … description there. Appetizing … well, it isn't the precise word I would use."

"That was how the Grays described it. Of course, we make ours with a replicator using the recipe file the Gray's provided."

"You're sure Earthlings eat this?"

"Oh yes, sir. By all accounts it is enormously popular."

"Well, as they say, when in an Earth-themed hotel, do as the Earthlings do, eh?" Pelham took a plate and dished on a slice.

He and Duncil found seats. Duncil picked up his spork and poked at the pete-za. He fingered his knife and looked askance at the food. "How do you suppose we dig into this thing?"

Pelham peered around to try to discover how other delegates were attacking the problem, only to find a decided lack of consensus. An Arsawan on the other side of the table was cutting the pete-za with his knife and picking up the bites with his spork. An Oecanthus beside Pelham was sucking up the red sauce through its thin feeding tube, leaving the crust and toppings behind. The Thomian who had earlier threatened the crowd with business opportunities held a piece of the pete-za in his fist and was taking bites directly from it. Another delegate, species unknown mainly because their face was buried in the pete-za, was, well, eating with their face buried in the pete-za.

"Golly, I don't know," Pelham said.

They decided at last on eating the pete-za from their hands, Thomian style. After one bite, they stared at each other, eyes bright with delight.

"I say, Duncil, this hits the old spot, what?"

"The flavors, the textures. Man."

"Earth food never disappoints, old sport. Did I tell you I've had waffles?"

"You did, in fact. Last night."

Pelham waggled his head in mock embarrassment. "Sorry about that. Sometimes the old bean gets a bit mushy."

"Think nothing of it. Waffles are worth mentioning twice. As is this pete-za."

The lights dimmed in the room. Delegates stuffed the last bites of pete-za into their mouths or equivalents. Those in line for seconds grabbed a quick slice and slipped back to their seats. A spotlight came up on the empty platform, followed by a *pop* and a column of smoke. The smoke cleared to reveal a Javidian, a chunky ocean blue reptile with a cavernous mouth, round eyes, and red spikes running down the back of its head. With a description like that, one could easily get the idea Javidians were the stuff of nightmares — monsters from under the bed — were it not for their broad toothy smiles, which exuded not malevolence but excited friendliness.

This Javidian's stout body was dressed in a maroon suit and puffy shirt. A tail sporting a ball of spikes bounced across the platform as the alien stepped forward.

"Good evening. I am The Amazing Mystico."

The magician raised one of her four arms and made a flourish with one hand. A wand flicked into it from nowhere. Mystico tapped another hand with the wand, and two white birds appeared. They fluttered around the room while the crowd applauded, settling over beside the pete-za, where they began to peck at the leftovers.

"And now," The Amazing Mystico said, "I need a volunteer from the audience."

Pelham shot his arm up in the air and waved it back and forth, jumping onto his chair to make himself seen over the larger delegates.

"Yes," said Mystico, "the Haplor there."

Pelham beamed and walked to the platform as Mystico rolled a glossy black box front and center.

"What is your name and where are you from?" Mystico asked.

"Pelham G. ..." Pelham flinched as he heard his name amplified through the room. He looked around and tried again. "Pelham G. Totleigh. I'm from Sonus."

"And would you like to visit your home on Sonus for a moment, Pelham?"

"What? Oh, no thank you."

Mystico whispered through a frozen smile. "Say yes. It's part of the act."

"Hmm? Oh. You said Sonus? Ah yes. Quite. Now that you mention it, I suppose I wouldn't mind popping back home for a moment or two. I forgot to pack my slippers."

Mystico waved a hand toward the box. "This, Pelham G. Totleigh, is the magical transporter chamber. This box can convey you across the galaxy in an instant."

"I say," said Pelham, "that sounds marvelous. Can it bring me back too? I have unfinished business here, don't you know."

Mystico flung open one side of the box. "It can. Please step inside. You may sit on the bench."

Pelham said, "One wonders why this isn't being employed in transport. It jolly well would have made my trip here nicer. I had to ride with a bunch of —"

"Please. Step inside."

"Ah. Righto." Pelham stepped into the box to a musty smell. He perched on a wire mesh platform in the middle of the box, his head pressing against the top. The door closed, plunging Pelham into pitch blackness, and he wondered, not for the first time in his life, what he had got himself into. Did he even want to go home? Sure, an evening with the old chums would be agreeable, but what would Aunt Agutha say if he ran into her?

A hatch in the bottom of the box opened. The spiky head of a Javidian like Mystico appeared through the hole along with a hand holding a light. "Come with me."

"What?"

"Hurry. We have fifteen seconds before Mystico opens the box."

Pelham slid through the hatch, finding a ladder extending through the platform and the floor below. He climbed down into a gray room lined with lockers.

The Javidian pointed to a staircase. "Go up those stairs and back into the meeting room. When the spotlight shines on you, tell everybody you just returned from Sinus."

"Do you mean Sonus?"

"Whatever. Tell them you went there."

"But I didn't."

The Javidian rolled its huge eyes. "Yeah, I know that. I'm the one who pulled you out of the box five seconds ago. Play along with the act, and you'll end up with one hundred credits to your casino account. Say you saw home, met friends, whatever, and then were drawn back here at Mystico's words."

"What words?"

"Go!" The Javidian turned and walked away, saying, "The package is out for delivery."

Pelham sauntered toward the stairs but stopped when he heard a door behind him slide open. He turned to see two Okcho slipping into the gray room. They wore wide-necked pullover tunics over pants. They moved toward the lockers, drew out casino uniforms, and stepped behind partitions to change.

Pelham moved toward the door from which the Okcho had entered. Beside it sat a uniformed Zurk lost in his electronic device.

"Pardon me," Pelham asked the guard, "but could you tell me where that door leads?"

The Zurk looked up from the device. "Sorry, little guy. I didn't see you there."

"Quite all right. About this door then?"

"Officially, this door goes nowhere."

"Nowhere?"

"That is the explanation I am authorized to give, sir."

"Well, I must say, such a thing hardly sounds likely. Doesn't every door lead somewhere?"

The guard considered it. "That is often the case, yes. And yet this one does not."

"Does it perhaps connect to the Okcho village?"

The Zurk's expression hardened. He stared at Pelham without answering.

"You see, I couldn't help noticing those two Okcho who came through as if coming to work. It stands to reason then —"

A voice came from behind Pelham. "Hey! I thought I told you to get back to the meeting room. You're holding up the act." The Javidian grabbed Pelham with all four arms and pushed him up the first few steps.

"All right, all right," Pelham said. "I'll go. Only one question. When is it I'm supposed to reach Sonus?"

Chapter 16

Fools Rush In

The stairs were not built for the likes of Haplors. Pelham had to take two steps on each tread. At least it wasn't a pneumatic lift, he thought. Reaching the top, he found himself in a hallway between the meeting rooms. A door on the left was open. He stepped through it and found himself immediately blinded by a glaring spotlight.

From the platform, The Amazing Mystico said, "Here is our friend materialized back at last from his fantastic transport. I had to call you several times, friend. Your world must be many light-years away. Tell us, how is everything back home?"

Pelham was startled by the floodlight and more than a bit confused by all this talk of transporting. He hadn't gone home or been enchanted into materializing anywhere. He had climbed down a bally ladder into a rather grim locker room where people kept yelling at him and treating him in a rude manner. Pelham, however, remembered the promise of one hundred credits. "Oh … um. Everything was fine. Same old same old, you know. Glad to be back."

The crowd applauded, and the spotlight flashed out. Pelham blinked in the darkness and fumbled his way back to his seat, guided by the dim light of his bracelet flashing a new higher balance, or rather a less negative balance.

"Nice trip?" Duncil asked in a whisper as he slipped into his seat.

Pelham tutted. "The whole thing was a trick. I only climbed down a ladder and walked back up a flight of stairs."

Pelham's bracelet dinged, and a message popped up: *Now you know the way out.*

He muttered to himself, "I may know the way out, but how the blazes am I supposed to pass through the door with that guard there?"

Pelham decided to ignore the message and focus on the rest of the magic show. The illusions, though, were ruined for him now that he knew they were all tricks. After yawning through a fellow trade delegate ostensibly being sawed in half, he stood and wandered out, thinking he might take one more peep at that door downstairs.

He slipped down the stairs and approached the guard, while his brain raced, trying to come up with a plan. "Excuse me," he asked the guard, "do you have the time?" He had a vague notion of dashing through the door while the Zurk checked on the current o'clock.

The guard eyed him. "You will find the exact time displayed on your bracelet, sir."

Pelham glanced at his wrist. "Ah yes. There it is. Dashed handy gizmos these bracelets." He stood smiling at the guard, desperately trying to think of another play.

"Is there anything else you require, sir?" While the words were polite, the tone was more like a slap across the face.

"Ah ... no ..." He directed his eyes to the blank wall over the guard's shoulder. "I was only trying to figure out what in the galaxy that thing is."

When the Zurk spun to peer at the wall, Pelham pivoted toward the door. He had his hand over the control panel when the guard's arm shot out and grabbed him by the shoulder.

"Excuse me, sir, may I help you?"

"Um ... yes. Um ... I was invited to a party at the house of an Okcho chum of mine. Casual get-together. You know the sort."

"I am sorry, sir, but no hotel guests are permitted entrance to the Okcho community. The Okcho deserve their privacy. I'm sure you understand."

"Ah ... but ..." But he couldn't think of anything else to say.

The veneer of deference fell from the guard's face. "Listen, sunshine, beat it."

Pelham climbed a few steps up the stairs, turned, and plopped down on a tread. From there he could see across the room to the mysterious door. An Okcho came through, pulled a casino uniform from a locker, and stepped behind a partition to change. Once dressed, the Okcho started up the stairs.

Pelham stood as the Okcho approached. "Pardon me."

The person stared at him, his face a question. "What are you doing here?"

"Long story ... having to do with magic tricks and ladders and all. But to keep the narrative moving along, I wanted to ask you about where that door leads." He pointed back toward the guard. "Is that the way to your town?"

The Okcho narrowed his eyes. "Why do you want to know?"

"Oh ... um ... I was supposed to ... well ... well ... I'm writing a news story on how the Okcho make this place work, don't you know. I thought it would be a great way to start the piece — a worker leaving home in the morning —"

"It's evening," the Okcho said.

"So it is."

"We work all hours."

"Right. Leaving home in the evening and checking in at the old Pink Mingo."

The Okcho said nothing.

"That's the door I want ... for my story, I mean, right?"

"Yeah." The Okcho moved past him up the stairs, calling back, "But I didn't tell you."

Pelham sat on the step as before, thinking about what to do next. Two Okcho came down the stairs past him, one of them carrying a bag. They opened lockers and pulled out open-necked tunics like the one he had seen the other Okcho change out of.

As they moved behind partitions to change, one of them called to the other, "What did you pick up?"

"Hmm?"

"In the bag."

"Oh. Bread."

"Zurk bread? That tasteless lump of starch?"

"Yeah, but it's cheap."

"You can make bread at home."

"Who has time with these long shifts? By the time I get home, all I ever do is fix some porridge and collapse in bed."

The Okcho left through the door, the guard shooting them a bored nod as they exited. Pelham wondered if he might be able to slip out as part of a group. He decided to wait and find out.

As he sat there, he gave more thought to the enigmatic messages. Who had sent them? What did they mean? What truth might he find in the village? He didn't come up with any answers.

A group of three Okcho descended the stairs. Pelham stood and followed them down, wandering nonchalantly toward the end of the lockers where he leaned against a wall while they changed clothes. As they moved toward the door, he casually fell in with them.

The guard stepped between him and the others, glaring down at him. "Sir, as I told you before, I cannot let you pass."

The door slammed shut behind the Okcho.

Pelham said, "You say this door leads nowhere?"

"That is correct."

"Then these people who passed through, where did they go?"

"I couldn't say. All I do is guard the door. Now please return to the hotel."

Pelham climbed the stairs out of the locker room. He wandered into the casino and accepted a proffered Amurru fizz in exchange for credits and a five-mingo rating.

He was watching the games and sipping his drink when two giant yellow birds came running through the doors, laughing like mammals. One of them bumped into Pelham, sending both him and the drink flying.

"I say," Pelham said.

To his surprise, the yellow bird removed its head, revealing a blue Rhegedian head underneath.

"Oops! Excuse me," the Rhegedian said. "I'm having difficulty seeing in this costume. Are you all right? Oh no! Is that empty glass there yours? Let me buy you another one."

"Think nothing of it, old scout. I was practically finished anyway. Costume, you say?"

"Yes, there's a costume party on floor forty-two. Everyone is dressing as a different species. You should come."

"Perhaps I will. Where did you obtain this disguise?"

"A store along the strip. They have everything."

"Thank you. Thank you indeed." Pelham headed toward the lobby.

The costume store had aisle after aisle of anything a cosplayer could want. Pelham wandered past piles of masks and wigs; huge displays of fake weapons; costumes with feathers, scales, fins, and skin. He recognized complete outfits to duplicate famous characters from vids, masks of species both real and imagined, and no end of decorations to transform anyone's home into a scene from another world.

"May I help you?"

A green, scaly Srathan face stared down at him. Pelham noticed it sat atop a thin body with yellow hands. The person pulled off the mask to reveal an Okcho head.

"Um ... yes. Do you have Okcho costumes?"

The sales attendant was quiet for a moment. "Why?"

"Costume party."

"And you want to go as an Okcho? You're not going to act like a slave, are you?"

"What? No. I ... um ... have a lot of respect for the Okcho people."

"Do you now?"

"I confess I don't actually know a great deal about your culture, but from the few I have met, my esteem could not be higher."

"Hmm. All right. Well, you're a little short to be an Okcho. How about a child's costume?"

"Sounds perfect."

It wasn't. The child's costume had a plastic face mask, held in place with a cheap elastic strap. It covered only the face, not the entire head. And the yellow body was simulated by a tacky yellow onesie that pulled on over Pelham's clothes. It lacked any green veining and looked far from convincing.

"Not a totally credible disguise," Pelham said, looking doubtfully at himself in the mirror with the salesclerk beside him.

"You could add a tunic and boots to look more realistic. And a floppy field hat to cover the back of your head."

"If you think it would help."

The sales attendant disappeared into another part of the store and returned with the clothes. Pelham slipped them on and liked the look much better. Yes, this might fool the guard ... provided the guard had poor eyesight ... and Pelham could slip through the door quickly ... and in a group.

And then what? His mind reeled with questions. How would he find what he was looking for in the Okcho village? How would it help Emer? Could he get back into the hotel afterward? What if he were arrested?

The sales attendant had said something. "Hmm?" Pelham asked.

"I asked if you were going to buy it."

Pelham swallowed or at least tried to. "Yes," he said with a cough. "I'll take it."

"Payment stick, please."

Pelham fished the electronic doodad from the pocket in his regular suit underneath the onesie and handed it over with a flourish. He was pleased to be paying for something the normal way instead of using credits on his casino bracelet.

He gasped at the price when he saw it. Still, if this succeeded in getting Emer released, he could turn it in on his expense report. If it succeeded, that is.

Dressed in his Okcho costume, Pelham strode back into the Pink Mingo. At the front desk, Urdi the Unfortunate gawked at him, leading Pelham to surmise that the costume might not be all that convincing to Okcho eyes. Oh well, he thought, he only needed to convince a Zurk guard for a few seconds.

Ignoring Urdi, Pelham headed across the lobby to the service hallway between the meeting rooms.

"You there. Wait."

Pelham took another two steps.

"You. Okcho. The short one."

Pelham flirted with the idea of making a dash for it but realized doing so would only call attention to himself. Better to try to pass muster with this person. Call it a dress rehearsal. He stopped and swung around to find an unknown Zurk waddling toward him.

"Why aren't you in uniform?" the Zurk asked.

"What? Oh … um … that. Well … um … the fact is, I don't work here."

"Oh. Too bad. I was looking for a drink." The Zurk scrutinized him. "You're a child. The casino doesn't employ children, does it? What are you doing here?"

"What I'm doing here is … um … well … it's Take Your Child to Work Day, don't you know. That's why I'm here."

"Your parent is employed here?"

"Certainly. Loves the place. Goes on and on about how enjoyable the job is. I had to see it for myself."

"What is his name?"

"Whose name?"

"Your parent. What's his name?"

"His name? Oh … Dad … Dad the … Dad the …" Pelham was drawing a blank on coming up with an Okcho-sounding name. Then one came to him. "No. Sorry. It's my mom, not my dad. Mom the Marvelous."

"Your mother's name is Mom?"

"Um … yes. Family name, you know. My grandmama wanted to name my mom after her own mother, and that's what she always called her."

The Zurk blinked, his proboscis curling up and down like a window shade. "Astounding. You're sure you don't sell drinks?"

"Sorry. Try the casino bar."

"Right. Right. Well, don't let me keep you."

The Zurk plodded off as Pelham leaned on a pillar for momentary support. A cup of tea would hit the old spot right now. But this was no time for refreshment. Pelham G. Totleigh was on a mission.

Chapter 17

No to the Handholding

It wasn't easy for Pelham to make his way down the stairs dressed in the Okcho costume. The eyeholes in the hard plastic mask blocked the view of his own feet and the steps, forcing him to cling to the railing and tread carefully, one step at a time. He finally reached the bottom of the stairs at the same time as an Okcho male coming down behind him. Pelham followed the Okcho to the lockers.

"Pardon me," Pelham said in a low voice. "I was wondering if I could pass through the door with you."

The Okcho looked Pelham up and down. "Who are you?"

"Pelham G. Totleigh. I have a friend who finds herself knee-deep in the soup, as it were, and I need to meet with someone in your village to help extricate her from said broth." He applied his most winning smile, letting it drop when he realized it couldn't be seen behind the mask.

"What are you playing at? Is our culture a joke to you?"

"What? No."

"This is our home. Our community isn't a costume party. We're not a local attraction for you to goggle at like the galaxy's largest ball of paint or something."

Pelham motioned to the Okcho to keep his voice down. "Oh, absolutely. Not, I mean. Absolutely not."

"What are you? What species?"

"Haplor. I'm here with the trade conference. My friend truly is in trouble. That's my only motivation."

The Okcho was silent for a moment. "You're not playing dress up? You're not making fun of us?"

"Of course not. I promise you. This disguise is merely for the purpose of sneaking past the guard." Pelham jerked his head in the direction of the door.

The Okcho's eyes flicked to the guard and back to Pelham. His body relaxed. Possibly the idea of fooling the guard had more appeal. "What exactly is it you want me to do?"

"Practically nothing, old chap. I only ask that you let me walk through with you."

"That's it?"

"You might also hold my hand."

"Hold your hand?"

"As if you were my parent."

"No."

"No to the handholding?"

"Definitely no to the handholding. Frankly, I'm not sure about any of this."

"But —"

"Look, whoever you are, let me be clear. I don't think this lame disguise of yours is going to fool anybody. Your little scheme is going to fail, and I don't want to risk losing my job by associating myself with it. You'll be arrested. And while they are dragging you off for interrogation, I plan to be home enjoying a cup of tea."

Behind the mask, a bead of sweat ran down beside Pelham's ear. Perhaps his scheme wasn't as sound as he had supposed. He could end up in the same pickle as Emer, or at least an adjacent, semi-related pickle, facing more questioning, more confinement. His brain told him to back away and scurry up the stairs to the casino, the bar, his comfy suite. To his surprise, however, his feet decided to stand pat. He glanced down at them, wondering what they were up to. Brain and feet fought it out, the line of battle running through his stomach, which went all fluttery and dropped away like in one of those dreams where you're falling.

Pelham blinked. Somehow his feet had won the argument. He was going through with it ... if he could convince this Okcho to help him, that is. "I have to do it. You don't have to hold my hand or pretend you know me. Only let me lurk near you as you pass through the door."

***

No to the Handholding

Up in their suite, Blandings set down the tablet with the book he was reading and re-checked the time. He had expected Mr. Totleigh to return from the conjurer's show by now. Of course, he might be having a drink with this Duncil person he had mentioned. More worryingly, he might have slipped back into the casino for more gambling. Blandings hoped he hadn't. Gambling was not a safe activity for someone with Mr. Totleigh's level of excitability. He would rely too much on luck and intuition and not enough on sound strategy.

But what could Blandings do? It would not be proper for a valet to simply go fetch his employer and drag him off like some truant schoolboy. Not without a valid reason. What Blandings needed was a ruse, a pretext for why Mr. Totleigh should return to the suite. He took a sip of tea and began turning the problem over in his mind.

***

As it turned out, Pelham had more than one Okcho to give him cover. Before the male had finished changing his clothes, Kiz the Chatty and Shay the Shorter both arrived on the scene.

Pelham flipped up his mask to greet them. "Hello. Pelham G. Totleigh."

"I remember you," Shay said.

Kiz the Chatty said, "Sure. It's Mr. Totleigh. How are you, Mr. Totleigh?"

"Oh, a bit warmish in this getup but otherwise doing fine."

"What are you doing here? And why are you dressed like that?"

He leaned in toward them and lowered his voice. "I'm supposed to meet someone in your town, and that blighter of a guard won't let anyone through except Okcho. Or should it be Okchos? Okchosen?"

Shay said, "It's Okcho, whether one or a thousand. Yeah, the guards don't let others through. They do let in a fair number of Zurk archaeologists to dig up our heritage, though."

"And Zurk guards on patrols," Kiz said. "Intimidation duty, as we call it. But not other species. Last year a huge Astridian came to Vogus. She was so massive she stepped right over the wall. It must have taken twenty guards to corral her."

Shay said, "Who are you supposed to be meeting, Mr. Totleigh?"

"Ah. Well, I don't … um … exactly know. It's all hush-hush. Cloak and dagger and whatnot."

"I don't follow you."

Pelham considered telling them about trying to find proof that Emer wasn't involved in the attack, but he worried they might construe what he was doing as an effort to identify the Okcho Lamination Force people and report on them to Zurk authorities. He nearly decided to show them the mysterious messages he had received. However, knowing he couldn't adequately explain them or even say who they were from, the Okcho might not react well to that either. Yet not mentioning the messages or his idea of proving Emer's innocence left him without much to say.

"As I was telling this gentleman here, I am trying to free a friend from Zurk security. To that end, I believe I can acquire the information I need in your village. I was hoping to slip through the door with a group."

Kiz said, "Well, aren't you a sweetheart for trying to help a friend? But you should go back to your room, Mr. Totleigh. You don't want to get on the wrong side of the Zurks, let me tell you."

The Okcho male harrumphed. "Maybe *we* should turn him in to the Zurks."

"Wait, you said you would help me," Pelham said.

"I did not."

"You seemed to be considering it, at least."

"I did. Now I'm not sure."

"I say it's too dangerous," Kiz said. "Both for us and for Mr. Totleigh."

Shay said, "I sympathize with what he's trying to do. We've all had friends held by the Zurks." She threw a meaningful glance at the male Okcho. "This might even work out to our benefit. You're always saying we need to raise awareness among other species."

"Oh, certainly," Pelham said. "I will be more than happy to spread the word far and wide."

"I don't know," said the male, rubbing a hand across his crests. "He looks like trouble to me."

"Come on," Shay said. "He's harmless."

"What makes you think so?"

"I know a nice person, a gentle person when I see one. Gort knows I deal with enough who aren't so pleasant. When we go through, we'll put him in the middle of us. Kiz the Chatty, you talk to the guard to distract him."

Kiz said, "You mean flirt with a Zurk? They're immune."

"Not flirt," Shay said, "just speak with him, get his attention. If the guard catches him, we can always say we don't know him."

"You don't seriously think he'll believe that, do you?" the male asked.

"Why not? Okcho move in from across the hardscape all the time looking for jobs."

"Despite our warnings to them to go back," the male said.

Kiz pulled a tunic from her locker and stepped behind the changing partition. "I need to change first."

Shay grabbed clothes from her own locker and stepped behind another partition. "Give us a minute, Mr. Totleigh."

"Take all the time you need." Pelham averted his eyes away from the partitions. "While we wait, could you explain to me how you come by your names? I mean the 'the' parts."

Kiz the Chatty called over the partition. "It's age-old, older than history. Our first names, Kiz and Shay and all the others, those are given to us at birth by our parents. Our other names — we call them our indicative names — are given much later. They may come from a nickname we pick up in school or a quality someone observes in how we approach life. If the name gains acceptance over time, it's formalized with a vote by the elders."

"Golly, fascinating." Pelham turned to the male. "And what's your name, if I may ask?"

The Okcho grimaced.

Kiz stepped back around the partition dressed in village clothes. "He's Bren the Bulky."

"Bren the Bulky? I say, you don't look bulky."

Another grimace. "I was a chubby kid. By the time I grew out of it, I already had the name."

Dressed, Shay slipped out from her partition. "Are we ready?" Everyone was. "Okay, Mr. Totleigh, when we go through, don't say a word."

They bunched together with Shay the Shorter in front, Kiz the Chatty and Bren the Bulky on either side of Pelham.

As they approached the door, Kiz said to the guard, "Woo! What a shift! You're lucky to be able to sit down here. We have to deal with all the customers. We had a Thomian tonight who lost big and started yelling and tossing tables around. He demolished one of the slot machines and nearly the guy sitting there. Can you believe it?"

The guard shook his head as he waved them through. "Thomians. Bunch of thugs if you ask me."

"Right you are," Kiz said. "Have a good night."

Crowded up against the others and unable to see well in the mask, Pelham stumbled on the raised threshold. He caught himself and hurried on out into cool night air.

***

Blandings was scrolling through the proposed Bononian trade agreement, his eyes intent. This was his fourth or fifth time through the document, but this time an idea had hit him, and he was looking for something specific.

He stopped mid-scroll, his finger still poised over the screen. Section seventeen, paragraph six, the one item in the agreement on which Mr. Totleigh might have a strong opinion — inspection terms. The Bononians wanted a guarantee that inspections would be completed within two Bononian days. Blandings knew how much Mr. Totleigh hated and tended to procrastinate on inspections, seeing as how they were time-consuming and tedious and often involved getting dirty. Mr. Totleigh would undoubtedly prefer to have the period extended.

Now all Blandings needed to do was bring the matter to his attention. Of course, with Emer in custody, the point was currently moot. Yet he thought he could persuade Mr. Totleigh that now was the time to prepare their response.

The first task was to locate his wayward employer. "VICTOR, where is Mr. Totleigh?"

VICTOR's genteel voice replied, "Pelham G. Totleigh is not in the Pink Mingo Hotel and Casino."

"Excuse me?"

"I said, Pelham G. Tot —"

"I heard you," Blandings said.

"Ah. Since you said excuse me, I naturally assumed —"

"Where could Mr. Totleigh be?"

"Technically, anyplace in the galaxy other than the Pink Mingo."

Blandings could almost feel the blood drain from his face.

Chapter 18

Are You Lonesome Tonight?

Between being surrounded by the Okcho and wearing an ill-fitting mask, Pelham at first couldn't see the place he was entering. He was aware only of stepping into darkness, his feet padding across uneven rock, a chilly breeze blowing in around the edges of his mask.

Then Shay, Bren, and Kiz spread apart, and Pelham pulled off the mask. He took in the scene around him. Gone was the glamour of the casino, the glitz of the hotel. In the sky, three small moons struggled to compete against the glow of neon from the Zurk strip on the other side of the high wall.

The ground below them was gray and rocky, the rocks split with fissures running like veins across the surface of the planet. And as if echoing the green veins in the Okcho skin, tufts of grass and delicate flowers grew from some of the cracks.

The small hamlet that stretched before Pelham was an irregular loop of tiny shacks roughly built from mismatched boards and castoff sheets of metal. In the middle of the village stood a circular structure constructed of uncut stones and large enough for community gatherings. Beyond the circle of huts, the ground rose into dark hills.

Pelham's first reaction to the place was shock at its poverty. No wonder the Zurks didn't want hotel guests dropping by. What must it be like, he wondered, for the Okcho to work inside the Pink Mingo, having their faces rubbed, as it were, in all the luxury and ostentation of the casino and then come home every day to so much less? It wasn't hard to imagine how the Okcho Litigation Force came to be.

And yet, he couldn't help but feel that here in this simple village he had at last stepped onto the real Vogus. In this place was a sense of ancient culture, of history. There was a "there" there.

The question was, what was he doing there? This place was beyond his frame of reference. What could he say to these people to relate to them? He felt out of place, like a spoon in the wrong drawer. Scratch that. More like a spoon in a shoe cubby. This simple gathering of huts was a completely different world from the casino. It was a separate reality from Sonus as well.

"Welcome to Baile Atha," Kiz the Chatty said. She took a deep breath and let it out as if cleansing her soul. "There are more cabins over the next hill built by newcomers, but this is the original village, most of it anyway."

"The rest of it is gone," Shay the Shorter said, a trace of bitterness in her voice.

"Gone where?" Pelham asked.

"Someone built a casino on top of it."

"I'm sorry," Pelham said.

"That's what the Zurks said, but they built there all the same."

Bren the Bulky said, "We got you here. Now what?"

"I ... I don't know," said Pelham. He had been so focused on getting through the door, he hadn't planned for what to do next. He had more or less assumed he would be contacted by someone. He glanced around as if expecting somebody to walk up then and there.

From out of the darkness came the bellowing of an animal. Pelham startled. "What's that?"

Sonus didn't have animals, and on his visits to Haplor, he had not strayed from urban areas into the wilder parts of the planet. A wave of unease swept over him, and Pelham found himself wishing Blandings were there with him. He thought with a tinge of guilt that Blandings didn't even know where he was.

"What's what, love?" Kiz asked.

"Those growling noises? Are there wild beasts here?"

Kiz laughed. "Those are only kludas. They're as tame as a ladle. Their lowing has been my lullaby since I was the size of a milk pail."

With the clop of approaching hoof steps, a dark shaggy animal with spiky horns much like the Okcho crests meandered across their path. After stopping to nibble at a patch of grass growing from a crack in the rocks, it looked up at the Haplor visitor and blinked.

Pelham jumped back. "Don't you pen them up?"

Bren shrugged. "They come and go as they please. As would we if we didn't have Zurk jobs."

The kluda dropped its head to munch another tuft of grass and wandered off into the night.

Shay said, "Are you hungry, Mr. Totleigh?"

"Hmm? Oh, now that you mention it, I am a bit peckish."

"Come to my house. I'll fix you something to eat."

"Wait, Mr. Totleigh." Kiz had a sort of twitchy look about her. Odd, Pelham thought, now that the danger had passed and all. "Um ... why don't I stay with you? I could tell you all about our life here, and you could tell me about your home."

Shay waved a hand. "You go on home and get some rest, Kiz the Chatty. You need it."

"But —"

"Don't you worry. I'll take care of Mr. Totleigh."

Kiz seemed to want to say more, but Bren said, "He'll be fine."

Kiz left with Bren, Kiz looking back a couple of times.

Shay said, "So food then?"

Pelham gazed around again, struck by the poverty of the shacks, and had second thoughts. "Oh, I couldn't."

She shot him a hard look. "What? We don't meet your standards of cleanliness, of refinement?"

"No! No, it's not that at all."

"Or are we too poor to offer you anything? Is that it?"

"I don't want to take —"

"The Zurks have not left us much in the way of dignity. At least allow me the honor of extending hospitality to a guest."

Pelham understood perfectly. More than once when a chum had been down on his luck, and Pelham had spotted him a few bills, the bloke would turn around and use a portion of the funds to buy Pelham a drink in thanks. He came to realize that people wanted and needed to give to others.

"Certainly," Pelham said. "I would be in your debt, and I would most enjoy seeing your home."

***

Blandings stood straight as a steel beam before the desk of Lieutenant Commander Mountjoy.

"Can't find him, eh?" Mountjoy said.

"No, sir. VICTOR said Mr. Totleigh is not on the premises."

"Have you checked anywhere else in the colony? We have some interesting shops up and down the strip. Also a few other casinos, though nothing as grand as the Pink Mingo. But you know how it is. Rumors spread about some other casino paying out better, and people flock to it."

"Then I will indeed check the other establishments. However, I fear Mr. Totleigh may have gone somewhere else."

"Where would that be?"

"The Okcho community."

"Poppycock."

"Is it?"

"It is." Mountjoy held up stubby fingers. "One, there is only one access point to the Okcho village, and it is guarded twenty-nine hours a day. Two, even if he could have somehow entered their hamlet, they would kick him right back out. The Okcho are extremely private people. They would alert us to come pick him up. Three, he wouldn't even like it there. The Okcho live in squalor. Zahn knows, we've tried to teach them better ways, but they still cling to their traditions. I tell you, it's like raising children. Totleigh would take one look at the place and hightail it back to the hotel. Excuse me, do you even have tails?"

"We do not," Blandings said gravely. He couldn't help but notice how Mountjoy's proboscis had flattened out to completely cover his mouth. Now what might that particular mannerism mean in his species?

***

Despite the occasional lowing of kludas, Baile Atha was overwhelmingly quiet. No buzzes or beeps of electronics. No humming of appliances. No clunking of machines. Pelham found it both peaceful and unnerving at the same time.

He followed Shay around the arc of shacks. Most of the huts were dark, but in others soft lights were glowing. From one, Pelham heard a single voice singing a song soft and low.

A light flashed at his feet, and Pelham jumped back.

"It's only a fire hamster," Shay said.

"A fire what?"

"A little rodent with bioluminescence. Earlier in the evening the children would have been chasing them around the commons."

"Odd adaptation," Pelham said. "Why would they want to glow in the dark?"

"They use it to attract mates."

"Wouldn't it also attract predators? Large hungry animals as well as small children?"

"Oh, it does. I guess that's why there aren't many of them."

From out across the hills some other animal howled. The fire hamster flashed excitedly and scurried off.

Shay stopped at a tiny shanty built from stones, thatched reed, and a section of pink board obviously scavenged from a mingo billboard. She pulled back a hanging mat to enter the cabin and moved to a small fireplace where she stooped to light a peat fire inside a grate. The flame flickered into life to show a single room with a stove at one end; a table and cot on opposite walls; and shelves filled with cooking utensils, a few clothes, and a handful of old-style paper books. A blanket woven in bright colors with intricate swirling shapes hung on one wall.

"Tea and toast?" she asked.

"That would be lovely, thanks."

Shay lit the stove, filled a kettle from a hand pump, and set it on to boil.

Pelham wandered around the room, taking it in. The cot was a simple, wooden frame covered with blankets. A mound of loose straw stubble was piled at one end. He poked it with a long finger. "Different sort of pillow from what we use on Sonus."

Shay drummed fingers on the spikes of her head. "You don't have crests that poke through fabric and get stuck in any kind of solid material."

"Ah. Right."

"Have a seat at the table."

Pelham complied.

Shay pulled a loaf of bread from a battered metal box, cut two thick slices, and lined them up carefully on a forked implement with a handle that Pelham had at first mistakenly thought might be some species of garden tool. She placed the implement with the bread on top of the stove beside the kettle to toast in the heat. "What do you know about the Okcho, Mr. Totleigh?"

"Not much. Assume I am a blank slate. Call me Pelham, please."

From a shelf she pulled a small jar of something thick and amber. She carried it to the table. "Honey. We make it ourselves. Well, the bees do. Centuries ago our civilization was as advanced as any. We built great cities along the rivers, created extraordinary technologies. We explored the moons and planets of our solar system. Ultimately, we walked away from all that."

"Willingly? Why?"

Shay sat down opposite him at the table. "That way of life was destroying our souls. We raised generations of children whose feet had never touched rock or soil, whose faces had never been kissed by a rainy wind. They spent their lives in buildings, in spacecraft. They were like greenhouse vegetables. Physically they were thriving, but cut off from the land, they were dying spiritually."

"So just like that, everyone decided to return to a simpler life?"

"Not everyone at first. It began as a movement. But it didn't take long for the advantages to become clear. I have been told Haplor is a world of vast forests. Tell me, Pelham, have you ever spent the night in one of them, sleeping under the stars?"

He answered quietly. "I ... I don't get to Haplor often. I was born on the moon Sonus. Our colony is doing terra-whatchamacallit. I lived my entire childhood under a dome breathing manufactured air. We can see the stars. They're beautiful, but something about viewing them through the dome separates us from them. Odd that it would seem that way since they are light-years distant in any case. It has only been recently that we can spend any time outside without pressure suits."

"Then I grieve for you and for your separation from nature."

"As I said, until not long ago, separation from nature was a matter of life and death. So we're doing all right, you know. We like it."

Shay paused as if considering this. "Perhaps you do. I shouldn't expect your people to be like mine. As for us, when we returned to a simpler life, we rediscovered ourselves ... until the Zurks came." She rose, poured the tea, and brought it and the toast to the table. "Would you like cream for your tea?"

Pelham cradled the cup in his long fingers and stared into it as the leaves in the bottom yielded their dark, rich flavor. "Yes, please."

She opened a trapdoor in the floor, reached in and pulled out a small ceramic jug, which she handed to Pelham. He removed the stopper and poured a dribble of orange liquid into his tea. He looked up at her in surprise.

"Kluda milk," she said.

"I've never had anything other than replicated milk, and it's always white." He took a tentative sip and nodded. "It's rich."

Shay drizzled honey on her toast and took a bite. "Mr. Totleigh, why don't you tell me exactly what you are trying to accomplish by coming here?"

Before answering, he took a sip of tea and a bite of toast, followed by another gulp of tea to wash the toast down.

"I told you. My friend is being held by Zurk security in connection with the attack."

"How does coming here help?"

Pelham hesitated. How could he explain it without it sounding like one more exploitation of her people? However, she had opened up to him. He believed he could trust her.

"I received a message on my wrist gizmo saying I could learn the truth here."

"What truth?"

"I suppose the truth that my friend was not part of the attack."

"In other words, you're trying to learn who *was* behind it."

"I'd like to talk to them."

"Who sent you this message?"

"I don't know."

"You came here, risking arrest, based only on that?"

"I want to help my friend." He took another long sip.

"More tea?"

"Don't mind if I do."

Shay stood and walked to the stove. She first picked up a tablet device and tapped something on it. Then she reached for the kettle, brought it to the table, and refilled the cups.

She sat down and took a sip before speaking. "You said you want to prove your friend isn't connected with the Okcho Liberation Force."

"Right. I'm hoping to get proof of her non-involvement."

"Then you need to infiltrate the Okcho Liberation Force."

"I do?"

"You do."

"I wouldn't want to do anything underhanded. Yet I suppose it makes sense. But how in the blazes can I slip in among them?"

One side of her mouth lifted into a half smile. "I can help you there."

Chapter 19

The First Item on the Agenda is the Split

"You think you can get me in with these Okcho Limitation folks?" Pelham asked.

Shay the Shorter leaned in over her teacup. "I happen to know they are meeting tonight."

"I say, that is excellent. But wait. What's the plan here? What I mean to say is, how do I find out what I need to know? Do I simply interrupt the gathering to ask them about my friend? Would they be kind enough to give me some sort of statement to the effect that she was not involved?"

Shay tilted her head. "Unlikely. Keep in mind these people are wanted by the Zurks."

"Yes, though clearly, I am not a Zurk."

"True. Still, they might suspect you are working for them."

"Working with Zurks? Hardly."

"They don't know that. These are wary people."

"I see. Golly. This is a stumper. What should I do then?"

She pointed at his mask on the table. "Wear your disguise. If you stay in the shadows, you might pass. Listen to what everyone says. They may mention your friend. Then you'll know."

"What if they don't?"

Shay patted his hand. "I'll come with you. If no one says anything, I'll bring the subject up myself."

"I wouldn't want you to end up in trouble."

A melancholy look moved across her face and was gone. "Don't worry. I won't."

"Righto! I'll do it. I say, this is a corking plan. I am well chuffed. Thanks awfully." Pelham pointed to his bracelet. "If I could, I would most certainly award you five mingos for this interaction."

Shay stood and quickly turned back toward the stove.

***

Blandings walked along the dark street in front of the Pink Mingo. He gazed into the sky, hoping for a reassuring sight of glowing stars. Instead, he found only a muddy purple haze. The glare from the lights along the strip obscured everything but themselves. He passed a souvenir shop and a clothing store. Both were closed for the night.

The next building had a flashing neon sign advertising the place as: *The Nugget*. Blandings pulled open the door to a cacophony of beeping and booping. The interior consisted of long aisles of slot machines stretched along a faded threadbare carpet. The low, well-lit ceiling gave a somewhat oppressive air to the place. He passed through the aisles, patrons of multiple species eyeing him as he moved along. A machine on his right began clanging. The Oecanthus sitting at it clicked excitedly as the payment stick inserted into the machine lit up with added bills. Once the clamor died down, the Oecanthus pressed the machine's red button to play it again. Blandings found no sign of Mr. Totleigh anywhere in the room.

He left The Nugget and tried two more casinos to no avail. The next place along the strip was a costume and party store that was closed.

At the end of the street stood a diner, still open for business. Blandings gazed in through the window. A Zurk stood behind the counter, wiping the surface with a rag. In a booth, two Yindi shared a beaker of something giving off steam, each of them with one tentacle submerged in the glass, another tentacle reaching out to each other, and their remaining appendages twitching across the tabletop. Otherwise, the diner was empty. Blandings entered and approached the counter.

"What can I get you?" the Zurk attendant asked, his proboscis flipping left and right.

"I was hoping you could supply me with some information."

"Information isn't on the menu. Bactaren burgers are on the menu. Maltese fruit pie is on the menu."

"How about a cup of tea?" Blandings asked, "with a side of information. I'm an excellent tipper."

"No tea. Kowfee. It's an Earth drink." The attendant pulled a cup out from under the counter and filled it from a carafe of black liquid. The Zurk slid it to Blandings along with a tiny pitcher of cream and a bottle of sweetener. "If this is your first time, you might want to doctor it up a bit."

Blandings poured in some milk and sweetener, took a sip, poured in more milk, took another sip, and looked up at the Zurk. "Fascinating. Bitter, robust … stimulating. Now, for my question. Have you seen someone like me this evening, another Haplor?"

"There hasn't been one in."

"Possibly one moving along the street?"

"You think I have time to stare out the window?"

"You might have noticed in passing."

The Zurk frowned. "Yeah. Now that you mention it, I think I did see someone like you."

***

Sergeant Humstuggle knocked on the doorframe to Lieutenant Commander Mountjoy's office.

Mountjoy looked up from the electronic device he was reading. "Yes, Humstuggle?"

"I'm calling it a day, sir, if it's all right with you."

"Is someone watching Totleigh's door?"

"I have a soldier on duty near there, sir. Corporal Fernsby, it is."

"I don't need the name. Have him report to me at once when Totleigh returns. What about the other Haplor, the valet?"

"He left the hotel for the strip."

"Right. Good. Is anyone on him?"

"We had someone tailing him, Private Dankworth, but he lost him."

"Again, I don't need the name. But here's the larger question, Sergeant." Mountjoy raised both hands. "What? How could our man possibly lose him? The strip is not that big."

"Sorry, sir. Dankworth doesn't know how it happened. Should I send out more men to find him?"

"It probably doesn't matter. Our money's on Totleigh."

"Yes, sir. Right, sir."

***

Pelham and Shay shuffled into the great stone structure in the middle of the circle of huts. Pelham peered around at it all. The chamber had the hallowed feel not just of history but of ancient pre-history.

Several other Okcho were already there, standing in knots of three or four or perched on the stone blocks that served as benches. In the center of the space stood a higher slab flanked by two torches. Shay guided Pelham to a seat where he would be blocked on one side by her and the other by a stone pillar.

"How old is this place?" Pelham asked Shay in a whisper.

"No one knows. Thousands of years. We meet here where our ancestors once stood, where their gaze remains."

Bren the Bulky entered the structure and strode to the center platform. The other Okcho found seats.

"Bren?" Pelham asked Shay. "Bren is in charge?"

She patted his leg. "Shh."

Pelham slouched on the bench and dropped his head, fearful Bren would see him and recognize the disguise.

Bren said, "I call this meeting of the Okcho Liberation Force to order. We have a lot to discuss tonight, including how best to follow up on our recent successful attack."

A voice from the other side of the room called out. "You call that an attack?"

"I do, Tud the Impatient," Bren said. "I call it a bold and impressive attack. When these guests return to their home planets, they will tell of the Okcho Liberation Force."

"There was no blood," Tud said, standing. "How can you call it an attack if there wasn't any blood?" Grumbles and groans surged through the crowd.

Tud was a solidly built man. He was also young, if the minimal amount of green veining running through his yellow skin was any indication. And the more Pelham peered around at the crowd, the more he was convinced the veins were a sign of age. He spotted a bent old man sitting near Tud who was practically as green as a Srathan.

"Not this again," Bren said, running a hand up his forehead and across his crests.

"Oh, there was blood drawn," another voice said. "The blood most near and dear to Zurk hearts. We bled their wallets."

"You *would* say that, Ned the Nerdy," Tud said. "This scheme was your idea, all your doing. And credit where it's due, your hack into their system was masterful. But costing them money isn't going to gain us our independence."

"It will in time," Bren said with irritation. "We take away their profit, and they'll be forced to listen to us."

Tud was undeterred. "We take away their profit, and they'll restrict us even more. They'll take away so many rights, we won't be able to move. No, we need to hit them hard the first time. We need force of arms. Who is with me?"

"I'm with you," said a thin person who rose to his feet. "I say it's time we took real action."

"Thank you, Lut the Rowdy," Tud said. "I knew you'd back me up."

"Me too," said a stout person who also stood, though with effort.

"Thank you for your support, Bob the Formerly Slim. It means a lot."

Pelham whispered to Shay, "Did he say Bob? You know, Bob is a Haplor name. Old Bobby Bicklesworth is a chum of mine."

Shay said, "Turns out Bob is a name in every known galactic civilization. Now be quiet. Things are happening."

Bren said, "The cyberattack worked a lot better than *your* last idea, Tud the Impatient — trying to burn down the Pink Mingo. Everyone knew the fire suppression system would kick in before any damage was done."

"That was Ned the Nerdy's fault," Tud said. "He was supposed to shut the system down."

"You keep talking, Tud the Impatient," Ned said. "You keep talking, I'll come over there and give you something to talk about … to the doctor."

"I'd like to see you try it, dork" Tud said.

Ned the Nerdy started from his seat. Other Okcho physically restrained him and forced him back down.

Tud said, "I say all like-minded people come with me, and we'll form our own group, a group that acts like a militia, not a tech club. Who wants to join the Okcho Liberation Army?"

Bren shook his head, "We can't keep doing this."

"Actually, there's already an Okcho Liberation Army," someone said. "They split off last year with Shik the Easily Provoked."

"You're right, Zed the Chronicler, you're right," said Tud. "Okay. We'll call ourselves the Real Okcho Liberation Force."

"Not that either," said Zed. "That's Arn the Not So Tall's group. Remember, they split off in the spring."

"I thought that happened in the summer," someone else said.

Zed said, "I'm sure it was spring."

"We've split enough," Bren said, "too much. There's strength in unity."

Pelham reached a hand up under his hat to scratch his head. The debate was growing increasingly difficult to follow. And no one had yet said a word about Emer. He glanced at Shay to see if she was ready to bring the topic up. She was biting her lip, her eyes darting back and forth between the speakers.

Tud said, "It doesn't matter when that split happened. If they have the name, they have the name. How about … I don't know … how about the New Vogus Army? Is that name available?"

Murmurs rolled across the room. Zed the Chronicler nodded.

"New Vogus Army it is," Tud said. "Come on, let's go develop some real plans for liberation."

A half dozen others stood and began moving.

Bren said, "You can't make plans for liberation. We're the Okcho Liberation Force. Liberation is our thing. You can make … army plans … arrange skirmishes and such."

"Oh, we will," Tud said. "You wait and see." He stormed out, followed by the others.

Pelham gazed around the room at the remaining faces, wondering what this schism would do to the group and to his chances of finding out what he needed to know.

Bren said, "Right, then. We have that out of the way. Now let's get down to business."

"Good riddance," someone called out, struggling to his feet.

"No need to stand up, Ren the Boneless," Bren said. "We can hear you fine."

"Much obliged," Ren said. "Anyhow, all that lot wants to do is fight for independence. Independence isn't even our main goal. It's regaining our rights."

Someone else said, "But how will we ever get rights without independence?"

The First Item on the Agenda is the Split

Bren held up his arms. "Please, everyone, let's not split again. Let's focus on matters at hand."

Ned the Nerdy stood. "I think I've found a way to take down the guest bracelets."

This was greeted by a chorus of moans.

"No, listen," Ned said. "This will hit them where it hurts — in guest relations, their image across the galaxy. We recently acquired a bracelet, and I have been examining the programming. All we need is for our contact to change one line of code, and they'll all crash with a division by zero error. Of course, getting past the system's security will be tricky, but …" Ned stopped talking as Bren raised both hands.

Bren said, "I think we have an even better opportunity before us. We're going to kidnap a hotel guest. Imagine how that will embarrass the Zurks and how news of the kidnapping will raise interstellar awareness of our plight."

Murmurs again swept around the room. Someone said, "But that's totally impractical. How do you propose we sneak a guest out of the casino right under the guards' long noses?"

Bren smiled. "We don't need to sneak one out. One is presently among us."

As if on cue, Shay stood. "Allow me to introduce to you all Pelham G. Totleigh."

Chapter 20

Pelham Makes the News

Pelham gaped as suspicious eyes from around the megalithic chamber turned toward him. Shay reached down and pulled off the cheap mask, revealing his Haplor face. All the eyes now narrowed.

Pelham stared up wide-eyed at Shay the Shorter. "I say, this is a bit of a betrayal, what?"

Shay pitched the plastic mask to the ground. "This Haplor has come here to expose us, to barter with the Zurks information about our plans and our leaders in exchange for rescuing an off-worlder friend."

Pelham said, "What? No, no. I ... I ... I wouldn't dream of bartering any of you. Mums the word, believe you me. I was only seeking a statement, a ... a communiqué, as it were, to the effect ... um ... well ... You see, my friend, Emer — she's a Bononian, don't you know — the security force thinks she was involved in the recent hack. If ... if you would only be so kind as to knock out some sort of official declaration dispelling that notion ... um ... I promise I would never breathe a word to anyone about your identities. I don't even know most of you. Well, I did happen to catch the name Bob there, of course. As it happens, I have a friend named Bob. But your secret is safe with me, Bob ... and Bren ... and Shay ... and ... um ... oh yes, Ned. It appears I picked up a few names. Quite unlike me. Generally, names float on past me like ... um ... um ... something that floats ... I don't know ... anything in zero-G, I suppose."

"Is there a point you're trying to make?" Bren asked.

"Yes. I'm sure I'll forget all your names in a matter of hours. And even if I didn't, I wouldn't dream of turning you in. The code of the Totleighs and all that. In fact, I would love to assist your cause. No one is more against oppression than I am … um … and I have had a lovely time here in your village … up until moments ago, at least. Heh-heh." Pelham swallowed. The narrowed eyes had not grown any more friendly.

"You *can* help our cause, Mr. Totleigh," Bren said.

"I can? Ah, splendid. Call me Pelham, I insist."

"When we publicize that we're holding you captive and explain the reasons why, the whole galaxy will be awakened to our plight."

The crowd erupted in cheers.

Pelham raised a feeble hand. "Oh. Hmm. Well, I don't wish to quibble, but I was rather hoping I could do my bit in some other capacity, something involving less, you know, rope and gags and loss of freedom. I'm supposed to be attending the trade conference sessions, you see."

"The Okcho have been gagged for decades, Mr. Totleigh," Bren said. "The Okcho have lost their freedom. The Zurks control this world, our world, but you're going to help us bring that all to an end."

More cheers.

"Could I just ask my question about my friend Emer? She wasn't involved with the attack, was she?"

Bren waved at two of the Okcho. "Take him to the hideout."

A bag was pulled over Pelham's head. Someone hoisted him to a shoulder and strode out of the stone structure, a fact Pelham realized only as the sounds of the meeting faded away. He was carried like that for some time, bouncing along as they covered rough ground. Finally, he was set down in a chair. His hands were tied together behind him. His legs were roped to the chair. Someone snatched off the bag. No lights were shining, but coming out of the bag, it didn't take long for his eyes to adjust.

He found himself inside a shack even smaller than Shay's and far less homey. The floor was dirt. In a corner a collection of rolled up mats leaned against the wall. The only furnishings were the chair where he sat plus a rough wooden table and three more chairs, two of which were now occupied by Okcho staring back at him.

"Now what do we do?" Pelham asked.

The Okcho said nothing. Pelham tried to match their silence, to return their stares, but it didn't work.

"I say, I hate to be a bother, but my nose has begun to itch." He wiggled the troublesome body part a couple of times. "I don't suppose you could untie my hands for a moment to give me a chance to scratch it."

The Okcho didn't respond.

"I only need one hand, in fact. You could leave the other one tied."

No response.

"Or you could scratch it for me. Of course, I don't want to be forward or violate any social norms of your people."

At last, there came a response, that is if one of the Okcho blinking could be called a response. Pelham didn't think it could.

To take his mind off the itch, he tried focusing on something else, anything else. There wasn't much inside the cabin, and none of it he found interesting. But through the window cut into the wall he could gaze out at billions of stars blazing in the pitch-black night sky. Not just individual dots of light, but a great swath of glowing starlight gashing across the heavens.

Hours passed. When the stars had faded and the dark sky began to lighten to an overcast day, the door to the shack opened. Bren the Bulky walked in, a satchel slung over one shoulder and a patronizing grin on his yellow face. "Have these guys been treating you well, Mr. Totleigh?"

"Well, they aren't much for conversation. Also, they had no compassion for the fact that my nose was itching like crazy." He wiggled it. "Blast it. Now it's started up again."

"This must be a difficult burden for you after your life of luxury."

"Well, I wouldn't so much characterize my life as luxurious. I live in a colony where we're trying to build up a dead moon. There's a lot of tubes and valves and suchlike all over."

Bren pulled a tablet device from the satchel, tapped on it a few times, and held it up. "Can you read this?"

It was, of course, written in a language alien to Pelham, but his translator bots soon converted the letters. He squinted and thrust his face forward. "Could you step closer? The print is a bit small. Ah, there. Yes, now I can make it out. 'My name is Pelham G. Totleigh —'"

"Save it," Bren said. "Here's what's going to happen. I'm going to turn on the camera on this device, and you're going to read."

"Ah, good. I was hoping for a light novel to pass the time. I don't suppose you have any of *The Adventures of Bongo*, what?"

***

Urdi the Unfortunate stood at his station at the reception desk. These early morning hours were his favorite. At this time of day, the only sounds were occasional bloops from the casino from gamblers winning just often enough to keep them at the tables or machines all night. It made for a brief respite in a day otherwise filled with difficult guests and demanding management.

The front door opened, and a Haplor walked in, his large eyes drooping. A new guest at this hour? No, this Haplor looked familiar. It was one of the ones who checked in the other day, the one who carried all the bags. The Haplor approached the desk.

"How may I help you?" Urdi asked.

"I beg your pardon," Blandings said, "I was wondering if you have seen my employer."

"The other Haplor?"

"Yes. Mr. Totleigh."

"The one with the bulging eyes?"

"He has been thus described."

"Gives him sort of a bewildered expression."

"On occasions, yes. The question is did you see him at any time last night?"

Urdi nodded solemnly. "Hmm. I did. Early in the evening I saw him exit the hotel toward the strip."

"Did you notice when he returned?"

"No, I did not."

Blandings heaved a sigh.

Urdi's head tilted to one side. "Unless …"

"Yes? Unless what?"

"Someone about your size came in later wearing an Okcho costume."

The Haplor raised one eyebrow. "Excuse me?"

"Not a particularly convincing costume either. More like something a child would wear for candy night."

Urdi the Unfortunate gazed off into the distance, thinking about candy nights long ago when he was a boy. It was a bittersweet memory. For some reason, he was never able to put together as good a costume as the other kids did. Generally, he had wanted to dress as a space cowboy. But somehow, using ribbons for suspenders, his dad's coat as a long duster, and a bent stick tucked into his belt as a blaster, he had never completely pulled off the look. People kept calling him a clown for reasons he never understood. Unfortunately, nobody on Vogus liked clowns. As a consequence, he tended to end up with less candy and more vegetables in his bag at the end of the night.

"Where did this person in the costume go?" Blandings asked.

Urdi waved a hand. "Back toward the —"

He was interrupted by chimes sounding from a video screen on the shop wall behind them. He peered up at it. People in the shops stepped into the lobby to check it out. A pair of Arsawans walking from the fitness center halted in their tracks and looked up.

Urdi pointed. "Ah, there's Mr. Totleigh now."

Pelham's features stared out from the screen, discombobulated, dumbstruck, eyes bulging like balls stuck on the front of his face.

He spoke in a slow voice. "My name is Pelham G. Totleigh. I am a captive of the Okcho Liber —" He squinted. "I say, what's that word?"

A voice off screen said, "Liberation."

"Of course. Silly me. The Okcho Liberation Force. The Okcho people have been oppressed by the Zurks, their land taken away, their aut ... autonomy crushed. I will be released when the following demands are met. One, all Okcho working for Zurks will be given a twenty percent pay raise effective immediately. Two, the Zurks must renegotiate leases for all land they control on Vogus. Three, the galactic alliance will dispatch a fact-finding commission to investigate the plight of the Okcho people. Four, a ransom of one million bills will be paid ... for me? I say, you want one million bills for me? I think you have vastly overestimated the ability of my little colony to pay, not to mention their desire to have me released. One million? You can't be —"

The screen went black.

Urdi glanced at the Haplor beside him. Now his eyes were bulging too.

***

"Who in your government do we contact about your ransom?" Bren asked.

Pelham thought it over. "Should it be who or whom? I wish Blandings were here. He knows these things."

"Forget the pronouns," Bren said. "I need a name."

"Well, the governor of Sonus is my Aunt Agutha, but I don't think —"

Bren rubbed a hand along the crest on his head. "Your aunt? Wonderful. An added incentive to secure your release."

Pelham chortled. "Wait until you speak with her."

"What do you mean by that?"

"I'd like to see her face when you ask for one million bills for my ransom. You'll be lucky to receive fourteen cents and a shiny rock. That's about how much my dear old aunt values me."

"We'll see about that," Bren said.

"Could you at least answer my question about Emer on the off chance I ever happen to be released?"

Bren shook his head. "Still going on about that, are you? Look, the Bononian is not our contact inside the hotel. Satisfied?"

"Thank you. That wasn't so difficult, was it? I still believe we can work together. You know, I could be of more help to your cause on the outside than I ever could be as a hostage. I don't mean to brag, but I do have a number of connections from my school days. My old pal Teddy Bracegirdle of the North Woolchester Bracegirdles, his uncle is in the senate on the Haplor home world. Or is it his aunt? We Haplors tend to produce strong women, you know. Oh, and my old chum Pongo Kissy-Wentworth. If I recall correctly, his father is on the galactic council. I ask you, one doesn't get more well-placed than that, what?"

Bren the Bulky smiled. "I think we'll stick to the ransom demand. Besides, as long as we keep you, we're on every news vid in this quadrant of the galaxy."

Chapter 21

Awkward Conversations

Bren the Bulky reached into the satchel and pulled out a fist-sized silver ball along with the cheap Okcho mask Pelham had worn to sneak into the village. "It's time I talk with that aunt of yours."

Bren sat in the one empty chair at the table along with the other two Okcho. He placed the silver ball on the table, pressed a button on it, and then tapped his tablet screen.

"Come on. Why won't this lamebrained device connect?"

That was the trouble with these little portable WoTCom devices, Bren thought. They never had enough power out here on the hardscape. But it was the only kind he could get smuggled out of the Zurk colony. He tried moving the unit closer to the tablet, which didn't help a bit.

"Hold this out the window," he said to one of the other Okcho.

His companion palmed the ball and stuck it, along with his arm, out into a cold mist.

Bren said, "Further ... further."

By now the Okcho had his head and both shoulders fully outside. "Hey, it's spitting rain out here."

"Hang on. I think it's working."

A deep rumble started up all around the cabin. The sound slowly rose in pitch to a shrill ringing. Then it fell silent as a blue pinprick of light appeared in midair, formed by the WoTCom unit creating a slender wormhole in a fold of space. Raindrops falling near that point quit falling and instead began to orbit around the blue dot before being sucked into it. The Okcho holding the silver sphere drew his head back from it as far as he could.

Awkward Conversations

Bren pulled the mask over his head, which took a minute since the elastic strap kept getting hung up on the points of his head crest. He tapped the screen. "Place a call to Sonus, the office of the governor."

The screen displayed a spinning circle. It spun and spun while telecommunication protocols were exchanged through the wormhole to establish the connection. The spinning circle of impatience was finally replaced by the face of a Haplor with black fur.

"Hello, is this the governor?" Bren asked.

"This is the governor's office." The Haplor leaned toward the screen. "Are you wearing a mask?"

"This is the Okcho Liberation Force. We're holding Pelham G. Totleigh captive."

"I see. And what can I do for you today?"

"What?"

"What is the nature of your inquiry?"

"As I said, we're holding Totleigh captive."

"Uh-huh. And?"

"I want to speak to the governor about ransom."

The Haplor tilted his head to one side. "Ransom? For Mr. Totleigh?"

"Who else?"

"Oh, I'm sure I wouldn't know. I'll see if the governor is available. Please hold."

The screen went blank, and Bren scowled at his hostage.

Pelham tried to shrug, though his bonds were too restrictive to fully make the gesture. "I told you there would be a certain lack of enthusiasm."

The screen came on again, this time displaying a wrinkled face fringed with sandy, dark-spotted fur and a hairdo that appeared every bit as rigid as Bren's own head crest. With a steely look in her eyes, she said, "What is this?"

"I am with the Okcho Liberation Force. We are holding Pelham G. Totleigh."

"What do you intend to do with him?"

"We only want the galaxy to know of our plight as second-class citizens on our own home world. That and a ransom of one million bills for his safe return."

The severe face broke into an open-mouthed cackle. "One million bills? One million … ooh … oh my giddy aunt. Let me tell you something, young man … or young woman — it's impossible to tell behind that ridiculous mask — I've never gained two cents worth of value from him. Good luck finding someone to give you one million bills. Ha!"

Bren, at first thrown by her reaction, recovered quickly. "If you don't pay, we'll execute him."

"No, you won't."

"We will."

"You won't, and here's why you won't. Since your little news flash went out, I've been contacted by the Alliance Council. They are, in fact, interested in learning more about your alleged plight. It isn't difficult for any of us around the galaxy to imagine the Zurks trampling over someone else's rights, all the while being terribly polite about it. Let's say the council is *currently* interested. However, if you kill an alliance citizen, you turn yourselves from victims into criminals. No one in the galaxy will lift a finger, wing, or tentacle to help you. So don't expect any ransom. You don't have the bargaining power."

"Don't push us, Governor. We are struggling for our existence. We are a desperate people."

"I'm sure you are. The question is are you stupid? Now, is it possible for me to speak with my nephew?"

"No."

"Then everyone in the galaxy will assume you've killed him."

"No. We haven't. He's fine."

"Then let me talk to him."

Who was this iron woman, Bren wondered? And how could Totleigh possibly be a relative? With reluctance, he pointed the screen toward his prisoner.

"What ho, Aunt Agutha," Pelham said.

"Well, I see you've stepped in it again, Nephew."

"Funny story that. Remember how you told me to do whatever I could to secure the release of the Bononian trade delegate? Well, I thought —"

"You thought. You thought. Pelham, you couldn't think your way out of a three-sided room."

"I say, really, Aunt Agutha. I mean ... gosh. A bit harsh, what?"

"You think that's harsh? You think I'm treating you poorly, my brainless relative? In many ways it is a blessing my late sister is not here to see this ... this ignominy."

"My present predicament is hardly my fault, Auntie. These people grabbed me. I was set up. I was tricked."

"Was this one of Blandings' schemes?"

"No. In fact, he was against it."

"I rest my case."

"But what are you going to do, Aunt Agutha?"

"Do? I have much to do. I have a meeting of the atmospheric enhancement committee coming up directly."

"I mean about me. What are you going to do about my … um … situation?"

"I don't intend to do anything. You thought yourself into this predicament, Pelham. I'll leave you to think yourself out. Now, I must get to my meeting. Tell your captor, good day."

Bren turned the tablet and saw the screen go blank. "She's gone."

"Yes, Aunt Agutha had to sign off," Pelham said. "She … um … sends her regards."

***

Before stepping into the posh office of Lord Bugzee, Lieutenant Commander Mountjoy took a moment to adjust his peaked cap and straighten his jacket. He wasn't doing it in deference to Bugzee. It was more of a self-defense move. Appearance mattered with Zurks.

It always aggravated Mountjoy that Lord Bugzee sat ensconced in this fashionable penthouse overlooking the strip while he, the highest-ranking military officer on Vogus, had been stuck down on level B2. It especially irritated him, as was the case now, when Bugzee summoned him as if he were a casino employee. Mountjoy forced his proboscis to uncurl, to give the appearance of one completely at ease. Intentionally neglecting to knock, Mountjoy opened the door and strode inside across the plush blue carpet toward the immense desk.

Bugzee looked up from something he was typing with two fingers on a tablet device. "Oh, there you are. Have a seat. Well, Mountjoy, you've made a hash of it this time."

"Have I?" said Mountjoy through clenched lips. He continued to stand. This was one place he did not want to get comfortable. "As I recall, Lord Bugzee, we both approved this plan."

The casino owner waved a hand. "I've told you before, Mountjoy. No need to be so formal. Feel free to simply call me m'lord."

Mountjoy forced a frozen smile to his face. He had no intention of addressing this money-grubbing merchant as m'lord.

Bugzee said in a mutter, "We should never have encouraged this Haplor to infiltrate the dissidents. We should have sent in one of our own, a professional."

Mountjoy patted a hand on his Zurk girth. "It would be difficult to disguise one of our own as an Okcho. As you yourself said, they might trust an outsider, especially someone as guileless as a Haplor."

"And yet your little scheme has ended up with this Haplor captured and news of the Okcho resistance splashed over the vids from one end of the galaxy to the other. Not to mention those ridiculous demands. This situation is intolerable. Who will want to visit Vogus now if people are afraid of being kidnapped?"

Mountjoy ran a hand down his proboscis, forcing it to stay relaxed and uncurled. "I rather think that was the point the Okcho were trying to make. They're trying to drive us out."

Bugzee grunted. His head rotated back to the tablet as if not engaging somehow made him less responsible for his next statement. "This Haplor must be rescued, and his captors brought to justice. And then an example will have to be made of them as a deterrent to others."

"Right. It is, however, a somewhat difficult task. We can't simply march troops into their community."

"Why can't you?" Bugzee pounded a fist on his desk. "Make a show of force. Have some backbone, Mountjoy." With a grunt he pulled himself from his chair and strode to gaze out the window to the strip below.

Mountjoy rubbed his forehead with one hand. "One would assume the OLF is employing scouts. We march in, and they'll simply rush Totleigh further out into the hardscape … or kill him. In short, rash action could make a bad situation worse. When the Haplor is released, as he will eventually be, I have no doubt I can extract from him all the information we wanted, including the names of the resistance leaders."

Bugzee spun around. "But you have a plan, right? You do have a plan to get him back, don't you, Mountjoy?"

"Of course," the commander lied. He had been racking his brain to come up with an idea when his lordship had summoned him up here like a common page boy.

"Then sort it," Bugzee barked. "We need this cleared up before it starts eating into profits. What are you grimacing about, Mountjoy?"

"Am I grimacing, Lord Bugzee? I hadn't realized."

"You are. What is it?"

"Oh, I was merely reflecting on the organizational chart."

"What organizational chart?"

"The one that shows me working for you, taking your orders. You know, the one that doesn't exist. I report to the chief of the Colonial Service."

"Yes, I know the chief. He's a friend of mine. We play cards together whenever I get back to Zurkannia. Or when he comes here. Hmm. I'm trying to recollect the last time he flew out for an inspection. He's probably due for one, don't you think?"

"I will do my job," Mountjoy said, "my duty. I am not impressed with threats."

Lord Bugzee plopped back into his huge, well-padded chair and leaned back with a smile half hidden under his proboscis. "Now who said anything about a threat, Mountjoy? We are but two citizens of the Zurkannian Empire doing our best to serve His Majesty."

***

Blandings stood in the hallway, rubbing his fingers together, trying to think of another plan. It was awkward asking a stranger for help. He had never met this person, and some of Mr. Totleigh's other friends back on Sonus were … well … a bit unreliable. For this scheme to work, he needed someone quick-witted and dependable. He took a breath, realizing this was the best ploy. He stepped forward, initiating a ding at the suite door.

From inside the room, a voice called, "Coming."

A moment later the wooden door swung open. A Cuneddan stood inside the doorway, drink in hand. "Hey, you're a Haplor. Are you a friend of Pelham's?"

"I am his valet. My name is Blandings. Are you Mr. Syd Duncil?"

"Something like that. Just call me Duncil … or Duncilrino if you prefer." He raised his glass and jiggled the ice. "Beverage?"

"Thank you, no."

"You're not like Pelham, are you?"

Blandings said nothing.

"What I mean is, you're more ... um ... formal."
"Indeed. This is not a social call. I am here about Mr. Totleigh."
"What about him?"
"You haven't heard?"
Duncil squinted. "Heard what?"

Chapter 22

Start the Revolution Without Me

In the little cabin out on the hardscape, Bren the Bulky sat at the table and stared at his prisoner. Pelham G. Totleigh, tied to a chair in the middle of the room, stared back with a vacant and impassive expression ... except for a nose that kept twitching.

"Stop that," Bren said.

Pelham blinked. "Hmm?"

"Stop doing the thing with your nose."

Pelham sniffled. "Frightfully sorry. The old sneezer is still a bit itchy. I don't suppose you could do anything about it, could you?"

Bren rolled his eyes. He stood, moved to the chair, and untied Pelham's hands from behind him. The Haplor swept both hands to his nose and rubbed, letting out a sigh of relief.

"Done?" Bren asked with an edgy tone.

"For now. Thanks awfully."

Bren retied Pelham's hands, this time in front of him so he could scratch to his heart's content. He doubted this little Haplor would get the drop on any of them.

"How about a drink?" Pelham asked. "I'm positively parched."

Bren grabbed a canteen from his gear and handed it over. Pelham took a long gulp. "Thanks. The water hits the old spot, eh? I don't suppose you could do me an Amurru fizz, could you? Or a cup of tea? Either really."

Bren responded with a glare. When this Haplor had fallen into his lap, it had seemed like his lucky day. This would advance the Okcho cause with awareness around the galaxy plus funds to carry on the struggle. Now it looked like it would only gain him a jail cell.

Pelham reached up and scratched his head. "What's the plan now that dear Aunt Agutha has turned you down flat?"

"That's not your concern."

"I beg to differ, old scout. It would be fair to say I am considerably invested in the turn of events. I'd like to return home soonish. I have a job and a flat and ... well ... a life."

"Sonus isn't the only group who might pay for your release. There are the trade conference people. Also, this kidnapping of a guest is a major black mark on the reputation of the Pink Mingo. They could pay."

"Theoretically. Not a million bills, I venture. I am at this moment in the hole to them for a few hundred plus the room, replicator charges, et cetera. It all adds up, you know."

The question was, Bren thought, how best to communicate with the Zurks. A call like he made to Sonus would be too dangerous. The Zurks could easily trace the wormhole. He could do another video drop as he had when they first announced the kidnapping, but that didn't provide a way for the Zurks to answer. What he needed was a safe way to send them a message and receive a response back.

He signaled to one of the other Okcho. "Fetch me Ned the Nerdy."

***

Mountjoy stepped into the interrogation room, pausing at the door to stop and scrutinize Emer at the table. Without a word he sat down across from her and again gave her the once over. Starting off with silence was one of his favorite techniques for getting inside a suspect's head.

Emer glowered at him. "What do you want this time?"

Mountjoy took a beat before answering. "What are your friends planning to do with Totleigh?"

The scowl dropped from Emer's face, replaced by raised eyebrows and a slack jaw. "What are you talking about? What's happened to him?"

"The Okcho Liberation Force kidnapped Totleigh after he went to them on your behalf."

Emer dropped her head into a hand. "I told him to stay out of this."

"Why? Because you didn't trust your co-conspirators?"

She shot him an if-looks-could-kill glare. "For the last time, I don't even know who these people are. All I knew at the time of the hack was that if you oppress people long enough, they fight back."

There was sincerity in her eyes. Mountjoy could almost believe her. Or else this Bononian was a good actor.

A knock sounded on the door. "Yes?" Mountjoy said.

The door cracked open, and Humstuggle's head poked through. "You have a call, sir. Some galactic alliance official."

Mountjoy's proboscis flicked back and forth in frustration. Not that this was a surprise. He had been expecting the galactic alliance to insert themselves into the situation. "Fine. Take our guest back to the cells."

Mountjoy returned to his office. He sat in his chair, swiveled around to face the view screen, and said, "Connect."

A voice said, "Yes, hello. Is this Commander Mountjoy?"

"Lieutenant Commander," Mountjoy admitted with annoyance. Fortunately, the screen stayed black, a voice call. It meant the other person wouldn't notice his irritation at having to deal with alliance bureaucrats.

"Sorry. This is Teego Martok. I am the Alliance Assistant Administrator for Economic Inequalities."

Gort help us, Mountjoy thought. He took a moment for a calming breath before answering. "How may I help you today ... Martok, was it?"

"I'm calling for an update on this hostage crisis."

"I wouldn't call it a crisis. We have matters in hand and expect a resolution soon."

"Wonderful. To which demands are you agreeing?"

Mountjoy tutted. "None of them."

"None? Not the raise in salary? Not the renegotiation of land leases?"

"The land leases are for His Majesty's Government back on Zurkannia to take up. As for salaries, they are a matter between employee and employer. It would be inappropriate for the military to intervene."

"I should say it is appropriate for you to intervene when it's a matter of public safety. Governments intervene in employment matters all the time —

health and safety issues, assuring a level playing field in contract negotiations, child labor laws."

Mountjoy leaned back in his chair, forcing his body to relax. "That is not the Zurkannian way."

"Well, then it appears the demand for an alliance fact-finding commission is in order. I will be talking with my superiors. Expect to hear more from us, Lieutenant Commander." The line went dead.

Fine, Mountjoy thought. At the normal speed of alliance bureaucracy, that would give him months. By then the perpetrators would all be tucked away in a work camp on Talso Four, and Vogus would be back to normal.

***

It was still sprinkling. Pelham watched through the window as a pair of kludas huddled against a moss-covered boulder that stuck up from the plain like a huge, perched bird. He stretched around in his chair, trying with tied hands to scratch a new itch on his backside.

The door crashed open, and Ned the Nerdy loped into the shack, heaving breaths. He dropped into one of the chairs and pulled off his wide-brimmed hat, dripping rain on the dirt floor.

"It's wet out there. Not to mention a fierce long walk."

"You should walk more," Bren said without sympathy. "Did they tell you what we need?"

"Uh-huh. A way to exchange secure asynchronous messages with the Zurks."

"I don't know what those words mean. What I want is to send them a message they can't trace but they can respond to."

Ned grinned. "That's what I said."

"Did you bring a gadget to do it?"

"You already have the gadget." He nodded toward Pelham.

"What?" asked Bren.

"His wrist device. Their VICTOR system sends and receives messages."

"It won't report his location, will it?"

"It can't, not this far from the hotel. The geolocation service is extremely localized."

"Again with the geek talk. You're sure about all that, are you?"

"It's what our contact told me."

"All right. How do we do it?"

"We can't, but he can."

Pelham's eyes darted back and forth between the two Okcho, who were now staring at him. "What? What?"

Bren said, "Tell VICTOR you want to send a message to Lord Bugzee."

"What do I say?"

"Tell him we need to know how they are coming along on meeting our demands. Tell him your life is in danger, and the casino needs to pay the ransom immediately — one million bills. Tell him to reply when they have it, and you'll send further instructions. You have all that?"

Pelham bit a lip. "They need to send the million bills in a message."

Ned said, "No, they can't put money in a message. Tell them to use a payment stick."

"Righto. Payment stick. Where do they send that?"

"We'll have further instructions on that," Bren said. "And don't forget the rest of the demands."

"What demands?" asked Pelham.

"Oh, for the love of Zahn. The pay increases, the renegotiation of land leases, the alliance commission."

"You want them to pay a commission in addition to the ransom? A commission on what? Is it a cut, a taste, a split as they say in the detective vids?"

Bren ran a hand over his crest. "Listen. On second thought, all you need to do is initiate the message. We'll tell you what to say."

Ned said, "Make it a text-only message."

"Righto," Pelham said. "Rally around, boys. Here we go. Hello, VICTOR."

The lilting voice sounded from the bracelet. "Oh, Mr. Totleigh, where are you? You have been out of sensor range since late last night. I was concerned for your safety."

"Ah yes. I am …" Pelham looked to the Okcho. "Where exactly am I, gentlemen?"

Bren answered with a shake of his yellow head.

Pelham said, "Can't say, VICTOR. Apparently, that information is not for publication. Anyhow, I need to send a message to Lord Bugzee."

"Text only," said Ned.

"A text message," Pelham said.

"What do you wish to say in the message, Mr. Totleigh?" VICTOR asked.

"The demands," Bren said.

"Um ... these fellows holding me want to know the status of meeting their demands. The ... um ... salary increases ... and the land lease thingamabob ... with the goats."

"Goats?" asked VICTOR.

"Re-goats, I think it was."

Bren said, "Not re-goats. Renegotiation."

"Ah. Sorry," said Pelham. "The land lease renegotiation. I got that one a bit mixed up."

Bren said, "And the galactic alliance needs to send a fact-finding commission."

"Oh, and the thing with the alliance blokes, the commission."

"And the ransom."

"And, of course, the ransom for my release, one million bills, if you can believe it, to be loaded to a payment stick with delivery details to be worked out later."

"Tell them to be quick about it."

"These chaps here expect an answer expeditiously and straightaway. Do you have all that, VICTOR?"

"I do, Mr. Totleigh. Are they treating you satisfactorily?"

"Oh, can't complain, you know. It isn't much worse than being interrogated by that blighter Mountjoy."

"I don't think I will pass that part along. Is there anything else I can do for you?"

"No, VICTOR. Send off the missive, please and thank you." Pelham lifted his eyes to Bren. "How did I do?"

It didn't take long to find out. The bracelet dinged, and Pelham raised his bound hands to look at it.

"What does it say?" Bren asked.

"It says, 'I'm afraid it will not be possible to proceed with those requests at this time. Sorry.' What's that mean?"

"It means," said Bren, "they refuse to negotiate with us."

"Ah," Pelham said. "Polite though, eh?"

Bren grumbled, paced around the cabin twice, and shot out the door.

Pelham smiled up at Ned. "So where did you pick up all your technical know-how?"

Ned eyed him suspiciously. "You're saying it's a surprise to find an Okcho who isn't fit only for menial jobs?"

"What? Hardly. Sorry if I gave that impression. No, I'm suitably impressed. All your hacking is much more than I could ever pull off."

Bren strode back in, a thick cloth bag in his hand. "I've had it with this guy. The longer we hold onto him, the riskier it gets. The Zurks could be flying overhead any minute with sophisticated tech to identify Haplor life signs."

Ned said, "I don't think such a thing exists."

"Yeah, well, you don't know for sure, do you? We're getting rid of him."

"Now, wait a moment, old chap," Pelham said, for the first time fearing for his life. "Let's not do anything rash. As I said, I have connections. Let's see what I can manage."

Bren didn't answer. He walked to Pelham and shoved the bag over his head. Pelham felt the bonds around his ankles fall away.

"Stand," Bren said.

Pelham rose with shaky legs. "You know, I believe I'm coming around to your way of viewing the situation vis-a-vis the Zurks. I say up with the revolution."

A hand grabbed his arm and walked him roughly out into the drizzle.

"Power to the people, what? Count me solidly as team Okcho."

"Button it," Bren growled.

Pelham was led across the rock to a place with the rustle of animals moving about. Bren, or someone, picked Pelham up and placed him onto a damp wooly back with an atrocious smell. The animal began moving. With his hands tied, Pelham was forced to lean forward, his head pressed up against the stinky animal's neck, to keep from falling off.

He rode like that for what seemed like hours, his mind racing. *So this is it. Death at a young age. I'm going to disappear out on a rocky, barren heathland on a distant planet alone … and hungry.* "I say, what about a last meal?"

Bren's voice came back. "Put a sock in it, would you?"

Despite the demeaning words, Pelham felt slightly relieved to know he wasn't alone. As he bounced along over the terrain, his mind went to Blandings, wishing his valet were there with him. Good old Blandings. He would have some words of wisdom, a tidbit of heartening philosophy, potentially even a scheme to get out of this scrape. Had he ever told Blandings how much he valued him? Yes, he had … on numerous occasions, in fact. That, at least, was a comfort.

It was also a comfort when in due course the rain at last stopped. Still, they rode on. Finally, the beast halted. Pelham waited for whatever would happen next to happen next. Nothing did.

"Hello?"

No answer. He had been abandoned. He tried to climb off the animal, which spooked it, causing the beast to skitter and Pelham to fall to the rocky ground.

Then someone pulled the bag off his head. Pelham blinked up into the twin suns, making out the face of Tud the Impatient.

"Well, what do we have here?" Tud said. "Looks like a present. I saw you on the news. Welcome, Mr. Totleigh. You are now a guest of the New Vogus Army."

Chapter 23

A Hunka Hunk of Busted Stone

"Where am I?" Pelham, his back flat on the ground, gazed up into the face of Tud the Impatient with a fair bit of confusion. "How did I end up here? For that matter, where did *you* come from? Where is Bren?"

Tud said, "You mean Bren the Bulky? Who knows? I haven't seen him since my group walked out of the meeting. As for how you came to be here, I assume you rode in on that kluda."

Pelham twisted his head in the direction Tud had nodded. A shaggy black kluda turned its head and made eye contact with him. It bleated.

Tud said, "He says you need to learn to balance your weight."

"You can understand what it's saying?"

"More or less. Kludas are more intelligent than you might think. We've learned to make ourselves understood, them and us. Those who live with us consent to share their milk and wool in exchange for food and protection and getting their coats trimmed now and then."

At this the kluda made a long throaty bellow.

"Yes," Tud said to the kluda, "this one is a stranger."

The animal twisted its head to one side and opened its mouth.

"No," Tud said, "it's not for eating.

Pelham sat up and scooted closer to Tud.

The kluda sniffed the air and followed its nose off across the rocky plain toward a patch of yellow flowers.

Pelham cautiously watched it go, then turned to Tud and held up his tied wrists. "If you could help me with these bonds and then point me in the direction of the hotel, I'll get out of your hair ... or horns ... or whatever you call those cresty things on your head."

Tud said, "You're not going anywhere."

"Oh, I say, now really. This is all getting a goodish bit old. You know, you may be asking yourself why Bren dumped me here. I can infer an answer. He found he couldn't trade me for ransom. As a hostage I appear to be of negligible value. Hence, you might as well let me go."

"I don't plan to use you as a hostage. I plan to use you as a shield."

"What? A what?"

"We're planning a raid tonight, and you're going along to make sure no one takes a shot at us ... or if they do, at least they'll hit you instead of us."

"Oh ... ah ... um ... don't you think you're being a trifle hasty? I mean to say, you might want to rethink this scheme. If you pay close attention, you will observe that I am more than a tad shorter than you. More than a tad, Tud. Ha! However, leaving aside my droll wit, my point, of course, is my size makes me less than completely effective as a shield."

Tud shrugged. "Eh, you'll do."

He grabbed Pelham's wrists and pulled him to his feet. Tud led him across the rock and down a hill toward a line of low concrete bunkers, the walls cracked and pockmarked, crumbling in spots, the metal doors covered with rust.

"What is this place?" Pelham asked.

"Abandoned military base. Back before the Okcho turned back to nature, this was one of our key planetary defense sites. Underground missile silos, command blockhouses, everything. My granny ran a boarding house for the guardians serving here. It's mine now. I figured what better place for the New Vogus Army than the location of the old Vogus army? Let me show you around."

Tud pulled at the door, which opened with a metallic shriek. They stepped inside to cooler, slightly clammy air. The huge room was dimly lit by shafts of sunlight shining through slit windows. They walked along, their footsteps echoing in the silence. Further in, a half dozen Okcho were sitting around a rickety table, playing a game involving dice. As Pelham passed, they stopped and stared at him with interest. He recognized one or two of them from the meeting.

"Is this the extent of your army?" Pelham asked Tud. "More like a patrol, I should say, a squad, a band."

Tud flashed him a savage look and pulled him on into the depths of the chamber where chunks of jagged concrete littered the floor. Pelham's eyes cast upward from the debris to corresponding holes in the roof from which a spider's web of rebar sprouted.

"Sit there." Tud nodded toward a pile of rubble along the wall.

Pelham stared up at the broken ceiling. "Are you quite sure this spot is safe?"

"It ought to be safe enough. Pieces don't break off all that often."

"Ah, but when they do, you see —"

"You'll be fine. The loose stuff's already fallen."

Pelham sat. He gazed up, inspecting the broken concrete overhead more thoroughly than he had ever inspected imports. He hunched his shoulders as if doing so would somehow protect him from a ton of falling cement.

He held out his bound hands, hoping they would be untied. Instead, Tud pulled a chain lock from a pocket and secured one of Pelham's legs to a loop of rebar sticking from a massive chunk of rubble.

Tud sat down on a hunk facing him. "Now, what's the OLF planning? What do you know of their next move?"

Pelham shrugged. "I rather think ransoming me was the scheme, and it didn't pan out. Oh, there was some talk about crashing the guest bracelets, but I don't remember it being seconded and voted on."

Tud rolled his eyes toward the fractured roof. "Guest bracelets. It's like their puny so-called demands. We don't want pay raises. We want the Zurks off the planet. Guest bracelets. What would that accomplish?"

"Search me. Embarrass the Zurks, I suppose."

"The Zurks are not going to leave Vogus out of embarrassment. What does the OLF think this is, a dinner party where someone dashes out mortified because they didn't dress properly?"

"That can be quite a problem."

"What?"

Pelham tutted. "One time I was invited over to Finky Weddelmeyer's place. Well, many a night Finky and I had hit the town, and it was never a big to-do. But in the meantime, old Finky had gone and got himself married. Little did I know this was to be a formal dinner party with the newlywed Weddelmeyers plus both sets of parents — who, by the way, were a quartet of stuffed squabs if I've ever seen any — and a couple of odd colonial muckety-mucks thrown in for good measure. Blandings had undertaken to persuade me to dress formally, but would I listen to him? No, I would not. Of course, no one is more formal than old Blandings. I wouldn't be surprised to find out he wears a necktie to bed. But I digress. I arrived at Finky's place —"

Tud cut him off. "You talk a lot."

Pelham waggled his head back and forth. "Oh, you know, I'm something of a storyteller. Many a time —"

Tud held up a hand. "Well, stop it. Two questions. Answer them yes or no. One, do you know what the OLF is planning?"

"Not as such."

"Yes or no."

"No."

"Two, do you have any idea what the Zurks are planning to do to rescue you?"

"Now, I ask you, how could I know of said plans when ipso facto they could only have been drawn up following my kidnapping."

"So no."

"Yes ... I mean, no ... I do not know what the Zurks are planning. However, this does all remind me of an interesting anecdote. See, one time a barrel of homebrewed hooch, which was made somewhere in the colony by persons unknown, was seized and then went missing. My Aunt Agutha — she's the head honcho, so to speak —"

Tud stood and called to one of the other Okcho, his voice echoing through the cavernous space, "Yon the Surly, gag him."

"Why do I have to?" the Okcho asked as he walked over, a bitter expression on his face. Tud ignored him and strode away. Yon untied a bandana from his own neck and secured it around Pelham's neck and open mouth.

The gag smelled like dirt mixed with kluda dander and marinated in sweat. Pelham started to say something but stopped when his tongue touched the gag, and he came close to gagging himself.

The rest of the day, Tud huddled with his men. Pelham couldn't make out what they were saying other than an occasional word here and there, none of which were encouraging. The list included attack, blasters, casualties, and most worrisome of all, Haplor.

After the discussion they left the bunker to complete assigned tasks, leaving Pelham alone. He gazed down at his costume, or rather the tattered remains of it. The yellow onesie was torn in spots, revealing his regular clothes underneath. Where it wasn't torn it was filthy.

For the second time that day, he contemplated his mortality. Should he have done more with his life, applied himself more assiduously as Aunt Agutha had so often admonished? After weighing it all, he decided no. On the whole, he thought he had done tolerably well. He had found friends and enjoyed their company. Surely that made for a life well lived. He had no regrets. Well, one regret — how he was likely to soon purchase that fabled one-way ticket out of the physical realm.

As daylight was fading through the window slits, Yon the Surly brought him a plate with a bit of bread and a portion of bean stew along with a cup of water. Pelham smiled in gratitude as the revolutionary ungagged him and handed him the plate.

"Thanks terribly." Pelham dug into the meal as best he could with his hands tied. The stew, though simple, employed unusual and flavorful spices. "I say, this is splendid. My compliments to the chef." He took another bite. "Is everything a go for tonight?"

"I'm not supposed to talk to you," Yon said.

"Ah, but you just did, see? So you might as well continue."

"I'm not supposed to talk to you."

"Am I going along on this raid?"

Yon said nothing.

"Are you the one who will take me?"

"Not me."

"Ah."

Yon's eyes swam with confused panic.

"You just confirmed that I'm going." Pelham handed the man back the empty plate and submitted to being re-gagged. He sat alone again, trying to come up with a daring plan to escape. He drew a blank.

Pelham was startled from his revels by steps echoing across the concrete floor. He spotted Kiz the Chatty. She waved and rushed over.

"Mr. Totleigh," Kiz said in a hushed tone.

"Mmm mmm mmm," Pelham tried to say through the bandana.

Kiz pulled the gag from his mouth.

"I say, thank you. That bally rag tasted awful. One wonders how long it has gone between washings."

Kiz glanced frantically over her shoulder. "Please, Mr. Totleigh, hold your voice down."

"These fellows here are talking about violence — armed insurrection — and putting me bang in the middle of it."

"Shh."

"Not that they don't have cause, I'm sure, but I ask you, all the hate, the anger, what is it doing to them … inside I mean?"

"Shh."

"This one time my cousin Gussie —"

Kiz stuffed the gag back in his mouth. She held up a finger. "Listen, love. I'll take the gag out, but only if you promise to be quieter."

Pelham nodded, and she removed the gag once more.

This time in a whisper, Pelham asked, "What are you doing here, Kiz?"

"Mr. Totleigh, you know it's Kiz the Chatty. But to answer your question, I sneaked out here to make sure you were okay. I'm so sorry this happened to you."

"How did you know where to come?"

"It's hard to keep a secret among the Okcho. Everybody knows everything. You're famous, Mr. Totleigh. You're on every news vid from here to Snuulia."

"Can you sneak me out?"

"I doubt it, but I'll talk to the elders on your behalf. I don't think it helps our cause to kidnap people."

"You believe these elders will be sympathetic to my plight?"

"Urdi the Unfortunate will. He knows you."

"Urdi is an elder?"

"Urdi the Unfortunate. Yes, he has a lot of influence."

"You don't say. However, I should point out, you may not have an abundance of time to plead my case. I rather get the impression they're planning to storm the proverbial castle tonight, and I'm scheduled for top billing on the program."

"They're idiots. They're all idiots."

"I take it you're not a soldier in this Vogon army of theirs?"

"No. I'm not a member of any of these stupid groups. They're all boys playing dress up, if you ask me."

"So you what? Stand with the Zurks?"

She spit on the floor. "I do not."

"What side are you on then, if I may ask?"

"I try to be on the side of pragmatic, realistic solutions to complex issues. Which means I stand alone most of the time. The Zurks and all these Okcho paramilitary groups, they all push overly simplistic answers to complicated problems. Most of them just want to break something."

Pelham blinked. He was finding this all a bit hard to follow and didn't know what to say.

Kiz sat back on the floor. "Look, the fact is the Zurks are here, and we'll never push them out by force. I don't care what tactics or strategy these groups use. The Zurks are simply too powerful and willing to do whatever it takes to back up their power. Neither Bren the Bulky's stunts nor Tud the Impatient's raids are going to change that. These splinter resistance groups can't even agree on what they want. Some want a better deal with the Zurks. Others insist the Zurks have to go home. Some want the strip demolished. Others want Okcho control of the strip."

"What do you want?" Pelham asked.

She looked up at the crumbling ceiling. "I wish the Zurks had never come. But even if we could make them leave somehow, I'm not sure it would be a good idea at this point. There's a reason Okcho move off the hardscape to come work on the strip. Zurk jobs pay money. Not much, but it's better than nothing. They support families, which is more than this bare rock does sometimes. But Okcho need a better deal than we've been getting. The Zurks make all the rules, rake in all the profits, tell us what to do like we're their servants, run the planet — our planet. It isn't right."

Pelham knitted his eyebrows. She had given him a lot to think about, more than he normally thought about at any one time. Mainly he kept thinking how he didn't have long to do anything before this skirmish would begin.

More footsteps sounded. Kiz's eyes met his with alarm. Pelham waved his bound hands toward a huge chunk of concrete a few steps away. Kiz pushed the gag back into his mouth and retreated to the shadows.

Tud approached. Wearing a grin, he ungagged the prisoner once more. "Guess what? Somebody is here to see you. Believe it or not, it seems like one of Bren the Bulky's schemes might have paid off."

Chapter 24

The Inimitable Blandings

"What?" Pelham asked.

Tud detached the chain lock from Pelham's leg but left the rope tied around his wrists. He led the Haplor from the bunker. Outside, the night was clear and cool. Three moons hung pale and low in the sky beneath a swath of stars.

The half dozen soldiers of the New Vogus Army huddled in a knot beside a rock outcropping from which hung a flickering torch. As Tud and Pelham approached, the knot loosened. There in the middle stood Blandings and Duncil.

Pelham couldn't believe his eyes. "Bl ... Bla —"

The valet interrupted him. "I presume what you are trying to say, Mr. Totleigh, is blessed evening to you. May I say, blessed evening to you too." Blandings eyed Tud. "How have you been treating this person such that he cannot even manage the traditional Haplor greeting?"

"We've treated him fine," Tud said defensively. "We had to gag him. The guy talks incessantly."

"Let me get those bonds off you, Mr. Totleigh," Blandings said. He wrapped an arm around Pelham and pulled him a few steps away from the group. As he untied the rope, he said in a whisper, "Sir, pretend you don't know me or Mr. Duncil. We are impersonating the galactic alliance delegation that was part of the Okcho demands for your release."

Pelham gaped. "You are? How did you get yourself appointed to that?"

"Perhaps, sir, it would be better to speak as little as possible until we are free of the encampment."

Blandings steered him back to the huddle where Tud was asking Duncil, "How does this fact-finding commission work?"

Duncil said, "Simple, man. You tell us your complaints about the Zurks."

In response, all the rebels began talking at once.

"They treat us like lower life forms."

"The Zurks dictate to us working conditions, hours, wages."

"My cousin works in the casino. He asked for time off to care for his mother, and they fired him."

"Yeah, well, my sister was docked pay because she had the sniffles."

"We have to work all day inside, away from the ground, the fresh air, the suns. When you can see the suns, mind you. When it isn't cloudy as a blanket or bucketing out rain."

Duncil made a calm down gesture with his arms. "People. People. Take it easy. Take it easy."

Pelham found himself distracted from the conversation by Blandings' fingers, which began twitching. He glanced up and noticed the valet staring at him intently. He had seen that look before. He gazed down the front of his yellow onesie and brushed off any clumps of dirt and kluda hair he could find. Blandings relaxed noticeably.

One of the Okcho said, "The Zurks push us around. They trample all over us. My friend got into an argument with a Zurk over some food he served. A guard came over and immediately took the Zurk's side. My friend ended up getting hauled off to the cells for the night."

Duncil bobbed his head gravely. "We will look into it. You shouldn't have to live like that."

Someone else said, "The casinos are killing our culture. We want them out now."

Another one answered, "Well, we want the Zurks out. It would be nice to keep the casinos and hotels. What we want is control of them, control of our economic destiny."

"No, those places are poison. We need to get rid of them all, get back to our traditional way of life."

"Yeah, but my dad works on the strip. If everything closes, then how does he eat?"

"We existed fine before they came."

"That was then."

Tud spoke up, cutting off the discussion. "I think it would be better if we spoke with one voice. I can answer your questions." He pulled a device from a pocket and glanced at it. "It's getting late. I think tomorrow morning would be a better time to handle this. We have a ... a meeting tonight. We'll discuss the situation and report back to you. We can find you rooms in the village."

Blandings said, "Rooms for the two of us and Mr. Totleigh?"

"We were hoping to take Mr. Totleigh with us to the meeting. It's ... it's a meeting of all the Okcho resistance groups, and they want assurances he is all right."

"I don't believe that would be wise. Mr. Totleigh has obviously been through a traumatic experience. We need to put him to bed and provide him with medical care as soon as possible."

"But the other factions —"

Blandings took a step toward Tud. "Sir, Tud the Impatient, our delegation is here to help you, to learn of your situation. However, we do expect your full cooperation."

"The thing is, he's our bargaining chip. We were asking for concessions from the Zurks, ransom."

"Yu have something better than ransom now. You have the open eyes and ears of the galactic alliance."

Tud grimaced. "All right. You can take him back to Baile Atha. But stay on this side of the wall. We will meet you there in the morning."

"Satisfactory. It will provide us with an opportunity to speak with the villagers and solicit their opinions." Blandings pointed toward a hill. "The town is in this direction, is it not?"

Tud nodded. Blandings ushered Duncil and Pelham away from the cluster of Okcho across the dark, rocky landscape. After putting some distance between themselves and the abandoned military base, Blandings halted.

"I suggest, sir, you take this opportunity to remove yourself from that ... costume. Yellow is not your color."

"My man Blandings," Pelham said with fondness as he shed the tattered remains of the Okcho-colored onesie. He held it awkwardly in his hands, not knowing what to do with it until Blandings took it from him and tucked it away somewhere. "I can always depend on you."

"I endeavor to give satisfaction, sir."

"And you have. That was some smooth talking you pulled off back there with Tud the Impatient, what?"

"Thank you, sir."

Pelham swiveled his head left and right. "Not much out this way, eh? Are you sure we can find our way back?"

"I am confident of it, sir." The valet looked to the sky. "Do you observe that grouping of stars? The arrangement is said to resemble an Okcho head crest."

"Looks more like a Rhegedian blue squid to me. Note all the tentacles."

"I see what you mean, sir, provided the squid is swimming upside down."

"Well, yes, there is that."

"Those tentacles, as you say, form the points of the crest. This is a famous constellation on Vogus. They call it the great Okcho in the sky."

"Fascinating lecture there, Blandings, but, if you recall, I asked about finding the village, not astronomy."

"Yes, sir. My point is that as long as we keep the great Okcho to our left, we should walk straight to the town."

"Ah, excellent. Say, why do we not see this great Okcho fellow over the skies of Sonus?"

"It is because we are in another part of the galaxy, sir. We are looking, for the most part, at the same stars but from an entirely different perspective. Much like entering a room from a different door."

"What? Oh right. Intriguing."

Duncil said, "It's incredible out here, man. I can feel the universe speaking to me."

"What's it saying?" Pelham asked.

"It's saying, abide, man. Be present and abide."

Conversation died away as the grandeur of the barren plain at night swept over them. They walked in silence until at last they crested a hill and found the town below them.

"Here it is," Duncil said, "Now where?"

Pelham said, "Well, there's a woman named Shay with whom I'd like to have a pointed word or two."

"Best not, sir," Blandings said. "For now, we should keep a low profile and maintain the ruse that Mr. Duncil and I are alliance envoys bringing you here to rest pending the return of the New Vogus Army."

"What are we actually doing?"

"We are waiting for a propitious moment to escape back into the hotel."

"Very good, Blandings. Carry on."

They descended into the village and began walking along the circle of cabins in the direction of the casino wall. The door of a stone shanty swung open, chatter and music exploding from inside. An Okcho staggered out and nodded at them as they passed on the path. "How ya doing, hey?" The scent of alcohol wafted on the air.

"Gentlemen," Pelham said, "I believe we have found a pub. Recent events call for a celebratory libation. My treat. What can I get you?"

"Excellent," Duncil said. "White Rhegedian for me."

"Not familiar with that one," Pelham said. "And Rhegedians are blue, as you may have noticed."

"The people are blue. The drink is white."

"What about you, Blandings?"

The valet stepped in front of him and began brushing Pelham's shoulders and running a hand across Pelham's hair. "Before we go anywhere, sir, we must make you presentable."

"It's a pub, Blandings. My appearance doesn't matter. Now, I want to buy you a drink. What will you have?"

"If you insist, sir, I will take a small sherry."

Sherry it is."

Inside, groups of Okcho huddled around most of the tables. In one corner a fireplace blazed. In another, a band was playing a jig on stringed instruments. The patrons laughed and joked with each other. Pelham waved his companions toward a tiny table near the door and strode to the bar. An older Okcho stood behind the counter, his face and hands substantially green with veining.

Pelham said, "Lovely evening, eh? I would like a white Rhegedian, a sherry, and an Amurru fizz, stiffish."

The barman grinned. "Sorry, lad. If you want fancy drinks, you'll have to go somewhere in the Zurk colony. Out here we have stout on tap. It's our own brew. Should I pull you one?"

Taken by the charm of the surroundings, Pelham winked. "Why not? Pull three if you please." He slid his payment stick across the counter.

"We're not set up for payment sticks either, I'm afraid. But that doesn't matter. We heard about you alliance delegates coming in to hear our side of the story. Your drinks are on the house."

Pelham hauled the mugs to the table. "Limited beverage menu, but you alliance chaps are here to study the local culture, and here's some of it in liquid form." He raised his mug. "To my release."

They were only a few sips into their drinks when a figure burst into the room, panting heavily. He leaned his hands on a table and looked around at the patrons as the music ground to a halt. Pelham recognized him as one of the rebels.

"You," the man said, pointing a yellow finger across the room at Pelham.

"What? What?" All eyes swung in his direction.

"How did you give away our plans to raid the hotel?"

"What? What?"

"They were all over us. They captured everyone. They kept Tud the Impatient."

A wave of murmurs swept around the room. Pelham spoke over them. "I didn't know your plans. Even if I did, how could I give them away? We've only now come in from our trek across the plain."

"That much is true," the barman said. "They've barely sat down."

The patrons surrounded the man, asking for details.

Blandings said, "I suspect now is the appropriate time to exit before any other rebels show up and there are further questions of us."

"But my stout," Duncil said.

Blandings shot him a look. The three of them stood and edged out the door. They made their way on around the path until they reached the high wall into the casino. They rushed to the metal door and punched at the controls. It wouldn't budge. Blandings beat on the door. After more than a minute of pounding, it slid open a mere crack.

The Zurk guard whom Pelham had sneaked past the night before peered through the opening. The guard looked them up and down. "What's all this then?"

Blandings said, "We have rescued the Haplor who was being held hostage by Okcho dissidents. We need to return to the hotel."

"I'm sorry, but only Okcho are allowed to enter."

"Beg pardon? Forgive me if I failed to make my meaning clear. You see, this is an escape from the Okcho resistance. We need to be admitted at once."

"I have my orders."

Blandings, who rarely looked confused, now appeared completely baffled. "We are the alliance commissioners you let through a few hours ago. If you remember, we had quite a long discussion at that time about our authority. You assured me we could return when our business was completed."

"Yeah? Well, he wasn't with you then," the guard said, glaring at Pelham. "That one was trying to sneak through last night."

"And now you can get him back where he belongs."

"Nope. I am not falling for any of his tricks. No one but Okcho may come through the door."

Through tight lips, Blandings said, "I wonder if it would be possible for you to contact your superiors — I might suggest Lieutenant Commander Mountjoy — to inquire if perhaps this might be an instance in which an exception to the rules should be made. I suggest you tell him you have Mr. Pelham G. Totleigh at the door along with two companions who have executed his rescue."

"What? Who was executed?"

Duncil said, "We're going to be if you don't let us in. For the love of Zahn, man, call somebody."

The guard squinted at them in disapproval, then disappeared back inside with a slam of the door. After some tense moments, it slid open again, this time all the way. The guard motioned for them to enter. Blandings pushed Pelham through the doorway and followed with Duncil. A couple of Okcho over by the lockers stared at them.

The guard said, "Wait here, please."

"Wait for what?" Pelham asked.

The guard said nothing. Minutes later footsteps sounded on the stairs. Thick green pant legs appeared, followed by a thicker green jacket. Coming down last was the scowling face of Sergeant Humstuggle. He stopped at the bottom of the steps and looked them over. "I hear you've all been outside the walls."

"You hear correctly, Sergeant," Pelham said. "Blandings and Duncil have rescued me from desperados."

"Commander Mountjoy would like a word with you."

"I dare say he would. For my part, I have things to tell him, including an assurance I received that Emer was not involved in the casino hacking thingamabob. You might pass that along. I'll be certain to come around in the morning ... not too early, mind you. However, first I need a shower followed by several solid hours of shuteye."

Humstuggle twisted his head. "If you don't mind, Mr. Totleigh, the commander would like to see you right away."

"As it happens," Pelham said, "I do mind. I have had a bit of an ordeal."

Humstuggle cleared his throat, schnoz twitching. "Excuse me if I gave the impression that it was a request."

"What?"

"Come along."

"What?"

Chapter 25

The Code of the Totleighs

"I say, Sergeant, now really." All Pelham wanted was to crawl into bed ... or perhaps take a relaxing shower and then shuffle off to bed ... or possibly have a calming cup of tea and maybe a piece of fruit and then a shower and then bed. In any case, what he most definitely did not need at present was another interrogation by the Vogus security force. Nevertheless, that's what looked to be happening.

Sgt. Humstuggle led him up the stairs with Blandings and Duncil in step behind them. When they reached the main floor lobby, it was obvious the situation had changed over the course of the day Pelham had been outside the walls. Zurk security guards now stood at the entrance to the casino, at meeting room doors, at the hotel entrance. Over by the reception desk, one of the guards was frisking Urdi the Unfortunate, an expression of resignation on Urdi's face.

"What's with the police state?" Pelham asked.

Humstuggle said, "The rebels attacked the place last night. We're beefing up security."

"A bit much, don't you think?"

"We aren't taking any chances."

An Okcho with a drink tray stepped from the casino, one eye on the guards. "Amurru fizz, Mr. Totleigh?"

"What? Oh yes. Thanks awfully."

"No," Humstuggle said. "His head needs to be clear."

The Okcho shrugged and returned to the casino. Pelham licked his lips in disappointment.

"Where do you two think you're going?" Humstuggle asked Blandings and Duncil.

Blandings said, "I am accompanying Mr. Totleigh."

Duncil said, "I'm with them."

Humstuggle said, "No, you aren't. I am sorry, but that is against regulations."

"Is it, Sergeant?" Blandings asked, one eyebrow cocked. "I believe you will find that by resolution of the galactic alliance council, everyone has the right for a representative to be present with them during questioning."

"That applies to attorneys."

"I am sure such is often the case, Sergeant. However, there is nothing in the wording that specifies a required occupation for the representative. It could, for instance, be a valet."

Sgt. Humstuggle's proboscis twitched left then right. "All right." He wagged a finger at Duncil. "But you go back to your room."

Duncil said, "This is bogus, man. This poor guy gets kidnapped. Now you're taking him away."

Blandings gave Duncil a quiet smile. "I'll take care of Mr. Totleigh. Thank you for your help."

"I still say it's bogus." Duncil shook his head and wandered off.

With Blandings in tow, Humstuggle led Pelham past the front desk and along the hallway at the front of the hotel. At the elevators Humstuggle scanned his badge, and they entered.

When the elevator door opened again on the lower level, Humstuggle led them down the gloomy hallway, through the security headquarters bullpen, and to Commander Mountjoy's office door.

Mountjoy looked up as they entered, a friendly-looking smile poking out the sides of his proboscis. "Take a seat, Mr. Totleigh. I see Mr. Blandings has joined us as well. Have a seat, please. I dare say you've had quite an adventure."

"He has," Blandings said, continuing to stand. "He needs rest."

Mountjoy widened the smile. "I'll try not to keep him too late. I only want a report of what happened and who he met. Have you heard of the Okcho attack this evening?"

"Heard of it? I was there when they were discussing it," Pelham said.

"Who? I mean … good. Good. Then you understand what we're dealing with. We need to put an end to this rebellion."

There it was, thought Pelham. Exhausted as he was, he was not so knackered that he failed to grasp what was going on. He had momentarily been grateful for the interview being conducted in Mountjoy's office rather than in a cold interrogation room. Now it made sense. This more comfortable setting had less to do with hospitality and consideration for him than it did with Mountjoy trying to manipulate him into spilling the beans on the Okcho. Which Pelham was not about to do. He had promised the Okcho he would not reveal their names. Granted, the promise was made under duress, but Pelham's word was his bond. It was the code of the Totleighs.

"How did you even get into the Okcho village?" Mountjoy asked, his face a mask of guileless curiosity.

"Ah, well, I purchased an Okcho costume, and thusly disguised, I was able to sneak past the guard."

"What kind of costume?"

"Yellow leggings and top. Mask. Hat."

"And that fooled the guard?"

"I slipped through in a group." Too late it dawned on Pelham what the next question would inevitably be.

"And what were the names of the people in this group?"

"Names?"

"Their names, please."

Pelham shrugged. "Hmm. I don't think we were formally introduced."

"Uh-huh," Mountjoy said with a skeptical tone. "This group of Okcho no doubt realized you weren't one of them."

"Oh, I don't think so. You see, the disguise made me appear to be an Okcho child due to my stature and all. I imagine it played on their sympathies to no small extent."

"Uh-huh. And they let you walk in with them ... no questions asked?"

"That's correct. Yes, Commander, you have the picture clearly in your mind."

"What happened next after you entered the village?"

"Ah." Pelham leaned in and waggled his eyebrows. "I was able to infiltrate a meeting of this Okcho Litigation Forts." He decided to leave out anything about Shay the Shorter. Being betrayed by her was no reason to turn around and betray her.

"You mean the Okcho Liberation Force. How did you find out about their meeting?"

"Sleuthing."

"Sleuthing?"

Pelham tapped a finger on the side of his nose. "Yes, Commander, I investigated. I spied, snooped, pursued clues."

"You don't say. In any case, you must have heard names there in the meeting."

"It may be that a few monikers were bandied about."

"Such as?"

Pelham made a clicking sound with his mouth. "I am afraid, Commander, I'm not frightfully good with names. No doubt they were all aliases in any case."

Mountjoy's jaw bulged out on one side. "Bren the Bulky?"

"Who? I say, these Okcho names are fascinating, what? So descriptive. So expository. Is expository the word I'm stabbing at, Blandings?"

"I feel sure it is, sir."

Mountjoy said, "Can you at least describe these people?"

"Oh, certainly, I can. Glad to. Let's see now. Well, they all were Okcho, of course. They had those funny crest doohickies on their heads. Yellow skin with the green veining. Tell me, Commander, is my assumption correct that they pick up more of the veining as they age?"

"We're not here to discuss aging, Mr. Totleigh." Mountjoy sucked in a long breath and let it out, his proboscis raising and lowering. "I'm feeling myself age considerably as this conversation progresses. What else can you tell me about them? I need specific details."

"Such as?"

"Height, weight?" Pelham could detect a hint of a snarl in the lieutenant commander's voice.

Pelham chuckled. "They were hardly going to let me measure and weigh them."

"Estimates."

"Oh, I'd say they all weighed more than I do, less than you. Does that help?" Pelham shot a grin toward Blandings.

Mountjoy glared. "Do you think this is funny, Mr. Totleigh?"

"I don't know. Personally, I found it amusing, but I couldn't help noticing neither you nor Blandings laughed. Of course, Blandings isn't much for chuckles."

Mountjoy pasted the smile back on his face. "You know, I think we may have gotten off on the wrong foot here. Tea?"

"Yes, rather. A good old cuppa might be just the thing to buck me up."

"Humstuggle!" Mountjoy called.

Behind Pelham came the squeak of a chair followed by heavy footsteps.

"Yes, Commander?" Humstuggle said from the office door.

Mountjoy waved a hand. "Tea, please. For three."

Humstuggle grumbled and moved off.

Mountjoy said, "What you don't appear to appreciate, Mr. Totleigh, is that these people are terrorists. Take the attack this evening. A group of them tried to break into the hotel safe. Thank Gort they didn't succeed, or they would have had enough in valuables to finance arms purchases. We have the leader in an interrogation room right now, and I'll be talking to him further once I finish with you."

"Ahem." The unobtrusive sound had come from Blandings.

Mountjoy shifted his gaze to the valet. "Did you have something to add?" The question dripped with derision.

"Oh no," Blandings said. "However, I might point out, Lieutenant Commander, what I observed in the short time I was in Okcho territory securing Mr. Totleigh's release. These people are desperate. They live in poverty. They feel they have been dispossessed of their own home world. Securing blasters may not be a requirement for a rebellion to start. They will use rocks and sticks if need be."

Mountjoy's eyes narrowed. "You saw them too? Can you give me a description of them?"

"Unfortunately, it was dark. Everyone was draped in shadows."

Sgt. Humstuggle returned with a tray full of replicated tea and a face full of scowl. He served everyone, then stomped out. Pelham took a sip and made a face. It tasted like warm water.

Leaving his own cup untouched, Mountjoy said, "How exactly did you arrange Mr. Totleigh's release, Mr. Blandings?"

"By way of a ruse. One of the other trade delegates, Mr. Syd Duncil, and I impersonated the requested galactic alliance delegation."

Mountjoy stared at Blandings for a moment with what Pelham took to be a look of admiration. "Listen, gentlemen, I'm trying to defend Vogus. I *will* defend

Vogus. I will crush this rebellion, and someday people across the Zurk empire will speak of what we do here."

"Oh, they'll speak of it all right, Commander," Pelham said, gesturing with his cup, "and they're going to call it Lost Vogus if you don't start listening to what the Okcho are saying. Blandings, what is that line about freedom in the end? I had to learn the ruddy thing at school."

"Possibly, sir you mean, 'In the end, freedom wins.' A rather saccharine phrase, but inspiring nonetheless, and more often than not true, historically speaking."

"Once again, Blandings, you've hit it right on the schnoz. No offence, Commander."

"What?" Mountjoy asked.

"Would it hurt, Commander, to sit down and listen to what they say they want?"

For a few beats Mountjoy stared at them in silence, his jaw feverishly working back and forth. "What they want is totally impractical. They want us to leave them on their own when they aren't prepared for it. These Okcho are ignorant of the ways of the modern galaxy. They are not equipped to handle independence or self-government or their own defense. They need us. If we left Vogus, the Thomians would swoop in the next day ... or someone worse. Without us, there would be no peace, no stability on this planet. If you truly want to help these people, Mr. Totleigh, I suggest you remember something that leads to the arrest of the rebel leaders who are steering them all toward disaster."

Pelham took a sip of tea, shivered, and pushed the cup away from him across the desk. "Well, I do recollect one thing, Commander. When this one group was holding me captive, the leader told me point blank that Emer was in no way working with them. I dare say then you should release her."

"What did this unnamed leader say exactly?"

"Exactly? You mean word for word?"

"As best as you recall."

"Well, I believe he said something to the effect of, 'The Bononian is not our ... our connection or whatever ... inside the hotel.' Something like that."

Mountjoy raised his head, his proboscis lifting like a trumpet. "He said the Bononian was not their connection?"

"Or contact or associate. I can't call the exact word to mind."

"Whatever. That implies they do have a confederate here, only not the Bononian. Is that how you took it?"

"All I took from it, Commander, was that Emer wasn't involved. As I say, why not release her?"

Mountjoy scoffed. "Because the terrorist might have been lying, that's why."

"And yet you act as if you believe him."

"Well, I do, and I don't. It's true we haven't gotten anything out of the Bononian. And I grant it is possible this Okcho leader may have been telling the truth. Or perhaps, knowing you would report to us, he fed you misinformation to send us off chasing our noses as we hunt for this alleged other collaborator."

"But it is evidence that she was not involved, is it not? That's what you said you wanted."

Mountjoy's jaw bulged again. "Tell you what, I will release Emer. You are probably right that the Bononian had nothing to do with the attack."

Pelham stood. "Thank you. I appreciate it. If there is any other way I can be of assistance, please let me know."

Mountjoy raised a hand. "You misunderstand. I am releasing Emer. I am not releasing either of you. I know you have further information about the Okcho resistance. You're not going anywhere until you are more forthcoming."

Chapter 26

The Advantages of Keeping Expectations Low

With an unnerving *clang*, the massive steel door to the cellblock swung shut behind Pelham and Blandings. To Pelham's surprise, the room inside was not lined with individual barred cells but with only a grid of yellow lines painted on the floor. At each spot where the yellow lines intersected, a pyramid-shaped bot topped by a spherical camera eye was bolted to the floor.

Inside one of the rectangles, Emer sat on the edge of a slab hanging from the wall. She waved to Pelham and Blandings.

"No bars?" Pelham asked Sgt. Humstuggle, who had led them to the cellblock. "What do you use? Force fields?"

Humstuggle tutted. "Do you have any idea how much force fields cost to operate?"

"Can't say I do."

"Well, it's a lot. And bars don't work for tiny aliens or those who can squish themselves through tight openings. Take it from me, we get all kinds here."

"So you use lines? How do these bally lines keep anyone in custody?"

"Watch bots. Step inside, and I'll show you."

Not having much choice in the matter, Pelham and Blandings stepped across a line into an empty rectangle of the grid. Humstuggle pulled out a tablet and tapped on it. The bots on the four corners of the rectangle lit up.

"All right, the system is armed," Humstuggle said. "Now let's say you try to slip past."

Digging in his pocket, the sergeant came out with a small piece of candy. He pitched it toward the Haplors, causing Pelham to duck reflexively. He needn't have bothered. As the sweet passed over the yellow line, the ball head of one of the watch bots rotated with the speed of logic circuits and fired a laser beam, disintegrating the confection to a fine mist of sugar. Humstuggle slid another candy along the floor across the line. In a frighteningly similar manner, this one also was destroyed.

"See how it works?" the sergeant asked with a smirk. "Takes much less power than a force field and more effective than bars. We'll see what a few hours of cooling off in here do for your story. Hope you don't sleepwalk." He chuckled at his own joke. He was the only one. Pelham was still gaping at the bots.

Humstuggle tapped on his tablet again and nodded to Emer. "You're free to go."

"I am?"

"Yeah. Get out of here."

She took a step toward the yellow line, then hesitated. "You have those killer bots turned off, right?"

"Sure," Humstuggle said in a non-reassuring tone.

Emer crossed the line without drawing fire. "May I have a word with Mr. Totleigh?"

The sergeant grimaced. "Keep it brief."

Pelham met her at the edge of his cell, leaning as near to the yellow line as he dared, which is to say not particularly close at all.

"What's going on?" she asked. "Why are you in here?"

"I am happy to report I was able to convince Mountjoy of your innocence."

"Thank you. But what about you? Why are you now locked up?"

"Ah. Well, in the process I stumbled into a few dodgy experiences, which Commander Mountjoy believes has given me inside information on the Okcho resistance." Pelham lowered his voice to a whisper. "In fact, I did learn a thing or two, but I'm not telling him."

Emer's eyes flashed, momentarily reminding Pelham of the way Aunt Agutha had often regarded him after some particularly boneheaded move on his part. It wasn't a pleasant sensation at all. He was relieved when her next words made it clear that he wasn't the one who was perturbing her.

The Advantages of Keeping Expectations Low

"This is disgraceful. First me, now you. The Zurks can't simply round up off-worlders on vague suspicions and hold them without charge."

Humstuggle stepped between them, looking stern. "Come along now."

Emer shot Pelham a strained smile and straightened. "Don't worry. I'm going to talk to the other trade delegates about this outrage. It will all work out." She followed Humstuggle out of the cell block.

Pelham sighed and crossed to the concrete shelf and bare mattress serving as a cell cot. He sat, shaking his head. "It appears we are well in it this time, eh, Blandings?"

"Our prospects do appear to be at an ebb, sir."

"I can only imagine what Aunt Agutha will say — me getting arrested again."

"The governor is not likely to be pleased, sir."

Pelham chuffed out a hollow laugh. "No, she will not. And try telling her I did it all to close the trade deal and to defend the honor of the Totleighs. Will she listen? Will she see reason? I think not, Blandings. I think not."

"It is a pity, sir. However, the good news is that Dame Agutha almost certainly does not know of this latest turn of events. It is doubtful Lieutenant Commander Mountjoy will be informing Sonus … or anyone … of your detention, since doing so could only put pressure on him."

Pelham looked up with raised eyebrows. "By Gort, you're right, Blandings. Which gives us time to think of a plan. Do you have anything?"

"I have not as yet put my mind to the task, sir."

"Well, do so at once."

"Yes, sir. I am starting on it now."

"It occurs to me, Blandings, if we could come up with some story that sounds convincing, then it might induce Mountjoy to release us without us having to spill the old beans about the Okcho. Did I tell you, Blandings, I gave them my word that I would not reveal their identities to the Zurks?"

"I inferred as much, sir, from your reticence in naming names."

"You know me well, Blandings."

"Indeed, sir."

"What we need is a story. Something that sounds credible enough to make Mountjoy think we are cooperating but without causing any harm to the Okcho."

"Perhaps, sir, the answer might be to tell the lieutenant commander about the recent split among the rebels. That single piece of information would not place any individuals in jeopardy."

"How in the moon do you know about the split, Blandings? That happened in the meeting before I was even captured."

"When Mr. Duncil and I were inquiring after you in our guise as alliance envoys, someone informed us how the Okcho Liberation Force had, as it were, transferred you to their new rivals, the New Vogus Army. As I understand it, there are several competing resistance groups."

"There are indeed, Blandings. They apparently pop up like mushrooms in the springtime, if you take my meaning."

"I do, sir."

"Well, you know, Sonus doesn't have mushrooms … or much of a spring for that matter."

"Yes. However, I am familiar with the fungus in question."

"So you reckon if I told Mountjoy about the New Vogus Army, he might be content with that?"

"I am certain he would press for names, the location of hideouts, and other details. However, you have previously established your failure to pick up on such specifics."

"I have indeed. But do you really think he would believe all those items had escaped my attention?"

Blandings dropped his gaze to the concrete floor and cleared his throat. "I think the lieutenant commander would find it plausible that you overlooked those facts."

Pelham beamed and shook a long finger in the air. "You see, Blandings, there is an advantage to keeping people's expectations of oneself low."

"Is there, sir?"

"Oh, rather. Take yourself, for example. You have performed such a great number of miracles in times past that now everyone positively expects it of you. Case in point, had you not come up with this present scheme to slip Mountjoy the bit about the split, I would have found myself somewhat disappointed in you."

"A circumstance most disheartening, sir."

"No doubt. However, as it turns out, you have once more come through with the goods. My point is that you, Blandings, have cultivated lofty expectations for yourself. Not that there's anything wrong with that. I, for one, certainly appreciate the high standard you have set. As for me, though, I enjoy basking in the soft sunshine of low expectations. Why, I doubt Aunt Agutha's estimation of me could sink any lower."

"Such a scenario would be difficult to imagine, sir."

"I say it's better to let people think you're an idiot. Then, on those occasions when I do manage to hit the target, everyone is astounded."

"Indeed, sir."

***

Gladiss scrutinized the lines of programming code while drumming her fingers on her desk. The Amazing Mystico had complained to housekeeping that if they didn't fix this so-called glitch, Mystico would take her act elsewhere. It wasn't a glitch, Gladiss thought. The cleaning bots were programmed to pick up litter from the floor. How were the bots supposed to know that the many shreds of paper and bits of straw in the corner of Mystico's room was, in fact, a Javidian nest? A nest Mystico had to reconstruct every night after the cleaning bot sucked it all up each morning.

As head of housekeeping, the problem fell to Gladiss, which meant she had to reprogram the cleaning bots. She enjoyed these little programming puzzles, though this one was going to be tricky. She was tempted to simply shut off the vacuuming service for Mystico's room. The trouble was that the magician would no doubt eventually complain about the accumulation of non-nest-related litter. Her only recourse was to add some logic to the program.

Gladiss sat back and stretched her arms, taking a minute to gaze out her window at the brightly lit strip below. Her view wasn't as grand as Lord Bugzee's, three floors above her, but it wasn't bad.

In her younger days, her travels across the galaxy had taken her to places far more beautiful — the great falls on Antares Five, the lava ocean of Delusia. Nowadays, she was content to settle down here on Vogus. At least here things were more glamourous than the remote aquafarm on Porta where she grew up. And here she could contribute, make a difference.

Her eyes moved back to the screen. What if the bot surveyed the size of the heap of litter before vacuuming it? It would be rare for a pile of scrap to be as large as a Javidian's nest. She wasn't sure of the exact dimensions of a Javidian's nest, but she assumed it had to rival a standard-sized bed. She opened a screen to the network to confirm the assumption, ending up learning not only that one fact but more about Javidians than she wanted to know.

Gladdis programmed a function to have the bot assess the piles of scrap before cleaning them up. She compiled the program and ran it through a simulator with satisfactory results. She sent it off to the squad of cleaning bots on Mystico's floor. She would test it there first before rolling it out through the entire hotel.

As she was finishing, a coded message popped up. Gladiss held her personal device up to the screen and used the app innocently labeled as File Inspector to read and translate the message. She nodded her head slowly. Then she logged in under a different account and opened another set of programmed instructions. She scrolled slowly through the code, again drumming her fingers. This tweak would require some finesse.

***

It was shortly before the first sun's rise when Kiz the Chatty trudged back to her cabin after a long, exhausting night in the casino. Her bones ached, but she wasn't ready to drop into bed. First, she needed to unwind. She threw some kindling into the stove and lit it. Fixing herself a cup of tea, she sat on the bench that ran along one wall, staring at the glow of the embers.

A shadow stirred on the cot, flipped over, and propped itself up on one arm. "You're home."

"As are you. I was afraid you had been arrested."

"No, that was Tud the Impatient's group. They're calling themselves the New Vogus Army. In any case, the Zurks released most of them. They probably wanted to be sure everyone could make it in for their shifts."

"Money beats politics every time, just like a flush always beats a straight. The Zurks have responded to the raid by posting armed guards everywhere. It's like a concentration camp inside the casino."

Bren the Bulky swung his legs to the floor and padded over to the bench. He sat down beside her, and she leaned against him. As they sat there in silence, he ran a finger gently along her head crest.

"What's on your mind?" Bren asked.

"Nothing."

The Advantages of Keeping Expectations Low

"C'mon. Do we need to change your name to Kiz the Not So Chatty? Kiz the Quiet?"

"I keep thinking about poor Mr. Totleigh."

"The Haplor? What a pain in the neck he was."

"He came here trying to help a friend, and what did we do to him? Betray him. Kidnap him. Swap him around like a sack of melons."

"He came here in disguise to infiltrate the resistance. We have it on solid authority that Mountjoy wanted him to get in and meet us. And I understand the Zurks picked him up for debriefing as soon as he returned to the hotel."

Kiz scoffed. "I don't believe it. If he had given them names and locations, a squad of security officers would have already swept through here and arrested you along with everybody else. No, Mr. Totleigh is a friend, and we treated him shamefully."

Bren was quiet. He stood and moved to the stove where he dropped tea leaves into a cup and poured from the still warm kettle. He turned back to Kiz. "I think you're blaming the wrong people."

"Who then? The Zurks? Are they the cause of everything wrong in our world?"

"Yes. Well, not all. But it's because of them that we're turning on each other and continually looking for spies under every rock. They're why we have resistance movements to begin with."

Kiz took in a breath and let it out. "You're not wrong."

"Is that the sound of a revolutionary being born?"

"No. You and your revolution. You and Tud the Impatient and all of them. The answer doesn't lie in hacking attacks or armed assaults. It's in talking, listening, negotiation."

"Talking does no good unless you can back up your words with action."

Kiz sipped her tea. "I'll tell you this for nothing. Something has to give. With this escalation, we're seeing the Zurks for who they truly are. I don't like it, and I'm not the only one. Every Okcho in the casino was muttering about the extra guards, the unrest, everything that's been going on. I sense an uneasiness among the guests too. This place is a powder keg."

Bren chuckled softly.

"What?" Kiz asked.

"Apt metaphor. The fuse may have already been lit."

Chapter 27

It's Now or Never

Hours later, Kiz the Chatty awoke to find the day already warmed and Bren gone. She pulled herself from the cot and re-lit the stove. Warming a pot of water, she washed herself and dressed. She ate a bowl of grains with kluda milk, savoring the thick, orange liquid.

Checking her casino-issued device for keeping track of her shifts, she saw she had time before she needed to report in. She wandered out of her cabin to see what was going on in the village.

What she saw there shocked her. Unlike other mornings, children were not playing in the commons. Old women and men were not gathering for tea and gossip. The space was deserted except for a squad of Zurk guards, who stood there with their fat hands resting on blaster holsters.

Trying to act as inconspicuously as possible, Kiz ambled along the path to the home of her sister, Enna the Uneasy. She found Enna sitting at a table, her fingers fiercely knitted together.

"So now they're extending security to our front doors?" Kiz asked.

"They came in shortly after the suns rose. Said it was for our protection from disruptive influences."

"Sure, it is. Who protects us from them?"

Enna eyed her but said nothing.

Kiz said, "They're looking for an excuse to arrest us. They're trying to intimidate us, to keep us in our place."

"And then what will happen after we're all locked up? Will the Zurks deport us from our own world? Are we going to lose our planet altogether?"

"Not a chance. They need us to work in the hotels and casinos."

"Do they? They can bring in anybody — Axans, Delusians."

"They wouldn't dare."

Enna raised a skeptical eyebrow. "Bren the Bulky is calling for a general strike. Someone inside the hotel is getting signs made for us. We can pick them up when we go into work."

Kiz's face dropped. "The Zurks will only clamp down harder."

"Sure, they will. But what else do you suggest? Wait until the Zurks start loading us on spaceships bound for Gort knows where?"

Kiz sighed and stared out the cabin window at the guards. "You're right. It's time we did something."

"It's past time," Enna said.

**

It had been a busy morning for Lieutenant Commander Mountjoy. Reluctantly, he had agreed to Lord Bugzee's idea to deploy guards to the Okcho village. He worried the presence of soldiers there would only make matters worse. But following the raid on the hotel, what else could he do?

After selecting the guards and giving them their assignments, he then found himself with a new problem. He was running out of men. Between the patrols beyond the colony walls and the added security around the hotel complex, his force was stretched tighter than the elastic in Humstuggle's pants.

He had placed a call to Colonial Command back on the home world to ask for additional guards. It had proved to be an unwelcome request. If a larger force were going to be stationed on Vogus on a permanent basis, then Mountjoy would be entitled to a promotion to full commander, and that was something his jealous comrades in command were hesitant to approve.

In the end, his superior had taken pains to make it clear the troops were to be assigned on a temporary basis only. He extracted from Mountjoy a guarantee that, with the troops, the civil unrest could be subdued within a dozen standard Zurkannian days.

At last the orders were given. The reinforcements would be here in two days, which was lightning fast by Colonial Command standards. Mountjoy hoped it would be soon enough.

A *beep* sounded from his electronic device. Mountjoy grabbed it. "What is it?"

He heard the voice of Sgt. Humstuggle. "Sir, you better get up here?" Sounds of chanting filtered in from the background.

"What's going on?"

"They're ... they're ... You should come right away."

Mountjoy pushed away from his desk and tottered out of the office and down the hall. He rode the elevator up. As soon as the door opened on the ground floor, the chants of the Okcho reached his ears. "Zurks go home. Zurks go home."

He moved down the hall as quickly as his fat legs could take him. There in the lobby between the front door, the casino, and the conference area was a group of Okcho dressed in village clothes, marching in a circle, and carrying signs.

Vogus for the Okcho

Zurks Out Now

Not Your Planet

Free Vogus

Hotel guests were standing around gawking at them. Mountjoy spotted Humstuggle and hurried over.

"None of these protestors are working," the sergeant said. "The casino is empty. The trade delegates are meeting and were supposed to have water and coffee served."

"Mountjoy!"

The lieutenant commander closed his eyes and took a breath. Lord Bugzee's voice was the last one he wanted to hear right now. He rotated his head to acknowledge the casino owner.

"This situation is intolerable, Mountjoy."

"Agreed," the commander said.

"Arrest this rabble immediately."

"If we do that, who will staff the hotel and casino?"

"Your guards can take over those jobs temporarily. Eventually, more Okcho will come off the hardscape looking for work. They always do."

"My guards are already spread too thin. If I reassign them to work in the casino, I'll have to move them out of the Okcho village and off hotel security."

"You can't do that. With this unrest, we need them in those places too."

Mountjoy threw up his arms. "I have more guards coming in two days. When they get here, we can cover everything. Until then, let's go easy on the arrests."

Bugzee scowled and listened to the chants. He shook his head. "No. This is bad for our image. Arrest the protestors now. Once these radicals are all locked up, everything will quiet down, and we can reassign your men. We must keep the business running."

Mountjoy scanned the crowd. He knew many of these people. They weren't radicals. These weren't leaders of dissident groups. What were they doing out here protesting? All that arresting these people would accomplish would be to fill up the cells and cause problems for everybody. But if he didn't do something, the powers that be back on the home world would blame him for inaction, with Bugzee directing the choir.

"Humstuggle," Mountjoy said, "arrest these people."

The sergeant nodded and passed the word to his guards. They moved in, grabbing protestors by their arms and pulling them out of the circle. The Okcho reacted, some by going limp so that they had to be dragged off, others by punching and kicking at the guards. The guards retaliated by pulling out their batons and swinging at the protestor's heads. Blood spurted. Points were broken off head crests. Cries and screams rang out. Some were knocked down unconscious.

Around the periphery, the faces of the hotel guests watching all this morphed into countenances of horror and disgust. Lord Bugzee, noticing their reactions, grabbed Mountjoy by the arm and yelled over the roar, "No. No. Stop them."

But it was too late. The genie was out of the bottle. The guards were in full backlash mode, and between those handcuffed and those knocked unconscious, the protest was soon crushed.

Mountjoy whirled on Bugzee. "It's broken up as you requested. Are you happy now?"

"No, I am not. This entire episode was badly mishandled. Your guards were far too aggressive, and they've alienated our guests."

"It was a volatile situation. What did you expect?"

"I expected guards under your command to act in the best interest of the empire." Bugzee swung around and stomped away.

***

Viva Lost Vogus

One hundred light-years around the arc of the galaxy, an assignment editor on the planet Avan was reviewing news copy when a *chirp* sounded from his wing device. He tapped it with the other wing, scrolled through the alert, and then yelled out. "Taj, in here now."

An Avanian with feathers as yellow as the editor's flew in and roosted on the guest perch. "Whatcha want, Boss?"

"You like covering galactic conflicts, right?"

"Sure. What's up?"

"There's a huge Okcho protest against the Zurks on Vogus."

The reporter smirked. "That's right up my branch. I'd like to see those Zurks taken down a notch or two. Remember when I spent three days in one of their cages while covering the riots on Neilara?"

"Sure do. Grab the first ship out that can jump you there."

"On it. Boy, this is gonna be great."

***

Pelham was pleased when Sgt. Humstuggle at last switched off the watch bots around his cell and brought him out for further questioning. After all, he now had a plan to give them a morsel of information in hopes of being released. And judging from the number of handcuffed Okcho being interviewed in the main security office, they would be needing his cell. Humstuggle took him to an interrogation room.

Pelham sat down in the chair and leisurely crossed his legs. "What's all that going on out there?"

"Never you mind," Humstuggle said. "We're here to talk about what you know about the Okcho resistance."

"Ah yes. Regarding that, something did spring to mind."

"Did it now? And what was that?"

"Well, while I was at the meeting of the Okcho Liquidation Forks, a flock of those birds —"

"Birds? What birds?"

"Merely an idiom, Sergeant. A number of Okcho is what I mean. They split off to form a new group. They called themselves the New Vogus Army. Sounds ominous, eh?"

Humstuggle studied Pelham's face. "Who is the leader of this New Vogus Army?"

"I ... I didn't catch the bloke's exact name. Something the something ... or something like that."

"Something the something."

"Righto. Tall fellow. Well, not all *that* tall. There were plenty of others taller. Hard to tell with the Okcho given their head crests and all, what?"

"I suppose that information is of some help," Humstuggle said. "New Vogus Army. Are you sure about that bit? It isn't the Blue Focus Barmy or the Too Bogus Mommy, is it?"

"Sergeant, those names make absolutely no sense. I know what I heard. Now surely this proves my willingness to cooperate, does it not? I expect you'll want to pass this vital piece of intelligence on up the chain of command posthaste. Speaking of said chain, I can't help but question why Commander Mountjoy isn't conducting this interrogation."

"He's busy interviewing someone else, someone from whom we expect to gather more reliable information."

Pelham's eyebrows shot up. "Who would that be?"

***

"Now," said Mountjoy in an adjoining interrogation room, "tell me who you spoke to in the Okcho village."

Blandings cleared his throat. "As you can imagine, Lieutenant Commander, I spoke to anyone who would listen, asking them if they had seen a Haplor. My goal was to secure Mr. Totleigh's release by any means."

"And you told them you and this Duncil person were the alliance delegation the kidnappers had demanded."

"We did. It caused quite a stir. They were pleased to learn their demands were receiving action."

"Though, in fact, they weren't."

"Yes. I regret the deception. But my priority was Mr. Totleigh. I promised myself that after he was released, I would do whatever I could for the Okcho cause."

"You mean their cause against us?"

"I would not characterize it as such, Lieutenant Commander. I believe the Zurks and Okcho can find common purpose."

Mountjoy made a harrumph sound. "Who told you where you could find Totleigh?"

Blandings knew this was the tricky part — to say little but still come across as credible and cooperative. "The gentleman was older and more slender than the average Okcho."

"His name?"

"He didn't say. He agreed to speak to me on condition of anonymity."

"Describe his crests."

"His crests? Are those distinctive enough among the Okcho to identify individuals?"

"Close enough. We can make a case with them."

"Sad to say, I failed to pay attention to such details. I believe the third spike back ... no, wait, perhaps the fourth ... in any case, it had a fork in it ... I think. The night was dark."

"Would you recognize this person?"

Blandings tilted his head. "Possibly. However, I do recall what he told me."

"What was that?"

"He said Mr. Totleigh was being held by a new faction called the New Vogus Army. Were you aware of the existence of the New Vogus Army, Lieutenant Commander?"

"No, I can't say I was."

"Feel free to verify the information with Mr. Totleigh. Trust me, Lieutenant Commander, we do want to help."

"Why didn't you share these details earlier?"

"Excuse me, are you referring to a few hours ago when you dragged us in here after a wearisome, sleepless night? Really, Lieutenant Commander, at the time we could barely think straight."

Chapter 28

One for the Money, Two for the Show

"Now, since we have cooperated, Lieutenant Commander," Blandings said. "I was hoping you might find a way to release Mr. Totleigh and myself as a gesture of goodwill?"

"Did you see all the Okcho out in the bullpen?" Mountjoy asked.

"I did. If I may ask, why were all those people arrested?"

"A protest."

"A violent protest?"

"It became violent when the guards went to break it up."

"I see." Blandings could imagine all too clearly what most likely happened.

"So you'll understand why I say this is no time for gestures of goodwill. You two can stay here along with everybody else."

"One might make the case, Lieutenant Commander, that this is precisely the time when your administration could use some goodwill."

"We'll worry about that later."

Blandings considered pressing harder but decided it might easily prove counterproductive. If Mountjoy's tightly curled proboscis was any indication, he was clearly feeling stressed.

A uniformed Zurk led Blandings back to the cells. He found them now occupied not only by Pelham but by several Okcho as well.

Pelham said, "Ah, Blandings, there you are. As you can see, the cells have got a bit crowded in here with all the arrests the Zurks are making. Allow me to make introductions. Have you met Kiz the Chatty? She's a fine Jack Black dealer, let me tell you. This is Zed the Chronicler. Brainy chap like yourself. He was at the meeting where I was captured. Hmm, I probably shouldn't have said that. Oh, and over there you'll remember Tud the Impatient, the leader of the New Vogus Army. And, of course, you know Urdi the Unfortunate. I haven't yet met the others. Everyone, this is my man Blandings."

"Wait," Tud said, "You're not a representative of the galactic alliance?"

Blandings dropped his head. He had anticipated this moment with a fair bit of disquietude. There was nothing for it but to tell the truth. "I confess I misrepresented my position in an effort to free Mr. Totleigh … for all the good it has done now that we all find ourselves confined here. However, I wish to assure you, all of you, your cause is near to our hearts. Mr. Totleigh and I intend to do whatever we can for your people."

"Hear, hear," Pelham said. "Truer words were never spoken. We plan to rally around you Okcho all we can."

Tud glared. "As if I would believe anything either of you say." He walked to the other side of his cell and leaned against the wall.

Blandings said, "At the very least, I hope you all accept that neither Mr. Totleigh nor myself have revealed any of your names to the Zurks."

"Then why are we in jail?" Tud called back over his shoulder.

"You know why, Tud the Impatient," Kiz said. "You were arrested as part of your crazy raid, and Zed and I were arrested at the protest."

"And I," Urdi the Unfortunate said in a monotone, "was swept up in the arrests even though I didn't march. Not surprising, of course. These sorts of things tend to happen to me."

Blandings said, "Kiz the Chatty, you have a cut on the side of your face. Please allow me to attend to it."

Tud scoffed. "You have Okcho medical knowledge? And supplies?"

For an instant, a smile flickered across Blandings' face. "A gentleman's gentleman should be prepared for all contingencies. Please come here under the light, miss."

Urdi shrugged. "It's not too bad in here really. I suppose they'll feed us … sometime."

***

One for the Money, Two for the Show

"Place your bets," the Zurk at the Jack Black table said without enthusiasm.

Syd Duncil stared back across the table at the dealer. He was finding it difficult to maintain his inner harmony with a uniformed and well-armed Zurk sulking at him, not to mention sighing. The dealer continually sighed and gazed off into the distance as if he wished he were anywhere other than here.

His Duncilness figured the Zurks thought it demeaning to perform jobs normally assigned to what they considered an inferior species. The upshot, though, was when it came to attending to a table of customers, these Zurks were clearly inferior to the professional and amiable Okcho.

For the fifth time Duncil checked his cards, still a six and a seven. The Arsawan to his left was showing fifteen. To have a chance at winning, Duncil had to take another card.

"Hit me," he said.

The Zurk dealer looked up with a sneer that seemed to communicate that the guard only wished he could.

"I mean," Duncil said, making a gimme motion with his hand, "I want another card."

The Zurk complied, dealing a ten. Duncil had busted. He finished his drink and left the table. The casino wasn't the same without the Okcho. The whole vibe of the place was completely out of harmony.

Through the casino doors, Duncil heard the sound of an Earth guitar and wandered in that direction. He found Elfus performing in one of the meeting rooms, belting out a song about a favorite pair of blue shoes. This Earth rock and roll had songs about the oddest things. Duncil slipped to the doorway, bobbing his head to the upbeat music.

A moment later a great rumble sounded from the hallway. Elfus stopped mid-lyric, though the canned music continued to play. Duncil leaned out the door and saw a mob of Okcho bounding up the stairs, sticks and clubs in their hands, a steely glint in their eyes. Duncil ducked back into the room to avoid the stampede. Elfus dove through an exit near the stage. Audience members dropped to the floor and hid behind their chairs.

As the mob swept past the doors, the electric *whump* of blasters and wooden *thwacks* of clubs filled the hallway. Then came another thunder roll of footsteps as the mob moved on.

Duncil peeked out into the hall. The corridor was now clear. Hesitantly, he slipped from the room and peered around the corner into the main hall leading to the casino and the front desk. That passageway was anything but clear.

A trio of Zurk guards sat collapsed on the floor, hands pressed against their heads and sides. An equal number of Okcho lay moaning with blackened wounds from blaster shots. Duncil stood and stared, too shocked to do much else.

One of the Zurks said, "After them. Quick." He started to move but instead groaned and sat back down.

"I can't see straight," another Zurk said.

A third one slapped a hand to his side and inhaled sharply. "They took my blaster."

"They took mine too," the second one said, patting himself with both hands. "There were too many of them."

"Where did they head?" asked the first Zurk.

"Past the shops."

He raised his head with a shocked expression. "Toward administration?" The guard tapped his badge, which responded with a *chirp*. "Commander, we were swarmed by a mob of Okcho. We took out a few of them, but they overwhelmed us and took our blasters."

"Where are they now?" asked Mountjoy's voice.

"I think they're trying to breach the administrative offices. Not that they will, of course. They won't be able to get past the security controls."

Mountjoy said, "They shouldn't have been able to get past *you*. And what is that blasted music?"

"I believe it's 'Blue Suede Shoes,' sir. One of my favorites. Rather snappy, don't you think?"

***

When news of the riot reached Lord Bugzee in his penthouse, he didn't hesitate. He bolted from his suite to head toward a more defensible location — security headquarters.

Stepping into the elevator, he found himself sharing the ride with other Zurks, underlings who worked in administration. From the looks on their faces, it appeared they were fleeing as well. He didn't want all of them crowding into the security office with him.

"Go to your homes," Bugzee said, trying to project a calm, in-control demeanor.

"But how?" asked one of his fellow passengers. "We can't get out at the ground floor lobby. That's where the riot is."

Bugzee glared at the Zurk questioning him. "Then get off at one of the higher floors and take the pneumatic lifts the rest of the way down. You can exit through the kitchen. Just get to your homes." He punched the button for floor three.

The elevator stopped, and he shooed them out. Alone at last, he took the car on to the security level and strode down the long beige hall in a mood to both give and receive — to receive a briefing from Mountjoy and to give him a piece of his mind.

He was nearing the security office when he heard a *ding* and looked over his shoulder to see the other elevator door open and a horde of Okcho stream out. Zurks aren't known for their running abilities. Nevertheless, Lord Bugzee put on all the speed he could, reaching the security office door and fumbling with his access badge to slip inside in the nick of time. He slammed the door behind him and looked wildly about the room. "They're outside!"

The guards in the office looked up with alarm, as did Elfus and The Amazing Mystico.

"What are you two doing in here?" Bugzee asked.

The two performers side-eyed each other. Elfus said, "I suppose the same thing as you, looking for a safe spot to ride this thing out."

The sounds of pounding thundered from the door behind him. Bugzee scowled. "This place may not be it."

Then a *buzz* sounded from the doorway, and everyone inside the bullpen froze. Somehow, the Okcho had successfully transmitted the security code. The door started to slide open. Sgt. Humstuggle ran to it and threw the emergency lock.

"That won't hold forever," Humstuggle called. "Drag over the desks and cabinets."

The officers grabbed desks, filing cabinets, whatever they could and pushed them across the room in front of the door.

In response to all the commotion, Mountjoy moved to his office doorway, alarm on his face. "Everybody inside the cellblock. Now."

They all crowded around the huge steel door. Sgt. Humstuggle shoved his way through them and unlocked it with a key. They hurried inside to a cellblock already full of Okcho plus two Haplors.

***

Pelham watched them all crowd in — Bugzee, Elfus, Mystico, Mountjoy, Humstuggle, and the handful of guards. Pushed by the bulkier Zurks, Mystico and Elfus ended up squeezed against one of the watch bots guarding Pelham's cell.

"A bit cramped, eh?" Pelham said. "This cellblock was overcrowded enough without being infested with all these Zurks. By the by, you might want to mind your step there."

"Where?" asked Mystico.

Pelham indicated the robotic guard. "Cross the line between any two of those bots, and they'll blast you to crumbs."

Both entertainers shuffled back. Mystico pulled the spiky tail up into an arm.

Pelham said, "I say, Mystico, I don't see that assistant of yours. I hope they're safe."

"Pardon?"

"The other Javidian person, the one who helped me through the hole when you allegedly made me disappear. Speaking of which, look here, old scout, I don't want to cast aspersions, but is your magic act all mere deception? I have to say I was rather disheartened."

"Why do you think we call them tricks? It's all illusion. Did you imagine I could make people disappear for real?"

"Well, no ... not really ... maybe."

Mystico's head dropped. "Well, I suppose I did make Ada disappear."

"Ada?"

"My assistant. I made my assistant disappear, and it required only a few magic words ... a few hasty, thoughtless words. At any rate, Ada's back on Javid now."

"Sorry to hear that, old sport."

"Still, the show must go on."

Elfus nodded his head. "That's right. The real Elfus said those exact words to me when I started out."

"You've met the real Elfus?" Pelham asked. "You've been to Earth?"

"No, no. Elfus hasn't been on Earth for years and years. The Grays offered him life-extending technology plus a long-term singing contract if he came with them."

"Well, what do you know?"

Tud the Impatient called out, "Hey, m'lord, are you planning to hide in here forever? Abandon your guests?"

"Who is this person?" Bugzee asked with a glower. "What are these Okcho doing in here with us?"

Mountjoy said, "Most of them are the protestors you had me arrest. That one there is the one who led the assault on the casino last night."

"And now others have joined the fight," Tud said, "trapping you in here like fire hamsters in a jar."

"We'll be fine," Mountjoy said. "Reinforcements will be here in two days."

"Will they now?" Tud asked. "I'm sure the Okcho would never think of shutting down the landing pad."

"You Okcho don't have the technical know-how," Mountjoy said.

"How much technical knowledge does it take to toss a bunch of rocks on the pad to make a safe landing impossible?"

"Then the troops will simply land out on the hardscape. There are plenty of flat places there."

"Sure. And they can march in," Tud said. "Meanwhile, our side will be inside the defensible walls of the colony."

The bracelets on the two Haplors, the only ones in the cellblock wearing bracelets, dinged.

"What's that noise?" Bugzee's head rotated to stare at Pelham. "Who are you?"

'Pelham G. Totleigh," the Haplor said. "I'm one of your hotel guests. Can't say much for the accommodations down here, though."

"Mountjoy, what's one of my guests doing in the cells?" Bugzee demanded.

"We believe he has information about the insurrection," Mountjoy said.

"Only I don't," Pelham said, "though I do have a bit of news coming in over this bracelet thingy. It appears the rebels have found a listing of the salaries of everyone who works at the Pink Mingo and are making it known to all the guests. Oh my! Can that be right? I say, Lord Bugzee, you do pull in an eye-popping sum."

Bugzee crossed his fat arms. "My pay is consistent with other —"

The bracelets dinged again. Pelham said. "Consequently, the rebels have changed their salary demands from a twenty percent raise to forty percent. All in all, I think that sounds tolerably fair given the wage inequalities at present."

"Without me, none of them would even have jobs," Bugzee said.

Voices sounded from the other side of the steel cellblock door. A minute later someone — or more likely, multiple someones — began pounding on it.

Tud the Impatient smirked. "If you aren't careful, m'lord, they may soon be testing the proposition of having jobs without you."

The bracelets dinged a third time. Pelham said, "And this just in, the rioters have apparently broken through the security on the elevators."

"You don't say," Mountjoy said.

Chapter 29

Jailhouse Rock (With Real Rocks)

"Mr. Totleigh, are you there?" The lyrical voice sounded through Pelham's bracelet.

"Yes, I am there ... or rather here, down in the cells, I mean. Is that you, VICTOR?"

"Yes, Mr. Totleigh. It is good to hear your voice. Hotel guest Emer had inquired about you. Would you like to speak with her?"

"I thought you couldn't do that."

"Oh no. Communication between guests is one of my specialties."

"You mean I could have ... Why didn't you suggest that when I was looking for her at the beginning of all this?"

"You asked for Emer's location, not to speak with her."

"But I ..." Pelham rubbed the back of his neck. "It doesn't matter. Put Emer on, please."

Emer's voice came through the bracelet with strains of music playing in the background. "Pelham?"

"What ho, Emer! Are you having a party up there?"

"Something like that. A traditional Okcho band is playing in the lobby."

Out in the middle of the cellblock, Lord Bugzee groaned. "They're taking over my hotel."

Emer asked, "What's going on down there? Are you safe in the cells?"

"Funny you should ask," Pelham said. "This is an altogether hopping spot as well. The cells are brimming with arrested Okcho protestors along with Blandings and me. Plus, we have a veritable troupe of professional entertainers and so many Zurks I doubt a fellow could toss an egg without hitting one. And if you can hear that pounding, that's a horde of Okcho outside the door hoping to join our little party and possibly pitch a few of said eggs. In answer to your question, yes, I am safe. In fact, I believe I might actually be on the safer side of the watch bots at present. And up there you have music, eh?"

"Music and food and a steady stream of reporters arriving from every known planet in the galaxy. Everybody is being interviewed — Okcho, hotel guests. Wait, what's that moaning?"

"That would be Lord Bugzee," Pelham said.

"Ah. Anyway, the trade delegates are eating it up, getting their moments of fame before the cameras."

Bugzee scoffed. "It'll turn to chaos up there. Without the Zurks, how will they manage?"

Pelham said, "Emer, Lord Bugzee has expressed a measure of concern about everything getting along without Zurks in charge."

She laughed. "Tell him to come see for himself. Some of the Okcho have volunteered to cook for hotel guests and reporters. Did you know Okcho don't use replicators? They cook from ingredients. They're organizing foraging parties to roam the hardscape for all the makings. Hotel guests are going out and having a great time collecting plants. Okcho cooking is fantastic, by the way. Have you tried it?"

"During my captivity I was given some excellent bean stew. If that's what a camp cook can scrounge up, I can only imagine what they could produce in a well-equipped kitchen."

One of the Okcho called out, "Ask her what they're fixing."

Another one said, "See if they'll send some down here. The guards can't feed us now that they're in the cells too."

Urdi the Unfortunate shook his head. "I don't think they'll be able to pass food through the siege. We probably won't be fed for quite some time."

Pelham said, "Perhaps we should change the subject, Emer, before we have food riots down here. Any ideas on how this situation can be resolved?"

"The Okcho leaders up here say Lord Bugzee needs to come out and open discussions."

Jailhouse Rock (With Real Rocks)

"Never," Bugzee said.

Pelham said, "His lordship appears at present unwilling to entertain the suggestion. I dare say he may change his mind if the chappies on the other side of the cell door manage to break through."

"Keep me posted," Emer said. "Do you need anything?"

"I could stand a stiffish Amurru fizz, but I don't see a feasible delivery method given the present circs. I'll hold for now."

"Okay. Talk with you later. Be careful."

"Righto. Toodle-oo."

Mountjoy muttered to no one in particular, "What I don't understand is how they slipped past the elevator security. The code changes constantly. It's our most secure system."

Humstuggle said, "When they overpowered the guards, they could have taken their badge authenticators."

"The authenticators only work in conjunction with biometric validation. No, they hacked the security system somehow."

"Impossible," Bugzee said.

"We heard rumors of a collaborator inside the hotel," Mountjoy said. "At first, we supposed the sympathizer was a Bononian, but in the end I couldn't pin anything on him."

"On her, you mean," Pelham said.

"You stay out of this. In any case, a guest couldn't have hacked into the security system."

"Then who?" asked Bugzee. "All the Zurks on staff are loyal."

Humstuggle said, "Do you think things actually are going well upstairs? And they have food ... and music?"

"No," Bugzee said with a growl. "I don't buy any of it. Someone is lying." He waved a hand toward Pelham. "You there, give me your bracelet."

"Me?" Pelham asked. "I'd rather not."

"Guards, take it from him."

"Stand down," Mountjoy said. "Nobody is taking anything."

Bugzee said, "I need to contact housekeeping, find out what the real situation is."

"Fine. We can do it through my badge." Mountjoy tapped his shield. "Housekeeping."

A voice sounded out. "Housekeeping. This is Gladiss."

"Yes, Gladiss," Mountjoy said. "This is —"

Bugzee talked over him. "This is Lord Bugzee. What is the situation out there?"

"Calm at the moment," Gladiss said. "Ships have come in with journalists. Some guests left when those ships departed, but most are sticking around."

"Has the alliance sent troops to quell the chaos?"

"No troops, only reporters. And what chaos? As I said, we're fine here."

"There's chaos down here in the cells. A mob of Okcho are trying to break in and assault me. What are the Zurk guards up there doing?"

"Now that they've been disarmed, they seem a little lost. Some of them are helping the Okcho with food preparation."

"Helping the ..." Bugzee's gray face changed to red. His eyes narrowed. "What about the casino?"

"It's shut down."

"But that's our profit margin! This will ruin me. Send the guards down here to attack the mob."

"Did I mention they were disarmed?" Gladdis said. "I don't think they'll go. Besides, I have my hands full trying to help everyone find a room and then keeping them all clean."

"Well, don't. Don't cooperate with the Okcho."

"You think we should let guests from across the galaxy stay at the Pink Mingo in dirty rooms?"

"Yes ... No ... I don't know."

Bugzee made a slashing motion across his throat. Mountjoy cut the connection. The casino owner was breathing so heavily Pelham thought he would hyperventilate. "Gladiss is not thinking about the good of the Zurkannian empire."

Humstuggle shrugged. "Well, Gladiss isn't a Zurk. I think she's a Porta, right?"

Mountjoy turned his head to give the sergeant a warning glance. Humstuggle said no more.

The banging from the door grew louder. The Okcho outside now seemed to be throwing things against it. Who knew what? Office chairs? Rocks?

Lord Bugzee's eyes grew wide, his proboscis stiff enough to have been starched. He looked to Mountjoy. "We're facing an apocalypse here."

Jailhouse Rock (With Real Rocks)

Tud the Impatient stepped nearer the yellow line. "Apocalypse, you say? We've already had one of those. Let me see, when was that? Oh yeah, it was when you lot came. Take my word for it, you'll get used to it." He called toward the steel door, "This is Tud the Impatient. Who's out there?"

A voice sounded through the door. "The Okcho Liberation Front."

"Never heard of you," Tud said.

"Formerly the Okcho Liberation Force. We rebranded."

Tud swept his head around toward Lord Bugzee, a worried look in his eye. "Those people out there are the most radical element. They're our enemies too. If they bust through that door, they'll slaughter us all. Let us out of these cells so we can defend ourselves."

Pelham blinked. The folks he met at the meeting hadn't seemed much like the slaughtering type. But then the intricacies of Okcho politics with their fluid alliances and splits remained a mystery to him.

"If we let you out, what's in it for us?" Bugzee asked with a sneer.

"We'll defend you too," Tud said.

"Sure, you will." Mountjoy said, sarcasm sounding in his voice.

"We'll join forces," Tud said. "You know you don't have enough guards in here to take on a mob."

Bugzee and Mountjoy exchanged doubtful expressions. Humstuggle joined in with a shake of his head.

"How can we trust you?" Bugzee asked.

"Make us an offer."

"What kind of offer?"

A loud clang came from the door.

Tud smiled. "Your best offer."

"All right," Bugzee said, "fight with us and we'll drop all charges against you."

"Not good enough," Tud said. "Grant those pay raises too."

Which surprised Pelham. Back at the bunker, Tud had told him they weren't interested in pay raises. They only wanted to expel the Zurks from the planet. "I say, Tud, didn't —"

"Sir," said Blandings, interrupting him. "I was wondering if I could have a word with you concerning a provision in the Bononian trade deal."

"What? The trade deal? With revolutionaries pounding at the door, this is hardly the appropriate time to speak of trade deals."

"You may be right, sir. Forgive me for bringing it up."

Bugzee stewed. He glared at Mountjoy. He glared at Tud. "Oh all right. Mountjoy, turn off the bots."

"You don't get to make that call," Mountjoy said. "This is my domain here."

"Turn 'em off."

"You trust these … these Okcho? This is the one who attacked the place last night."

"What choice do we have?" Bugzee said.

With a grimace, Mountjoy waved a capitulating hand at Humstuggle, who pulled out his tablet and made a few taps. The lights on all the watch bots blinked off.

Tud the Impatient said, "All right, all you Okcho, when they come through that door, some of you need to join me in meeting them head-on. The rest of you, hang back to take care of the Zurks. Do you understand what I'm saying?"

He was answered by nods from around the room.

Tud looked to Lord Bugzee with pleading eyes. "If we wait until they knock the door down, they'll have the advantage. I say we surprise them by opening it on them now. Have one of your men unlock it, and we'll rush them."

"Do it," Bugzee said.

"Are you kidding?" asked Mountjoy. "You want us to open it for them? No, this is crazy. Let's not be … well, impatient, impetuous. We don't even know they'll be able to breach the door."

"We could use some weapons too," Tud said. "Hand us your blasters."

"Absolutely not!" Mountjoy said.

"Suit yourself. We'll fight them hand-to-hand. Only get that door open. If I know the Okcho Liberation Front, they'll be bringing up explosives right about now."

"Open it," Bugzee said, his proboscis curled up like a ball. "Open it."

Mountjoy nodded to Humstuggle. As the sergeant approached the clanging door, the other Zurk guards trained their blaster pistols on it, ready to fire.

Tud, trailing behind him, said, "Hey, don't shoot me."

Mountjoy held up a hand to the guards. They lowered their weapons. Humstuggle inserted a key and twisted it. As the door began to creak open, the sergeant stepped behind the protection of its metal bulk. Tud the Impatient, along with a handful of other Okcho, surged forward and threw the steel door

Jailhouse Rock (With Real Rocks)

back, pinning Humstuggle to the wall. He let out a groan followed by a high-pitched whimper.

Expressions of shocked surprise registered on the faces of the Okcho outside the door when their first glimpse inside the cell block was one of another group of Okcho sprinting toward them. Their shock turned to smiles as their compatriots greeted them with an open-armed embrace. The Zurk guards inside the crowded cellblock were even more surprised to find themselves unexpectedly grappling with Okcho protestors who had jumped them from behind.

"What's the meaning of this?" Mountjoy demanded as four Okcho took him to the floor.

"You lied!" Lord Bugzee screamed.

"Yeah," Tud the Impatient said, "like when you first came here and lied about how Okcho would be treated as equals."

"I say, Lord Bugzee," Pelham said, "it appears you've been bamboozled."

Chapter 30

Don't Be Cruel

Pelham's head swiveled left and right as he tried to take in all the action around him. Through the doorway, Tud the Impatient and Bren the Bulky were smiling and congratulating each other. Inside the cellblock, groups of Okcho wrestled with Zurk guards, trying to overpower them. The air was filled with the sounds of fists punching, bodies falling, grunts of pain, and a few wild blaster shots from the surprised guards.

Kiz the Chatty grabbed the arm of a guard holding a blaster, forcing it up toward the ceiling while Zed the Chronicler flew in from the side. Together they took the guard down to the floor. All three rolled across the concrete in a blur, the slender Okcho bodies first above, then below the hefty Zurk. Pelham jumped on top of a disabled watch bot to avoid being rolled over by the bodies.

The blaster, now flat on the floor but still gripped in the Zurk's hand, shot a beam of blue light across the cellblock. It struck a toilet in a far cell, which erupted in a shower of bits of porcelain along with what Pelham sincerely hoped was water. A third Okcho ran in, kicked at the blaster, and sent it skittering across the floor. Lord Bugzee edged toward the weapon, but Blandings glided to it more quickly, snatched it up, and slipped it into a vest pocket.

Mountjoy, wrestling with four Okcho, managed to get off a shot that struck Tud the Impatient in the arm. The blaster must have been on a lower setting because, fortunately, Tud didn't explode like the toilet. He dropped to his knees with a moan and a dazed expression on his face, grabbing at the black spot that appeared on his arm. Before another shot could go off, The Amazing Mystico reached down and snatched the blaster from Mountjoy's grasp. With the flick of a hand, the blaster disappeared. Pelham's estimation of Mystico rose appreciably. Now that was a trick.

Two Okcho were struggling with another guard, the blaster weaving back and forth in the air. Elfus approached the scuffle and wrenched the blaster from the guard's hand, saying, "Thank ya vury much." He stuffed the weapon somewhere under his cape.

With a *creak*, the heavy steel door swung away from the wall. Sgt. Humstuggle crawled out on hands and knees, a red spot spreading across his schnoz. He eyeballed the brawl for a few moments then reached back, fumbling for his blaster.

With the dexterity Haplors are known for, Pelham sprang from the top of the bot onto the sergeant's back, plucked the blaster from its holster, and jumped to the doorway. Holding the pistol awkwardly by the handle, Pelham handed it off to Tud the Impatient.

As the blasters were wrested from Zurk hands, the fighting continued with fists, elbows, and kicked feet. The Okcho, who had been outside the cellblock trying to get in, either rushed in to join the fray or tossed their sticks and clubs to the Okcho inside. Before long, all the Zurks were subdued with everyone else standing around looking at them. Urdi the Unfortunate sat rocking on the floor holding his side.

"Are you all right, Urdi?" Pelham asked.

"The Unfortunate," Urdi said. "Oh, I may have cracked a rib or two. Only to be expected at my age."

Tud the Impatient scanned around the room. "Do we have all the blasters?" The Okcho clutching firearms held them up. "That's not all of them. Where are the rest?"

Elfus and The Amazing Mystico cast stealthy glances at each other.

"Hand over the weapons," Tud said. "We may need them if any of the colonists try to resist."

Blandings stepped to the massive steel door and extracted the set of keys still hanging from the lock. He handed them to Tud. "With respect, you now have access to the entire contents of the security force's arms locker. I am sure everyone only wishes to be able to defend themselves in what I'm sure you will admit remains a volatile situation."

"It depends." Tud scowled at Blandings before shifting his attention to Elfus and Mystico. "Whose side are you on?"

Elfus raised his hands. "I'm not taking sides. This is your planet. Do whatever you want. I only want to sing my songs."

"That's right," said Mystico. "I only care about entertaining ... and not getting shot."

Kiz the Chatty said, "Let them keep the blasters. They aren't against us. Can you blame them for wanting some protection?"

Tud made a face but nodded.

"What about us?" Lord Bugzee asked with a sneer. "Will you be ordering summary executions? That's what you revolutionaries do, isn't it?"

Tud put on a fake expression of surprise. "Executions? Hmm. I hadn't considered that. Now that you mention it, they might be justified given the way you Zurks exploited this planet and its people. What do you think, Bren the Bulky? How do you feel about firing squads, hangings, shooting people into space?"

Bren answered with a grin. "Well, I'm not normally pro execution as such. For one thing, it's not easy getting concessions from a dead person."

"Good point," Tud said. "Not to mention we'd have the entire Zurk navy flying in here hunting us down. No, I think this is a time for diplomacy, not retribution."

"I agree. Diplomacy it is," Bren said. "But I believe in negotiating from a position of strength." He eyed one of his followers. "Lock them in a cell. By the way, Tud the Impatient, you ought to have that blaster wound attended to."

Tud raised his arm to look at it, wincing as he did so. "It will make a thrilling story to tell the grandchildren someday."

"Let's get it looked at, if only to make sure you're still around to tell it to the grandchildren yourself."

The Zurks — Bugzee, Mountjoy, Humstuggle, and the handful of guards — were herded inside the yellow lines of a cell. An Okcho relieved Humstuggle of his tablet, studied the screen a minute, and then made a few taps. The watch bot lights blazed into life. All the non-Zurks departed through the steel door to the outer security office.

***

As the cellblock door clanged shut, Lord Bugzee strode across the cell, proboscis proudly unfurled, and commandeered the concrete shelf cot. The other Zurks watched him, some with angry glares. The ones with cuts and wounds probably needed the bunk more, but this wasn't about need. He was a lord, and they were not, and that was the end of it. Besides, it wasn't like any of this was his fault. Bugzee directed a scowl toward Mountjoy and said, "Well, Lieutenant Commander, you clearly bungled this situation."

Mountjoy's eyes narrowed to slits. "I bungled it? You were the one who believed the promises of that terrorist."

"Well, what choice did we have with an angry mob pounding at the door?"

"I'll tell you what choice we had. We could have waited two days for the reinforcements to arrive. The rioters weren't getting through the door, not with the weapons they had. The ones they had then, that is."

"Two days? You expected us to hunker down surrounded by enemies for two days without food or water?"

Muttering to himself, Sgt. Humstuggle turned his back on both of them and sat on the floor, rubbing his sore proboscis.

Bugzee wasn't finished. He was determined not to lose this argument. "They broke through all the other doors. They would have broken down this door eventually."

Mountjoy let out an exasperated grunt. "That was different. Someone hacked the security system. You can't hack a steel lock with a key."

"Yeah? What about a lock pick? What about a torch for Zahn's sake?"

Mountjoy crossed his arms. "It doesn't matter anyway. The question is what do we do now?"

"Now we wait for the reinforcements."

"Except Tud the Impatient is correct. They'll force the ship to land out somewhere on the hardscape. The troops will have to march in and try to attack the colony's defenses from the outside. And those defenses are solidly built. By then, all those reporters will be taking the Okcho side. You heard the reports of how everybody loves Okcho cooking and music."

Lord Bugzee's voice dripped with venom. "What do you suggest then? Negotiating with terrorists?"

Mountjoy inclined his head and flipped over a gray palm.

***

In contrast to the bickering and recriminations inside the Zurk cell, the mood in the outer security office was festive. Okcho laughed while rifling through desk drawers, distributing weapons, posing for pictures wearing colonial security berets. In Mountjoy's office, Tud's injured arm was being wrapped while Bren paced and talked excitedly about their next moves. Amid all the commotion, Elfus and Mystico excused themselves and made a discreet exit.

Pelham, watching it all from a corner with Blandings at his side, leaned over to his valet and said, "What do you say we pop upstairs for a few bushels of that Okcho food I keep hearing so much about?"

"It would depend, sir, on how much you wish to contribute to the pending discussions down here. I believe the next few hours will be critical."

"You think so? Dash it all, Blandings. Now you've presented me with one of those con thingies. You know, a puzzle, a dilemma, a stumper."

"A conundrum, sir?"

"That's the chap. You've handed me a vexing conundrum. My stomach, indeed, my very essence, is calling me upstairs to join the party, as it were. But after my experiences of the last few days of being bandied about from one rebel camp to another, bouncing from luxury hotel rooms to jail cells, I can't help but want to see this thing through. That is, if you think our presence will be of assistance."

"Often in highly charged situations such as this, an outside voice, a mediator, if you will, can be advantageous in guiding the parties to agreement."

"All right, Blandings, we'll stay for the nonce. But find out if you can have a bit of that celebrated grub sent down."

"As you wish, sir."

Before Blandings could move, a knock sounded on the door to the hall, and everyone froze. Bren the Bulky gestured to one of the other Okcho, who opened the door, blaster in hand. Gladiss took an anxious step back before walking in.

Tud the Impatient smiled broadly at the gray-skinned Porta. "Why didn't you just enter using your security hack?"

Gladiss made an aw-shucks face. "The hack was for you. Besides, I couldn't be sure your people wouldn't start shooting at anyone coming through the door long before they knew who it was." She nodded toward the Okcho holding the blaster to back up her assertion.

Blandings said, "Ah, so you, Gladiss, were the collaborator?"

Pelham gaped. "What? I would never have suspected your interests extended beyond cleaning bots."

Gladiss said. "My interest is in housekeeping. Seemed to me this planet had a mess that needed cleaning up."

"You Haplors don't know Gladiss," Kiz the Chatty said. "She has a history. She ran blaster rifles to the Antareans when the Thomians tried to overrun their planet. She fought on the loyalist side in the Delusian civil war."

"And let me tell you, that was a big mistake," Gladiss said. "Among those little Delusians, I stood out like a giant. Everybody kept taking potshots at me."

Bren said, "Somehow, she always ends up fighting for the little guy, and I don't mean short people like Delusians."

Gladiss shrugged. "Listen, it was a side hustle. I always got paid."

"Yes, but the other side would have paid better."

"Now you tell me. I don't suppose your people will pay much either."

Bren said, "Do you want to stay while we talk to Bugzee?"

"No, I do not. He and Mountjoy may suspect me by now, but I don't want to confirm those suspicions. I may need to keep my job here. That is, unless you lot kick them all off the planet."

"Yeah, that's the question," Bren said. "What do we want out of this?"

Chapter 31

Heartbreak Hotel

"What do you think they're doing in there?" Pelham asked Blandings as he eyed the closed door to Mountjoy's office. It had been some time since Lord Bugzee, Mountjoy, Sgt. Humstuggle, Bren the Bulky, Tud the Impatient, and, apparently in honor of his age, Urdi the Unfortunate had entered it and closed the door behind them.

Going into the office had been the second attempt at negotiations. The first attempt, conducted in the bullpen, had been something of a disappointment in terms of reaching agreement, what with the crowd of Okcho and reporters, who had trickled in, lobbing questions and comments from the sidelines. Unfortunately, the change of venue left Pelham in the dark as to what was transpiring.

"I am sorry, sir, but seeing through solid walls is beyond my abilities."

"Oh, think nothing of it, Blandings. One can hardly expect you to exceed your biological limitations. What we need is one of those … those x-ray bats from … um … what planet has those rummy creatures, Blandings?"

"The x-ray bat is native to Sratha, sir. However, since the creature lacks a translator bot compatible language, having one would not, in fact, aid us in this instance."

"There you have it then. I guess we'll just have to wait and find out."

They didn't have to wait long. The muffled voices from inside the office rose in volume, and a few isolated words could be made out.

An Okcho voice said, "Unfair."

A Zurk voice said, "Ludicrous … never."

Pelham made a face. "I dare say the discussion is not going swimmingly."

"That is most likely a fair assessment, sir, given the evidence at hand."

At that moment, the office door opened. Tud the Impatient stuck out his head. "You, Totleigh, get in here."

"Me? Certainly, but ... why?"

"It has been suggested we need a moderator."

"Ah. Righto. However, I suggest Blandings come in as well. He's the other half of my team, and ... well, when it comes to brains, he's more like two-thirds at least."

"Fine. Both of you then. Bring a couple of chairs."

The two Haplors scooted into the office, Blandings pushing along desk chairs for them both. Mountjoy's office had, on Pelham's previous visits, seemed spacious. There was nothing roomy about it now. Mountjoy and Lord Bugzee were jammed together on the far side of the desk, elbowing each other for position. Bren the Bulky, Tud the Impatient, and Urdi the Unfortunate were lined up in an arc across the desk from them. Sgt. Humstuggle stood guarding the door. Blandings squeezed the chairs into a cramped spot between a bookcase filled with bric-a-brac and a pole hung with an unfurled Zurkannian flag, a blue number with white wavy lines and a mythological lobster man holding a sword.

"So, how are negotiations coming?" Pelham asked, rubbing his palms together as he sat.

Everyone in the room faced him with grim expressions.

Bugzee said, "This is not a negotiation. The Zurkannian Empire does not bargain with terrorists."

"Then call it a business meeting," Bren said. "We want to discuss plans for the Pink Mingo and your colony going forward."

"It's not their colony," Tud said. "Not going forward anyway."

Bren made a calm-down gesture. "We're only talking. We should weigh all the options."

"Here's an option," Tud said, "the Zurks all leave and give us our planet back."

Mountjoy said, "You know, the might of the Zurkannian navy is currently protecting you. If we leave, you'll have someone else worse on your doorstep the next morning. Thomian gangs. The Lir Dynasty. The Lir would find you all quite tasty."

"We'll take our chances," Tud said. "We have friends in the galactic alliance."

"Temporary friends," Bugzee said, "Friends who will be extremely hesitant to commit themselves to a war on your behalf. But it doesn't matter because I will never leave Vogus. This colony was my dream. I'll be a martyr to the cause before I let it fail."

Pelham couldn't help but scoff. Lord Bugzee met his gaze with an annoyed glare. Pelham said, "Well, I say, really. That's a bit shortsighted, what? Lose your life for a bit of real estate? The galaxy is full of the stuff. Granted, it's much fuller of empty space, but there are plenty of moons and uninhabited planets, enough for loads of new dreams."

Mountjoy cleared his throat. "You were invited here, Mr. Totleigh, not to promulgate your own opinions but to mediate ours. Do you understand?"

"Ah. Righto. Wouldn't want to step out of line. But dash it all, the man was talking drivel, twaddle, utter nonsense. And I dare say I know nonsense when I hear it, don't I, Blandings?"

"I can attest, sir, you have had more than your share of acquaintance with theory and practice of the concept."

"There you have it."

Bren said, "Look, I don't see why the Zurks have to leave. This is a big planet. What we want are better working conditions, more autonomy, a say in our future. Give us a voice in how our planet relates to the galaxy instead of everything being run by the Zurk military."

Mountjoy said, "What has the military ever done wrong here? The planet lives in peace."

Tud lowered his head, pointing his spiny crest directly at the lieutenant commander like a kluda ready to charge. "A peace imposed at blaster point."

"Well, if you expect us to stand down after what you lot have done the last few days, you are mistaken. Our first duty is to protect the citizens of the Zurkannian Empire."

Bren said, "It is my understanding Okcho are also considered citizens of the Zurkannian Empire, are they not?"

"Technically," Mountjoy muttered.

"So we should be protected too."

Tud glowered at Bren. "You want to be a Zurk? I'll have no part of that. We are Okcho. We are independent."

Pelham frowned. Following the discussion as best he could, he reckoned they all had some valid points. Well, not Bugzee with his idiotic talk of martyrdom.

But the others, yes. Why couldn't the Okcho have more rights? Or why couldn't they be independent if that's what they wanted? However, Mountjoy was correct about the galaxy being a dangerous place. Sonus had been threatened a few times in its existence. It definitely helped to have the Haplor home world behind them.

Bren said, "You haven't said much, Urdi the Unfortunate. What do you think?"

Urdi scratched his head. "Oh. Well. Of course, I think the lieutenant commander makes some fair points concerning security. Bad things do have a way of happening. Don't I know it! Then again, I remember how it was before the Zurks came. I was only a tyke, sure, but I have memories. Pleasant memories they were too. Times were simpler then. Of course, it's possible they only seemed simpler because Mam and Da took care of me. But we didn't have all this conflict. I don't know why we can't all just get along." Urdi didn't so much stop talking as merely trail off, leaving everyone shooting awkward glances at each other.

Pelham said, "Forgive me if I'm overstepping again, but I have a suggestion. I had occasion earlier to discuss some of these issues with Kiz the Chatty. She had an interesting viewpoint on this whole Zurk vs. Okcho situation. Plus, I can't help but notice how all the rest of you — the rest of us, in fact — are male. Well, of course, all Zurks are male or what you call male. You are what you are, what? But anyhow, mightn't a female perspective be helpful?"

Pelham noted how the Zurks shivered at the word female and glanced away with obvious discomfort. Despite that, he felt strongly he was right about this. He may not know much, but he could recognize when somebody else knew something, and Kiz was sharp. He looked to Blandings for reassurance and was encouraged by a miniscule nod of the valet's head. By Zahn, he might have said the right thing for once. Too bad Aunt Agutha wasn't there to hear it. No, strike that. On second thought, he couldn't imagine a situation that would be improved by the presence of his irritable relative.

Bren the Bulky said, "I don't know, Mr. Totleigh, I think we have too many opinions in the room as it is."

Tud the Impatient said, "We're the rebel leaders, not her."

Lord Bugzee said, "It is totally inappropriate and out of the question. Zurks do not recognize the … female gender." He said the word like it had crawled out from under his sandwich.

"Now wait a minute," Bren said, evidently goaded by Bugzee's words, "there's nothing wrong with females. The Okcho have a long tradition of female elders."

"Yeah," Tud said, "I won't have you excluding half of our population. I say we listen to her ideas."

Mountjoy said, "You just said you were the leaders."

"We are. And as leader, I want to hear what she has to say."

"I agree," Bren said. "If the Zurks are against it, there must be something to the idea. Let's bring her in."

Bren hopped from the chair and left the office. After a few minutes of awkward silence, he returned with Kiz, waved her to his seat, and perched himself on the corner of Mountjoy's desk. The commander stared at this affront with a stiff proboscis.

Bren said, "We asked you in here, Kiz the Chatty, because we want your opinion. What do you think? Should we make the Zurks leave Vogus, or should we let them stay and negotiate with them for more rights and better working conditions?"

Kiz's eyes scanned the room. When they met Pelham's, he gave her a smile and a nod.

"It's not that simple," she said. "It's not a binary, black-and-white choice. Our people are dependent on the jobs —"

Bugzee interrupted. "Dependent on the Zurks, you mean."

"No," she said flatly, "the jobs … for the money they bring. But it is an insult to our culture for other species to come here from across the galaxy and find us acting as servants, as minions to Zurk employers. We need improved working conditions, all right, but better hours and better pay won't change the fact that the nature of those jobs demeans us. We're losing our identity as Okcho and becoming extensions of the Zurks."

"It's too bad you don't like your jobs," Bugzee said, "but there aren't any other jobs. We're a hotel and casino. The jobs we have to offer are in running games and food service. Take them or leave them. We don't have jobs in science and arts."

Tud said, "What she's saying is the jobs themselves are the problem. I agree. That's why I say we need to send the Zurks away. Yes, it will hurt for a few years, as it did when our grandparents stepped away from technology, but it will be better in the long run."

Kiz shook her head. "No, it's not the jobs in themselves. Dealing Jack Black doesn't harm me. In fact, I enjoy doing it. It's being on display as a second-rate species that damages us. It's hurting us as much or more as having the money is helping us."

"You exaggerate," Bugzee said with a sneer.

"Do I?"

"We have done nothing to label you as a lesser species."

Kiz shot him a look. "Everything here labels us as a lesser species. We are a part of the Pink Mingo only in the same way that the carpet and the slot machines are part of the place. To you we are tools to be used."

From the side of the room came a gentle clearing of the throat. No one noticed it except Pelham, who was familiar with the sound and knew it boded a helpful proposal. "A thought, Blandings?"

"Yes, sir, if I may offer a suggestion. We have heard reports from upstairs of people around the galaxy embracing Okcho cooking and music. Perhaps one or more Okcho owned and operated establishments, celebrating Okcho culture, would be a welcome addition to the strip. I mean, in addition to the current Zurk-owned establishments, of course. It might feasibly bring even more tourists to the colony for the benefit of all."

A light came to Kiz's eyes. "Yes."

Mountjoy looked up as his proboscis uncurled.

Tud said, "You mean let the Zurks stay but go into business beside them?"

Bren the Bulky said, "You know, that has possibilities."

Bugzee smacked his hand on the desk and glared. "No, it doesn't. Don't be ridiculous."

Urdi the Unfortunate sighed. "Oh dear. Just when things were looking promising. I guess it was all for naught."

Chapter 32

Carry On, Blandings

Lord Bugzee stared around at a roomful of gaping mouths and disappointed eyes.

"Excuse me?" asked Pelham. "You mean to say you don't like Blanding's idea for Okcho-owned businesses, Lord Bugzee?"

"I do not. Of course, I don't."

"Let me assure you, Blandings' ideas are consistently top of the line, head of the class."

"Thank you for saying so, sir. You are too kind."

"Think nothing of it, Blandings."

Bugzee pointed an angry finger at Pelham. "Look, this is a Zurk colony. People come here for what we Zurks have built. I won't have it diluted with Okcho ... culture." The word seemed to stick in his throat.

Mountjoy said, "You mean you won't have your profits diluted by letting new businesses open on the strip."

"You stay out of this."

"I am the ranking government representative here."

"And I am personal friends with people on the home world who outrank you."

Tud the Impatient said, "I'm not so sure about this plan either. I don't trust the Zurks. I want them off our planet."

"That is not going to happen either," Bugzee said. "The Okcho are going back to work. I'll give them a ten percent raise. That's my final offer. Of course, I can only speak for the Pink Mingo. You'll have to bargain separately with the other casino and shop owners along the strip."

Blandings said, "If I might make one more suggestion."

"You've suggested enough," Bugzee said.

"Perhaps," said Blandings, his calm face showing no reaction to the rebuff, "we might take a brief recess to think over the issues."

"Yes, let's," Mountjoy said, glaring at Lord Bugzee.

The suggestion sounded good to the casino owner. He figured all he needed was for the Okcho to have a quiet word together, and they would find a way to disagree among themselves as they always did. Then things could go back to the way they were.

The group filed out of the room into the outer security office, finding it now overflowing with alien reporters.

An Avanian flew up to Bugzee's face. "How are negotiations progressing?"

"How many times do I have to say this?" Lord Bugzee snapped. "Zurks do not negotiate with terrorists."

"Then what would you call what was going on in there?"

He pulled himself up straighter. "We were listening to the concerns of the indigenous people of Vogus. As you know, the Zurkannian Empire takes seriously its obligation to native people within its domain."

Bugzee detected a smirk growing on the reporter's feathered face. He reviewed his words, realizing with a chill that an unsympathetic ear might misconstrue them as paternalistic, imperialistic. He thought it best to avoid saying much more. "Other than that, I have no comment." Scanning around for a way to escape, he disappeared into an interrogation room.

***

Guided by the scent of something delicious, Pelham shuffled through the crowded office until he found a tray of buns on a side table. He grabbed one and began nibbling on the yeasty bread, delighted to find pieces of fruit inside and even more delighted to detect that the fruit seemed to have been soaked in a species of alcohol. He looked up toward a Kolrabie reporter towering over him, "I say, is this some of that Okcho cuisine? Tickles the old taste buds, eh?"

The Kolrabie, bent its long pliable body down toward Pelham. "A few questions, if you don't mind."

"I was hoping to grab a nibble actually."

"First, what's your name, and how are you involved in the discussions?"

The question prevented Pelham from getting another mouthful. "Pelham G. Totleigh from Sonus. I'm merely trying to help things along."

"By doing what?"

He stared longingly at the bun in his hand. "Oh, you know, a suggestion here, a word of encouragement there. Outsider's perspective and all that."

"Are the Zurks and Okcho reaching consensus?"

Pelham took a quick bite and answered with his mouth full. "Well, not as yet. It's a tricky-ish situation, you know. The Okcho bring up some fair points. Of course, the Zurks have their way of thinking as well."

Pelham found his attention drawn away from the interview to Blandings and Kiz, who were conferring in the corner. Now what the blazes were they talking about? Kiz nodded, and they both headed out the security office door.

"Excuse me," Pelham said to the reporter. He scooted through the crowd, munching on the bun as he maneuvered his way. He got himself out the door in time to see Blandings and Kiz disappearing into one of the elevators at the end of the corridor. "With nary a by your leave," he muttered to himself. He was annoyed but only for a moment. He recognized this as one of Blandings' schemes, one of Blandings' marvelous schemes.

Pelham returned to the bullpen to hunt down either a cup of tea or a replicator to make one. He was still searching in vain when Mountjoy called the group back into his office.

They took their previous seats. The lieutenant commander surveyed their faces. "What happened to the other Haplor and the other Okcho … the female?"

"Oh, ah," said Pelham. "They went off on some errand or another."

"What errand?" asked Mountjoy with suspicion in his voice.

"I didn't catch that part. They slipped away while I was chatting with a reporter."

Bugzee shuddered. "What did you tell the reporter?"

"Nothing. Not much. You know."

Bugzee stared at him for a moment before turning his gaze to the Okcho. "Have you three come up with any more reasonable proposals?"

Bren the Bulky said, "I'm still thinking about what Mr. Totleigh's companion suggested."

"Blandings," Pelham put in. "My valet. My gentleman's gentleman."

"Right. Whatever. Blandings. It's true our people love feeding and entertaining people. We could open restaurants, performance venues. We could give visitors something to do on Vogus besides gamble."

Bugzee's brow furrowed. "You're missing the point. Gambling is precisely what we want them to do here. That's where we make our money."

Pelham raised a finger. "I understand your position, Lord Bugzee. I've seen firsthand how the casino makes money. I'm a bit in the hole to you myself at present. However, I've done a smidgen of traveling around this fair galaxy of ours, and in my experience the hottest hotspots are those offering a variety of activities. You know, with some additional attractions, as it were, you might entice a whole new clientele to visit, what?"

"Rubbish," Bugzee said.

"Families, for instance," said Pelham.

"Complete rot."

"Cultural travelers. I think that's the term. Blandings would know. You know, the blokes who strive to experience the customs and traditions of other cultures."

"Poppycock."

"Now wait a minute, Bugzee," Tud the Impatient said. "You can't dismiss this out of hand."

"It's *Lord* Bugzee, and I can. I have."

The conversation raged back and forth. The casino owner refused to budge despite Bren, Tud, Urdi, and at times even Mountjoy and Humstuggle trying to pry him loose from his position.

Having already put in his bit and seeing no need to further engage with an obstinate person, Pelham detached from the discussion. Once or twice, he came close to nodding off, but raised voices always brought him back to consciousness with a start. After a while, he found himself thinking about those delicious buns in the outer office and wondered if he might slip out to grab another one. It seemed as if the meeting — or by now more nearly an argument — would go on indefinitely, and Pelham was definitely growing hungry.

Mountjoy said something about conflict, triggering in Pelham a flood of memories as he reflected on past squabbles in his life. He had not had many, with the exception, of course, of periodic clashes with Aunt Agutha. No, he thought, Pelham G. Totleigh was considered by one and all a person of peace, an all-round easy-going, fun-loving chap.

"Hmm," he murmured out loud.

The others stopped quarreling momentarily to turn their attention in his direction.

"Did you have something to add, Totleigh?" Mountjoy asked.

"Who? Me? Well … I don't know. I was ruminating over an experience I once had with a chum of mine by the name of Freddy Atchison-Atchison. You see, old Freddy and I ended up in a bit of a tiff over a matter of ninety-five bills he owed me. Normally, I wouldn't say a thing about it, but one night we were out on the town with the boys, and Freddy was absolutely spreading it around thick as butter. He was buying drinks for all and sundry. Naturally, I thought he had come into some funds and was expecting to be paid off. But no! At the end of the evening, he tried to put the touch on me again to pay for his largess. Well, I mean, really, I ask you?"

Lord Bugzee butted in. "Excuse me. How is this at all relevant?"

"Oh, you know, I had a notion it might be instructional how Freddy and I resolved our little spat."

Bugzee looked to the ceiling. "And how did you?"

"Foot race."

The Zurks and Okcho all stared at Pelham, none of them saying anything. Finally, Pelham muttered, "Sorry. The anecdote popped into my mind. I may just step out and see if they have any more of those scrumptious buns."

***

Lord Bugzee continued to hold his ground, wagering on the likelihood the Okcho would eventually find a way to splinter apart. When it became clear to everyone that nothing would be decided, Mountjoy suggested they adjourn for the day.

As they left the office, Lord Bugzee was relieved to find only a few reporters remaining in the outer room. He headed for the security office door, intending to return to his suite, assess whatever damage those savages had done up there, and have a quiet drink to help him gather his thoughts.

Instead, a Srathan reporter pigeon-holed him. "Lord Bugzee, what's your reaction to the announcement?"

"Announcement? What announcement?"

A leer swept across the Srathan's face as it turned a tablet device toward him and tapped. A video began playing of an Axan, the one in charge of the trade conference, J-something Jadarite. The Axan stood behind a lectern flanked by a Bononian, a Cuneddan, that Okcho female who had briefly upended their meeting, and that other Haplor — not Totleigh — the one who wasn't an imbecile.

"Good evening," the Axan said, looking pleased with himself. "We are here today to announce an agreement that was approved a short time ago by the delegates of the G42 Interstellar Trade Conference. Over this extremely long and trying day, we have learned much about how the Okcho have been treated unjustly on Vogus by their Zurk overlords."

Bugzee groaned. "No. No. No. No."

The Axan continued. "At the same time, we have been sustained and entertained by Okcho hospitality. The plight of these people has moved us all. Therefore, we have voted to petition our respective planetary governments as well as the galactic alliance to impose sanctions on the Greater Zurk Protectorate in general and the Zurk colony on Vogus in particular."

Bugzee's proboscis fell slack. How could they do this? His mind began spinning, desperately trying to come up with measures for damage control.

The Axan concluded his remarks with the others around him nodding in agreement. "Specifically, we recommend all alliance planets boycott Zurk businesses on Vogus until such time as the Zurks allow competing Okcho businesses to open and invest in those businesses in the interest of rectifying past abuses of power. Thank you."

Bugzee turned to find that Totleigh fellow right beside him. He had been standing on tiptoes watching the video, wearing a stupid grin on his face. "What do you want?" Bugzee growled.

"Hmm? Oh nothing. As I was saying earlier, marvelous chap that Blandings. Always hatches the most tremendous schemes. Mostly, I just sit back and say, 'Carry on, Blandings. Carry on.'" The Haplor strolled off, his head swaying merrily side to side.

Chapter 33

Return to Sender

"Again, Lord Bugzee, what is your reaction to the announcement?" the Srathan reporter asked.

"To the ... um ... announcement ... that announcement?" The casino owner had to think fast. How could he get ahead of this? How could he spin it to paint himself and the Pink Mingo in the best possible light? "Well, I ... I, of course, ... applaud this breakthrough. I, myself, sent the Okcho representative whom you saw on the video to the trade delegates' meeting with the proposal ... my proposal."

"You're saying you're in favor of boycotting Zurk businesses like your own until Okcho businesses open?"

"Well ... um ... the boycott is but a means to ... ensure the other business owners comply. I, myself, am absolutely in favor of Okcho-owned businesses on the strip." Bugzee coerced a smile into existence. "Yes. Yes. It is a great step forward."

Bren the Bulky slid in beside Bugzee. "We, the Okcho people, wish to express our gratitude to Lord Bugzee for his leadership in this matter. We look forward to a day in the near future when the strip will feature Okcho eateries and Okcho entertainment venues."

"Will there be Okcho casinos?" the reporter asked.

Bugzee reinserted himself. "No, we have agreed they will leave the gaming industry to the Zurks." He congratulated himself for his quick thinking to at least maintain a monopoly in gambling.

Bren clapped an arm on Bugzee's shoulder and held on despite the casino owner trying to slide away. "Sure. Of course, constructing and launching these new enterprises will require money, which the Okcho have until now had in short supply. And though he is far too modest to mention it himself, I am pleased to announce to the galaxy that Lord Bugzee has pledged to invest in Okcho businesses as a silent partner."

"Impressive, Lord Bugzee," the reporter said. "What motivated you to get involved in this plan?"

"Well ... um ... I thought it was the least I could do for the Okcho people to help them regain their identity —"

"And dignity," Bren put in.

"And dignity, of course," said Bugzee. "The interests of the Okcho have always been forefront in Zurk minds."

Bren said, "We also worked out an agreement for a joint council with equal representation by both Okcho representatives and Zurk colonial leaders to resolve all issues for the planet going forward."

Bugzee stared at Bren open-mouthed.

The reporter asked, "One last question, Lord Bugzee. What about the question of the credits in the gambling hack? Have you decided what to do about them?"

Bugzee shook his head in surrender. "After all this, who cares? It doesn't matter. We'll pay them. Now if you'll excuse us, my ... colleague and I have much to discuss."

Bugzee and Bren turned away from the reporter and took a step. Bugzee leaned in and whispered, "If you think this investment scheme and this so-called council —"

Bren said, "Oh, I do think. It's all going to happen. You just went on record confirming all of it."

***

Pelham, meanwhile, after getting another of those delicious buns inside him and despite almost choking on it as he listened to Bugzee's coerced statements, took the elevator back to the lobby in search of Blandings. He spotted Urdi the Unfortunate at the reception desk and wandered over.

"What ho, Urdi, back on the job, I see."

"It's Urdi the Unfortunate, Mr. Totleigh."

"As you have said on numerous occasions. But it always sounds, I don't know, so formal."

"It is our custom, Mr. Totleigh."

"As I have learned." Pelham scratched his head. "It's just difficult for me. I'm used to shortening names, you know. Ask my friends Binky, Corky, Finky, and Pongo. However, I promise to try my best, seeing as we seem to be at the threshold of a new era when Okcho customs will be respected, celebrated even."

"I don't know, Mr. Totleigh. It all sounds too good to be true."

"What about you, Urdi ... um ... the Unfortunate? Will you be moving on to a new career? Taking the stage? Launching a business?"

"Oh, I don't think so," Urdi said in a deadpan, "I figure I've found my niche right here, brightening people's day as I welcome them to the Pink Mingo."

Pelham coughed. "Well, you certainly are a ray of sunshine."

"If I started a business, any number of things might go wrong and probably would. Besides, you know what they say, you can't teach an old kluda new learned behaviors."

"Is that what they say? Doesn't exactly roll off the tongue, does it? And, not to put too fine a point on it, but that is squarely where I believe you're mistaken. There's always another you inside you, so to speak. Don't be afraid to reinvent yourself. Take my granddad, old Phineas R. Totleigh, may he rest in peace. After he had made his fortune and was at an age when other Haplors were looking forward to spending their days watching vids and hitting the restaurants with the sun still shining, he uprooted his entire life to help plant the Sonus colony. He was their first governor. And though not precisely the same sort of thing, only a few years ago my drink of choice was jem and tonic, and then a pal of mine bought a round of Amurru fizzes, and I enjoyed it so much I switched then and there and never looked back."

"Inspiring stories, Mr. Totleigh. Quite rousing. So you think I should start a business? I confess I did have an idea for a restaurant — Unfortunate Lunch. What do you think?"

"You ... um ... might want to workshop that a bit."

A Zurk serving drinks lumbered through the lobby, stopping to ask in a gruff voice, "Amurru fizz?"

"Don't mind if I do," Pelham said. "This is an occasion for celebration."

While pouring the drink, the Zurk sighed as if this was all a great inconvenience, leading to him receiving a mere four-mingo rating.

Pelham lifted his glass. "To the new Vogus. Now, Urdi the Unfortunate, I don't suppose you've seen Blandings around anywhere, have you?"

At that moment, Blandings and Emer emerged from the hallway leading to the meeting rooms.

Pelham called out, "What ho, Blandings!" He headed in their direction.

"I am pleased to tell you, sir, Ms. Emer and I have concluded talks on the Bilateral Bononia Sonus Free Trade Agreement, pending your approval, of course."

"Blandings, after that deal you pulled off with all the delegates, how could I doubt you?"

"Thank you, sir. I must say, Kiz the Chatty was responsible for most of what transpired in the meeting. She needed only a suggestion. The ultimate success of the gambit, however, will depend in large part on how Lord Bugzee receives it."

"Ho. Let me tell you, Blandings. He received it, all right. He choked it down as if he were eating a raw egg. In fact, after some sputtering and throat clearing, he claimed the scheme was his idea all along."

"Of course, he did, sir. Most gratifying, I must say."

"It is. Bren — I mean, Bren the Bulky — even conned him into committing to providing financing. All in all, I would say clouds are gathering at last."

"Excuse me?" Emer asked.

"Hmm? Oh, old Sonus idiom. See, we're trying to build up the atmosphere back home, so cloud formations are a sign of hope."

From the direction of the meeting rooms came the sounds of Elfus back at work once more, crooning a soft, melodic tune requesting that someone love him tenderly. The lyric was all about dreams fulfilled and lives made complete. Pelham found himself swaying to the music.

Emer said. "Personally, I'm astounded at Blandings here."

"He is a wonder, is he not? Don't know what I'd do without him."

A *bloop-bloop-bloop-bloop* sound erupted from the casino.

"I say, are they open for games again?" asked Pelham.

"More or less," Emer said.

They entered the gambling hall. Trade delegates and even some reporters were spread through the room once more enjoying the thrill of risking it all on the flip of a card.

Emer said, "Some of the Okcho have returned to their jobs for now to earn money. The rest of the games are being staffed by Zurks, which is clearly not the same experience, Zurks being Zurks."

"What will the casino do when the Okcho move on to other pursuits?" Pelham asked.

Emer shrugged. "That's their problem, though I suspect some Okcho will stay at their jobs. I was talking to Gladiss —"

"The housekeeping person? Turns out she has a past."

"Really? Anyway, she thinks they could attract Porta like herself to leave the farm and come work here. I wouldn't be surprised if some Bononians ended up taking jobs here as well. We're in a recession right now, and people are looking for work. Listen, I'm going to leave it to you two. I've had quite a day."

Pelham and Blandings bid goodnight to Emer, then approached the Jack Black table where they found Duncil staring at a ten, a six, and a pile of holographic chips, trying to decide what to do.

"What ho, Duncil, old sport," Pelham said.

"Hi, Pelham. Glad to see you out of jail." Duncil nodded to the dealer. "Hit me."

Pelham's eyes went to the dealer, who was none other than Shay the Shorter. She flipped over a five card and slid it to Duncil.

Pelham guffawed. "Twenty-one. I say, Duncil, well done."

The Cuneddan grinned, "The universe is favoring me, Pelham, probably for rescuing you from captivity."

With her eyes not moving from the table, Shay said, "Mr. Totleigh, I'm sorry. I …"

Pelham held up a hand. "Say no more. All's well that ends well. Let it not be said that Pelham G. Totleigh is not one to forgive and forget. I am, in fact, hugely forgetful, eh, Blandings?"

"I have on occasion noted it, sir."

"Say, Blandings, a teensy thought concerning that trade agreement with Bononia."

"Yes, sir?"

"How about the workers? What I'm saying is, as the Bononians rush to fill orders, will the employees be treated fairly? We aren't contributing to anyone being exploited, are we?"

"We are not. Bononia has an exemplary record on that score."

"Excellent. Then everything is wrapped up nicely." Pelham's head jerked up. "Wait. Oh blast."

"Sir?"

"Not everything is resolved, Blandings, I'm still deep in the hole to the casino. I hate to think what fireworks would erupt should a charge for gambling losses appear on a bill to Aunt Agutha."

"I do have an idea about that, sir."

***

Lieutenant Commander Leopold Mountjoy sat in his office, relieved to have the place to himself once again. He stared at a framed picture on the wall of his academy graduating class and counted all the full commanders represented in his year. They were going places. He was headed in the opposite direction.

He spun his head at the sound of someone at his doorway. Sgt. Humstuggle stood there holding a steaming cup. "Tea, sir?"

"Yes, thank you, Humstuggle." Mountjoy appreciated the consideration, though he knew without doubt the brew would be far too weak. He received the cup, took a sip, and dredged up a smile. "Ah. Well, Humstuggle, it has been nice working with you." The statement wasn't altogether true, but this was no time for pettiness.

"What do you mean, Commander? Are you going somewhere?"

"I expect as much. Lord Bugzee is doing his best to spin all these recent developments as a positive thing. However, the fact remains that the empire will regard these concessions as something of a blot on the Zurkannian reputation. We've lost, Humstuggle. We've lost the planet. Oh, we'll still be here, but it's difficult to call it a colony if it's under joint authority. Someone will have to be blamed, and it won't be a lord."

"You mean you?"

"I am the highest-ranking military authority on Vogus."

"What will they do to you?"

"Who knows? Stick me on a dreary moon somewhere. Assign me to mining surveys. Park me behind a desk reviewing the Grays' reports from Earth. It could be anything. But nothing enjoyable."

"Sorry to hear that, sir." A glint rose in Humstuggle's eye. "And ... um ... who will take your place here?"

"Well, they won't promote a sergeant, if that's what you mean."

Humstuggle's proboscis curled up. "Oh, no ... um ... of course not. I wasn't suggesting ..." His voice trailed off.

"I would imagine the most politically expedient thing to do would be to bring in someone whom neither the Zurks nor the Okcho like. That seems fair, or at least it would to some desk pilot back on the home world."

"What about Lord Bugzee?"

Mountjoy scoffed. "The rich and well-connected will always come out right side up. Granted, he is embarrassed at present, and he is unlikely to make any trips back to Zurkannia for some time. But assuming he can find a way to make money from this new arrangement, everything will blow over eventually."

"I expect he *will* make money," Humstuggle said, "as an investor in Okcho restaurants, I mean. Have you tried their cooking? It's fantastic."

Mountjoy answered with a silent glare.

Chapter 34

Leaving Lost Vogus

Blandings tipped up the corner of the two cards in front of him. His eyes darted to the four faceup cards in front of the dealer. With the practiced art of a gentleman's gentleman, he made his face a mask of tranquility. "Sir, please tap in a wager of twenty."

"Twenty. Righto." Pelham tapped his bracelet, and the holographic chips appeared beside Blandings' cards alongside what he had already bet on this hand.

The Delusian sitting beside Blandings stared at the valet for a minute before saying with a grin, "Raise another thirty."

The Arsawan around the table pushed his hole cards toward the dealer. "I fold."

Blandings glanced at Pelham. "Sir, please match the thirty raised by our Delusian friend."

"Are you sure, Blandings?" Pelham's eyes darted toward the Delusian. "She seems a goodish bit confident."

"Yes sir. Please place the bet."

Pelham typed it in. The pile of chips grew taller.

"Final card," the Okcho dealer said. He dealt it in line with the other four. In front of him now sat a nine, ten, two, six, and king.

The Delusian's grin widened. "Raise twenty."

Blandings said, "Twenty ... and raise thirty, sir."

"Blandings, I have all the confidence in the galaxy in you. However, if this all goes amiss ..." A confident glance from the valet silenced him. Pelham gulped and tapped it in.

The Delusian bet another thirty to call and then turned over her cards with a flourish, a nine and a ten, matching the nine and ten in front of the dealer for two pair. She smirked at the Haplors.

Blandings hesitated a moment, then turned up two tens of his own. The smile slid from the Delusian's face as Pelham's bracelet sounded an exultant and excited *bloop-bloop-bloop-bloop*.

"Three of a kind," the dealer said. "The Haplor wins."

Blandings looked to Pelham. "What is your balance now, sir?"

"We're on the pleasant side of two hundred!"

"Then I propose we retire to our suite."

"But you're doing so well, Blandings."

"The precise reason I suggest we quit. This is a fascinating pastime, and it has been most enjoyable calculating the odds. But it is, after all, a game of chance. We have taken enough of Lord Bugzee's money and can walk away ahead, as they say."

Pelham yawned. "You're right, of course, Blandings. And I'm done in from … from everything. You know, I just realized I haven't slept in my hotel bed this entire trip." He yawned again. "It's time to make up for it. Let's go." He stood to leave, awarding the dealer five mingos for his service.

"Mr. Totleigh! Blandings!" The voice shot across the casino. Kiz the Chatty, wearing village clothes, bounded through the crowd toward them waving a hand. She leaned down to greet Pelham with a hug. She gave Blandings a peck on the cheek, bringing a warm flush to the valet's face. "I wanted to thank you both for everything you've done for us."

"You are most welcome," Pelham said. "It was a pleasure to do our bit. Well, come to think of it, some parts were not so pleasurable, but I do look back on it all now with a good deal of satisfaction."

"You should. You did great, both of you. I've just come from the village. The people there are more excited than I've ever seen them. This is a real chance for us to join the galactic community while still maintaining our culture."

"So, I take it, you're not going to copy the Zurks. No space armadas and far-flung colonies?"

Kiz laughed. "Unlikely. No, this is our home … or it will be once we tear down the walls around the colony."

"Do you think you can make everything work here with the Zurks?"

"Most of us are willing to give it a try. We'll see how everything goes. Come back in a year or two. Maybe by then I'll have my own tea shop open."

"That sounds delightful. Good luck with it."

"Excuse me, Kiz the Chatty?" It was a reporter.

"Sorry. Have to run. Everything is happening at once." Kiz walked off with the reporter, waving goodbye to the Haplors.

They watched her go, then Pelham turned to Blandings and blinked … twice … three times."

"If I recall correctly, sir, you decided to head back to the suite."

"Correct as usual, Blandings. That I did." He yawned again. "All right. I'm headed for bed. And Blandings?"

"Sir?"

"Whatever I have on the calendar for tomorrow, clear it off. Take the eraser to it. Delete the entry. I believe I will have a proper lie-in."

"Very good, sir."

***

Late the next morning, Pelham G. Totleigh, in pajamas and dressing gown, sat on the couch in his suite sipping one of Blandings' perfect cups of tea. He breathed in the warm scent of the brew and exhaled a deep sigh. "I say, this is more like it, eh?"

"Are you referring, sir, to the tea or to relaxing in our suite or possibly to something else?"

"All of it, Blandings. All of it. I am feeling quite content this morning, serene, well chuffed."

"Things have indeed worked out well, sir."

A *ding* sang out from the door. Blandings answered it. "It is Ms. Emer, sir."

"Show her in," Pelham said. "Tea, Emer?"

"No, I can only stay a minute. My ship takes off soon." She perched in a chair. "I wanted to tell you about the Okcho elders."

"What of them? Elderly, one would presume?"

"That they are. But the news is that they have appointed their representatives to the new Vogus council, the one with both Zurks and Okcho."

"Ah. Let me guess. They selected Bren the Bulky and Tud the Impatient. I predict those two will end up fighting among themselves."

"They won't have the chance. The council shied away from appointing any former partisans."

"Do tell," Pelham said. "That must have reduced the field considerably, given all the various groups. Who did they pick then?"

"They selected Kiz the Chatty because of her recent prominence in resolving the crisis and Urdi the Unfortunate due to his age and experience working with the Zurks."

"Wise choices, I would say, especially Kiz the Chatty."

"I agree. Though, don't you think Urdi the Unfortunate is kind of a pessimist?"

Pelham flipped up a palm. "Well, if you had the life he's had ..."

"I have to rush off. Come see us on Bononia sometime, both of you."

"That sounds delightful. And believe me, if I come, I will most certainly bring along Blandings. Couldn't get by without him, don't you know. Toodle pip."

As Emer left, Pelham took another sip of tea. "Do you concur, Blandings, with the selection of Kiz and Urdi?"

"I do, sir. Kiz the Chatty brings great insight and a bold forward-looking energy. Urdi the Unfortunate has ... well, to his credit he possesses a certain hard-won world-weariness, a jaded, skeptical perspective, which can often be useful in making sure things move forward judiciously."

"He's a worrywart, is what you mean."

"One could put it that way, sir. I dare say, they both have a difficult job ahead of them. They are bound, no doubt, to receive criticism from all sides. Some will think they are moving too quickly, changing too much. Others will undoubtedly feel the opposite, that they are conceding too much to the Zurks, not being aggressive enough."

"You're saying Kiz and Urdi are in for it."

"I am afraid so, sir."

"Well, that's unfortunate, what?" Pelham said with a wink.

"I couldn't have said it better myself, sir."

The screen on the wall beeped and the face of Aunt Agutha appeared. Pelham nearly did a spit take with his tea and immediately found himself wishing he was drinking something a bit stronger to buck him up for this impending inquisition.

"Well, Nephew," she said with a frown, "still in your pajamas at this hour?"

"What? What?" asked Pelham, his mouth gaping.

Blandings said, "Good morning, Dame Agutha. If I may correct a misconception, it is, in fact, quite early here in local Vogus time."

"Is it?" Agutha asked. "All right then."

Pelham met Blandings' gaze and mouthed a thank you.

"What in the name of Gort has been going on there?" Aunt Agutha asked. "Everything on the news vids has been Vogus this and Vogus that. Leave it to you, Pelham, to disrupt an entire planet."

"So much has been going on, Auntie. Protests, assaults, tense negotiations, a veritable revolution of sorts. I, along with a few others, have been endeavoring to improve life on this planet, to give the Okcho back their independence."

"Sure, you have," she said with a sarcastic eyeroll.

Pelham plastered on his best smile. "I am also pleased to report we have concluded the trade deal with Bononia per your request."

"You did?"

"We did."

"I'll have to review it. You probably gave away too much. No doubt they played you like a harp."

"Ah, that's where you've misjudged things, Auntie. I promise you the terms are remarkably fair. Blandings says as much himself, don't you, Blandings?"

The valet gave her a dip of his head. "I find the particulars to be most equitable, ma'am."

"Hmm," Aunt Agutha said. "The last time we talked, you said they were demanding to be our exclusive supplier."

Blandings said, "They have since dropped that demand."

"What about them wanting to transport everything on Bononian ships?"

"Mr. Totleigh was able to negotiate it down to thirty percent of all shipments."

"Well, that's reasonable."

"I thought so, ma'am."

"Sounds like you know more about the agreement than Pelham. Which of you actually conducted the talks?"

"Let me assure you, Mr. Totleigh was intimately involved … when he wasn't engaged in crafting a new geopolitical future for Vogus. It is merely that I have a better head for remembering details."

"I can believe that," Agutha said. "It's a wonder he can keep track of his own name. I'm not sure what Pelham's head *is* good for … other than a place to park hats."

Pelham tried to take it in stride. "Blandings is like my personal offline memory storage. He stockpiles the trivial details, while I focus on the big picture."

"The trade deal is truly all completed then?"

"It is."

Aunt Agutha eyed him suspiciously across the connection. After a moment or two, her scowl began to fade. "I suppose, in the end, it doesn't matter who did what. The point is somehow you pulled it off." She paused to take a breath and let it out. "You astound me, Nephew. I don't know what to say."

"You don't?" Pelham asked. "Thank you springs to mind. A hearty well done would not be amiss."

"Hmm. All right, good job … for once. Is the conference over?"

"Yes. After everything that happened, they voted for an early adjournment. Blandings and I can return home any time."

"Fine. I'll arrange travel for you."

"Not on a Donovian military vessel, I hope."

Agutha frowned. "What's wrong with them? They got you there, didn't they?"

"In a manner of speaking. Whereupon, as I said, we secured the trade deal for Sonus as well as peace for the planet Vogus. I think that calls for a small reward, don't you?"

"Hmm. Well, perhaps you do deserve an upgrade in arrangements." She raised a tablet and tapped on it a few times. "There is a freighter from Tucana Three due to deliver supplies to Sonus."

"A freighter? I mean, really."

"It's not Donovian."

"True. Still, I was hoping for something a bit more upscale."

"Here's an Avanian cruise ship."

"Sounds better."

Blandings cleared his throat.

Pelham turned to him. "Yes, Blandings?"

"Given the small size of Avanians, sir, it is unlikely the accommodations will be comfortable."

"Sound reasoning, Blandings. Tell you what, Aunt Agutha, anything from a larger species?"

Her mouth tightened. "What about a Dieren passenger ship, the *Queen Scythia*?"

Pelham glanced at Blandings, who nodded.

"We'll take it. Thanks awfully."

"Then you'll be back at work tomorrow? And, by the way, don't infer from my inflection at the end of the sentence that I was asking a question."

"It will be my pleasure to report for duty, my dear aged relative."

"Aged? Watch it, Pelham." She glared at him with narrowed eyes as the screen went black.

Pelham sat back on the couch and sighed once more. "Yes, Blandings, this is indeed much more like it."

How would you like to make my day?
Please review this book on Amazon and on Goodreads.
Your honest words would mean the world to me.
Follow me on Instagram at garyrandolphstoryteller
and Facebook at GR Storyteller.

Last Word and Something Free

Thanks for reading *Viva Lost Vogus*. I hope you love Pelham and Blandings as much as I do. They are a tribute to the *Jeeves and Wooster* series of books and stories by the great P. G. Wodehouse. If you've never read them, consider checking them out. Perhaps the best introduction would be the 1990s British television series *Jeeves and Wooster*, starring a young Hugh Laurie and Stephen Fry, who are both always wonderful and even more brilliant when paired together. As of when I'm writing this, you can find episodes on YouTube.

I would love to hear what you think about the book. Leave a quick review on Amazon and/or Goodreads. Every review moves the book up the algorithm.

I want to thank Kameron Robinson for another great cover design. And, of course, a big thanks to you the readers who keep me going.

Follow me on Amazon, to know when I have new releases. To do so, click the Follow button beside my picture on the Amazon page for any of my books. You can also follow me on Instagram at garyrandolphstoryteller and Facebook at GaryRandolphStoryteller.

Check out my website at grstoryteller.com. It has summaries of all my books and links to my blogs. I also do storytelling, and you can watch some videos of me singing songs and reciting poems.

While you're on the website, please sign up for my mailing list at the bottom of the home page. Then I can tell you when I'm releasing a new book, having price promotions, or doing a storytelling performance. I promise I won't abuse the privilege of having your email address. Nobody hates spam more than I do.

And something free for you. If you sign up for my mailing list, I'll send you *The Jewels of Eca*, a short story that tells how Zastra (one of the characters in my Galactic Detective Agency series) joined up with Oren Vilkas. If you're a fan of that series, it's a tale you'll want to read

Other Books by Gary Blaine Randolph

Pelham and Blandings

Pelham G. Totleigh is an unlikely hero. His species, Haplors, are smaller than most others in the galaxy. And as his Aunt Agutha constantly reminds him, he is hardly the smartest or most industrious of Haplors. He also has an unfortunate habit of stumbling his way into the most outrageous and hilarious predicaments. Fortunately, his faithful valet Blandings has enough brainpower for both of them and is always there with a brilliant idea and an excellent cup of tea. This series is a loving tribute to and re-imagining of the Jeeves and Wooster stories of PG Wodehouse. Join Pelham and Blandings on their comic misadventures through space.

The series is available in both paperback and e-book formats on Amazon at https://www.amazon.com/dp/B0BYPLWPBV

Book 1 – Viva Lost Vogus
Book 2 – The Importance of Being Pelham
Book 3 – The Code of the Totleighs

The Galactic Detective Agency

Gabriel Lake is just a regular computer guy from Indianapolis ... until he is recruited into this series of lighthearted murder mysteries in space. Under the guidance of the brilliant Oren Vilkas, the Galactic Detective Agency hops from one weird world to another to take on quirky aliens and solve interstellar crime.

The complete series is available on Amazon at amazon.com/gp/product/B08XN1BL1G

Book 1 – A Town Called Potato
Book 2 – The Maltese Salmon
Book 3 – Return of the Judy
Book 4 – The Big Sneep
Book 5 – Murder on the Girsu Express (this is the one with Pelham)
Book 6 – The Cormabite Maneuver
Book 7 – Trouble in Paradox
Book 8 – The Wrath of Kah-Rehn

Alien World

If you were stranded, all alone on an alien world, if you had to hide your identity and try to blend in, how would you do it? What would it cost you? What would you long for most?

Not a comedy — well, there are some funny bits — *Alien World* is an exploration of what it would be like to be a stranger stranded on another planet and forced to live out decades there, trying to blend in while staying one step ahead of the authorities.

Available on Amazon at https://www.amazon.com/dp/B085SYG3L7

Made in the USA
Coppell, TX
17 May 2025

49489812R00138